Haunted Melody

Secrets of Roseville • Book 2

Betty Bolté

Copyright © 2017 by Betty Bolté
www.bettybolte.com
ISBN-13: 978-0-9981625-3-9
ISBN-10: 0-9981625-3-1

Digitally published as *Remnants* October 2014 by Liquid Silver Books, an imprint of Atlantic Bridge Publishing, 10509 Sedgegrass Dr., Indianapolis, Indiana 46235.

First print edition of *Remnants* published 2014 by CreateSpace.

To my children,
Danielle and Nicholas,
who are the songs in my heart.

Chapter One

The enormous orange jack-o-lantern faced the long driveway, challenging visitors to Twin Oaks with its glowing toothy grin. Paulette O'Connell propped her fists on her hips and assessed the rest of the decorations gathered on the wide front porch of her younger sister Meredith's antebellum plantation home. Gratitude and disquiet filled her chest along with the crisp fall air. Standing at the bottom of the three brick steps, she scanned the clusters of corn stalks propped against the two center columns, the gourds and pumpkins scattered about, and the wisps of fake spiderweb stretched between two of the large white columns. A forbidding black spider waited among the gossamer strands. A white sheet ghost danced in the brisk breeze, rattling the dried corn stalk leaves. With a chuckle, she clapped her hands together. "Perfect. Mer will love it."

Their next B&B guests might include several young children who would love the spooky yet fun décor as much as she did. If only trick-or-treaters in town came out to the country. But of course, the trek to Twin Oaks wouldn't yield enough return on investment for the children's parents to make such a journey. The memory of Halloween parties from her childhood made her smile. Costumes. Games.

Telling tales and singing songs about monsters and spooky things. They needed a reason to venture so far from town. Perhaps she could lure them to the plantation with some form of entertainment. Hmmm.

Halloween remained her favorite holiday, at least for the fun props. Ever since discovering she possessed the ability to see ghosts a few months before, the approaching holiday had taken on new meaning. She had grown up with "dreams" about a lady in a blue gown. Who knew she was actually a ghost, her Great-great-great-aunt Grace. Later, she learned from Meredith that Grace's brother, Great-great-great-grandfather Joe, also hung around the family cemetery, apparently waiting for his sister's return. Meredith had figured out the identities of the ghosts, but the sisters realized they possessed the ability to see ghosts at the same time.

Thankfully, the ghosts weren't scary so much as sad and a little spooky. After burying Grace's remains beside Joe's, the house held no more spirits, as they finally rested in peace. Knowing the plantation no longer hosted spooks made enjoying the tricks and treats of the season more fun. Although she rather missed Grace's friendly presence in a gorgeous blue dress replete with sparkling sequins, a dress which had inspired Paulette's own childhood designs.

Rubbing a hand over her protruding belly, she lingered in the fading afternoon light. She surveyed the expanse of pale grass reaching toward the distant road winding past. The glittering water of the fenced lake where ducks paddled about. Low clouds covered the sky, obscuring the sun. Several trees sported jagged trunks, remnants of the tornado they'd survived six months ago. Hunkered in the storm shelter within the stone foundation of Twin Oaks, she'd feared the destruction of the plantation once and for all. Thankfully, they'd suffered only minor damage, except for the old gazebo. Rebuilding it had been Meredith's first priority. Its new design proved very popular with the guests, who frequently enjoyed its shady quiet on a hot summer afternoon, or the soft lighting in the evening.

The baby shifted, a tiny foot or perhaps a fist bopping her hand where it rested. "Soon, little one. Another six weeks, give or take, and we'll meet properly."

Tires crunched on gravel and she recognized her sister's glaring yellow Camaro approaching. The sports car shouted its owner's status. Successful. Independent. Confident. All the attributes Paulette wished she could ascribe to herself. She waved as Meredith drove behind the house to park, and then Paulette hurried up the front steps and inside as fast as her bulk allowed.

Pregnancy increased her weight significantly from her normal slender build and made keeping her balance difficult. The baby couldn't come soon enough for her liking. Uncertainty spider crawled down her back. If she and Meredith had not made peace between them, she'd be on the street without any means of providing for her child. Good ole Johnny had fled to Alaska rather than face his fatherly duties. Alone and lonely, she'd had no choice but to come begging to her sister. The timing worked out for both of them, as did their renewed relationship. Otherwise, where would she have turned? She squared her shoulders and pulled open the heavy wooden door. No matter. Her baby would know love and laughter and never, ever be alone.

Pausing inside the closed door, she let out a breath. The grand entrance never failed to bring her pleasure. Hardwood floors reached across the space, inviting visitors to its interior rooms. As their grandmother, Mary O'Connell, had done before them, Paulette and Meredith utilized the small room toward the back of the house as a sitting and sewing room while the parlor at her immediate right served as a more formal place to greet guests. To the left, the double parlor waited for after-dinner gatherings, with their pipes and conversations. A flight of stairs, dressed up in dark brown treads with white fronts, led to the second floor and its rabbit's warren of bedrooms and baths. The distant rustling of paper bags and cabinet doors closing summoned her down the hallway and through the swinging door into the kitchen.

"Hey, Meredith, I was thinking…" Paulette hesitated to share her idea with her business oriented sister. How should she phrase her vision in such a way as to be convincing?

Meredith snagged a bunch of celery from the brown paper bag, sidestepping Grizabella as the calico twined about her ankles, to drop it into the crisper bin in the refrigerator. Dressed in tan jeans and a mulberry sweater, Meredith appeared ready to settle down to work in her home office despite the late afternoon hour. Paulette glanced out the small kitchen window. Sunshine stretched across the yard, creating long shadows in preparation for nightfall. Her gaze lit upon the gazebo with its white spindled railing and wooden posts supporting the peaked shaker shingled roof. A collection of metal chairs with colorful cushions surrounded the matching round table in the center. The rebuilt gazebo caught the light and threw it down as a lacy silhouette of the wrought iron gingerbread edging the roof. Beyond the gazebo the family cemetery lay under towering magnolia trees, safe within the confines of a metal fence. She dragged her attention back to smile at her sister.

"Yes?" Meredith shut the fridge and blinked at Paulette. "You were saying?"

"Sorry." Paulette shook her head, a grin curving her lips as she sifted through possible phrases. "Is Griz helping you with the groceries?"

"Always." Meredith cocked her head. "She's hoping I'll take pity on her and feed her early tonight."

"Any word from Max?" Anything to stall for time until she could land upon the right way to approach the subject. Meredith balked at large group activities, and the party she had in mind definitely qualified. "Will he be back from Atlanta soon?"

"He texted me that the preservation case will be heard tomorrow, then he'll know how much longer he needs to be in court." She lifted items from the bag and set them on the counter before dropping the bag on the floor. "I had no idea when I met him that lawyers traveled so much."

Grizabella hunkered on the floor, her tail twitching, before lunging into the open bag and pouncing on an imaginary mouse with a clatter of brown paper.

"I don't suppose there are very many lawyers who specialize in preservation law." Paulette folded her arms over her tummy and hiked one hip. "I'm glad you two found each other. You're good together."

Meredith flicked a glance at her, then shook her long strawberry-blonde ponytail. "Thanks. It still amazes me how things worked out."

"Unlike for me." Paulette laid her hands on her belly, her baby. "But we'll be fine now that I have you to back me up."

"And one day, you may find a man worthy to be your husband." Meredith scooted around the island counter and hugged Paulette in a quick encouraging movement. "But you'll always have a place to call home."

Paulette considered Meredith's words as her sister strode back to the other side of the island. "You may be right, but somehow I doubt I'll ever find anyone who'd want to take on responsibility for another man's child."

Meredith paused in the act of emptying another bag. "Blended families happen all the time. I'm sure if you want to have a husband who will be a father to your child, you'll find the right man."

Paulette shrugged and shifted her weight to the other hip. "Anyway, a husband is not in the cards right now. But tell me, what did you think of my jack-o-lantern? And the other decorations out front?"

Surely her sister had noticed the effort she'd made to enliven the house for the season. Her decorating skills had to be good for something. Since moving in, Paulette had tried to employ her limited creative talents wherever possible. She'd secured several clients, designing and creating authentic period costumes for them to wear in battle reenactments and ghost walk tours around the nearby cities of Nashville and Huntsville. She'd also redecorated several rooms to use as guest quarters for hire. Meredith hadn't wanted strangers around all the time, so they'd compromised. The six bedrooms stayed occupied most weekends, which helped with Paulette's efforts to build and promote her costume business. Currently, they only had two rooms not rented out for the coming weekend, but she remained confident they'd fill soon.

"No, sorry." Meredith reached for a box of orzo and strode to the pantry to put it on a shelf. "I was thinking about the challenge of tying together the various elements of the estate east of Roseville. The Bancroft's place."

"Oh. Well, I—" Disappointment swept across her shoulders, weighing them down, at Meredith's dismissal of her efforts. But then, she did have a lot of irons in the fire what with planning her wedding to Max, and the many clients with demanding particulars, as well as supervising the repairs around Twin Oaks. "What's the matter with the Bancroft place?"

"They expect me to work magic, pure and simple. Three buildings, and they want one common porch to unite them." Meredith shook her head and grabbed two cans of soup, moving them in time with the motion of her strawberry-blonde ponytail. "What the heck are they thinking?"

"You'll figure it out." Paulette smiled. Her sister's renown as an architect stretched around the world. She designed multi-million dollar mansions and other showcase buildings. Which proved more comforting than her previous desire to destroy things after the horrific deaths of her husband and unborn child. Twin Oaks' very existence had been threatened by her grief. After Max entered her life, her despair and anger had morphed into hope and love. "You always manage to beautify the jobs you take on. Anyway..."

Meredith placed the cans in the pantry and pushed the door closed. "Yes?"

She took a deep breath and let it out in a rush. "We should throw a party. Our guests will love it!" Her words spilled from her mouth. "A costume party, with masks and everything. We'd have to do it the weekend before Halloween, since the actual holiday is on a Friday. We could advertise it as a special event, with a special price, and..."

"Wait. A party? Are you kidding?" Meredith folded up the paper bags, leaving the cat's on the floor with Grizabella's calico tail sticking out and slowly swishing from side to side, and shoved them into a cabinet. "Your hormones must be out of whack."

"No, I—" Paulette searched for a compelling reason in the face of her sister's frown.

"We don't have time for a party. We've finally finished rebuilding the gazebo, and I have this Bancroft wizardry to complete before the winter weather interferes. And, more importantly, you're due soon. You don't need stress and worry. No parties. Not now."

"I thought I'd design some new costumes for us, show off my abilities. And..." She snapped her fingers as an idea popped into her head. She envisioned a grand affair, the house filled with pirates, ghosts, witches, princesses, even Barack Obama and George Bush look-alikes. "We could promote our planned Civil War encampment reenactment at the same time. Invite folks to attend in period costumes and uniforms. You could dress as Grace, if you'd like, even wear the jewelry she gave you. Come on. It'll be great!"

Meredith swiped a hand across her forehead. Grizabella had tired of her hiding place and now munched on her dinner. "I don't know. Seems like a lot of work. All to dress up and playact for an audience. What will Meg say? Just because she's the housekeeper and cook doesn't mean she'll be willing to do this."

"I think she'll love the idea of seeing Twin Oaks glowing with light and echoing with laughter. Put some life back into the old place." She gripped the back of a chair situated at the small glass-topped table tucked into the bay window overlooking the rear of the property. Urgency unexpectedly flowed through her, creating an increasing tension in her shoulders. "It'll be fun. I really want to. Please?"

Meredith sank onto a chair, propped her elbows on the table, and rested her chin in her palms. Her scrutiny made Paulette squirm. "Will there be music? Perhaps you could sing something? I used to love to hear you practice the tunes for the high school choir."

Not a chance. "I'm really not in the mood to sing, but we can have a DJ and dancing for the guests to enjoy."

Meredith frowned and tapped a forefinger on her cheek, regarding Paulette. "That's a good point. But why haven't you been singing? You used to all the time."

Why indeed. She shrugged. "Too much on my mind with the baby about due and me trying to feel like I'm contributing to the household finances. A litany of thoughts, tasks, reminders loop in my head to the point I think of nothing else. Maybe after the baby is born, I'll feel happy enough to want to share music again. But not until then."

"If you say so. Where would we find a DJ?"

"I'll figure it out. Come on. Let's have a party. Please?"

She held her breath, waiting for Meredith to say something. Anything. A shrug sparked hope.

"Meredith?"

"I'm going to regret this." Meredith shrugged again and sat up straight. A grin eased onto her lips. "The weekend before, you said?"

Paulette clapped her hands and grinned. "Yes, we'll kick off the festivities leading up to the holiday."

"Is two weeks enough time to plan a shindig?" Meredith pushed back to her feet and slid the chair in place under the table. "An awful lot will have to be accomplished in a short period of time."

"Don't you worry. I can pull it off. You'll see." She hugged her baby. "As long as someone doesn't decide to make an early entrance into the world."

The pale blue flame licked the bottom of the clear beaker. Zak Markel leaned closer, the gas-fueled heat warming his stubbly jaw. He sniffed, wrinkling his nose at the hint of sulfur. Using rubber-tipped tongs, he lifted the glass, flat-bottomed bulb by its slender neck and swirled the red mixture. *Perfect.* He'd succeeded in advancing another step in the process. He returned the beaker to the heat, picked up a pen, and jotted his observations into a lab notebook as his dad had taught him. Be precise and meticulous and success follows. Failure was for losers.

Most of his experiments worked flawlessly. Of course, his father's advice probably had been an attempt to encourage his son. Instead, Zak ended up choosing the safe route in order to appear successful in his father's eyes. Thus he experienced few challenges or obstacles in his work. Some days, he longed to risk experimenting with cutting-edge compounds. Until he'd recall the look on his dad's face when his teenage attempt to make his own soda machine fizzled. The censure and disappointment he'd detected in his father's countenance prompted him to shelve his ambitions.

But then he'd discovered those damn alchemical puzzles he desperately wanted to unravel but had as yet failed to do so. Failure frustrated him even more than his father. Made him want to hit something. He had failed to replicate seventeenth-century chemical processes, which called into question his high-priced education. He didn't want to transmute metal into gold. What he most hoped for was finding the secret to unlock the mysterious formula for the Elixir of Life. His little brother's future rested on whether a cure could be found. The legend surrounding the Philosopher's Stone, one of many aliases for the elixir, suggested the fine, red powder the formula purportedly created could heal all forms of illness. If only he could replicate the formula, perhaps he could save his brother's eyesight. Grant wasn't in any pressing danger from the slow-growing meningioma tumors, so Zak had time to work on solving the puzzle. His brother had demonstrated his uniqueness by managing to contract a disease rarely afflicting men, and almost never someone thirty-five. Zak would do *anything* to erase the headaches and pain lines etched on his younger brother's face. While the doctors stewed about proper medical treatments to slow or stop the growths, Zak had to do *something*, even if it ultimately proved futile, to help Grant fight the inoperable tumors wrapped around his optic nerves, threatening his eyesight and his future as a geologist.

Memories of their childhood together flitted through his brain. He pictured the two of them roaming the mountainside in search of exposed layers of earth, revealing the stratification of the land, the equivalent of tree rings showing the age and diversity of the climate over time. Grant had collected rocks and gems until his closet had no room to hang his clothes without draping over the boxes and tubs. During their search, they shared more than lunch. They shared their hopes for the future. They cemented their brotherhood in a deep and loving friendship.

He couldn't sit by and wait. Hope couldn't be the only strategy. He'd promised his mother he'd watch over his brother, and he always kept his word. But all he'd managed to prove so far was that he'd missed some key step or nuance to the precisely penned instructions. But what? He'd followed the directions to the letter. Though maybe some ingredient's physical properties had changed over the centuries. A thought worth pursuing.

Zak slid off the high stool and made his way across the room, heading for the bookcase situated by the back window of his basement laboratory. Outside, identical houses lined the sleepy street. The small ranch house in the quiet suburb surrounding Battle Creek, Michigan, had been his mother's idea so he'd live close by. The place remained a house, not a home. He never felt comfortable driving down the wide street with young trees scattered along the way, pulling into the concrete driveway, walking into the brick building. Truth be told, he hated living in the neighborhood. Hell, he hated living in the town. Although he loved his parents, he craved something different. In a new place with new opportunities. No chance of that, though. His life and work as a professor waited for him, a treadmill of boredom. No change in sight.

Scanning the room, a sense of claustrophobia settled about his shoulders like a jacket sized for a child. He'd fitted the lab with everything necessary to pursue his own experiments, even if he rarely chose to do so. He paused and mentally inventoried the room's accoutrements: work table with array of beakers, Bunsen burner, tongs, long handled spoons, sharp knife, acids and bases. Running water and a propane gas supply flowed to either end of the work space. Beside the window sat a square white table holding his closed laptop, carafe of water, and a half-filled tumbler, flanked by white wooden chairs. Everything right where it belonged. Combined, the lab and its contents did nothing to satisfy his longing for something out of his reach. Nor did any of the items assuage his fear of his brother succumbing to the illness, possibly even dying.

On a sigh, he strode to the bookcase. The case held few books, but those he possessed he'd chosen for specific purposes. He pulled a metal box containing the ancient yellowed journal from its place on the top shelf of the cedar bookcase. Laying it reverently on the table, he eased onto a chair, wiggled the tight-fitting lid off, and regarded the alchemist's journal housed within.

Fortune had led him to an out of the way antiques mall in Massachusetts the year before. He'd wandered through the menagerie of stalls, searching out old books and papers. Reading about past lives and experiences made his own better by comparison. The contents of ancient tomes and pages typically led to new insights into old problems, or at least a fresh perspective on how to approach solutions to them. He'd spotted the water-stained binding and a shot of anticipation, a thrill of expectation, lanced through him.

The cover revealed he'd struck figurative gold from a historic perspective. Scrawled across the battered front were the words LABORATORY NOTES OF XAVIER STARLING. He had resisted the urge to flip through the fragile pages. Instead, he gently opened the cover and read the first dated entry from 1676. The ancient alchemist's notes proved to contain a host of what had been groundbreaking formulas for everything from cleaning fluids, to wrinkle creams, rich dyes, forgotten recipes for delicacies, and even medicine created from herbs and metals. One specific formula Starling had labeled as the elusive Elixir of Life, something too valuable and notoriously difficult to create and definitely not to be trusted to just anyone. Zak's hands had trembled until he nearly dropped the volume. He inhaled to steady himself, releasing the breath on a count of five. Closing the book, he'd sauntered to the register at the front of the building, paid for his purchase, and emerged into the winter sunlight. He'd forced himself to remain calm, to not release a whoop of joy, but he couldn't stop the ear-to-ear grin.

Ever since buying the book, he'd tried to recreate the transmutations and formulas, but the directions employed mysterious symbols. Over time, he'd figured out some of the cipher elements, but most of the secrets remained obscured. Some key to the cipher must exist, but it eluded him. After Grant had been diagnosed with the tumors, the contents had become even more valuable to Zak as potentially holding the secret to a possible cure.

He opened the lab notes to the one recipe he thought he'd figured out, but had yet to achieve the results listed by the alchemist. Instead of a dry red powder, the elusive Elixir, he created a lump of doughy mass. Something went wrong with either his ingredients or his process, but damn if he knew what.

Considering how faint the spidery writing appeared on the page, he retrieved a handheld magnifying glass from the drawer in the table and hovered it over each ingredient. As he read through the list for what seemed the hundredth time, he noticed a faded symbol he'd missed in the margin. *Fascinating.* What could it be? Holding the book up to the light with one hand, he examined it, angling the page first one way and then another for a better look through the glass. He discerned a tiny sketch of what appeared to be an owl, with pointed ear tufts, perched on crossed sticks or branches inside a downward pointing triangle. A thin bar ran along the inside of the shape the width of the hypotenuse at the top. Zak sat back, gazing at the ceiling as he pondered the symbol's purpose.

The triangle could mean a triad or trinity of some kind. But three what? Days? Years? Owls? Since it pointed downward, might it represent a female or something feminine? Or nothing, simply a random occurrence by the alchemist? He linked his fingers behind his head. The other notations indicated the man who had kept the journal did nothing randomly. He also needed to decipher the presence of the bird, or more specifically, the owl. He'd have to research owl symbolism in order to determine the true significance.

Perhaps an Internet search would yield the answer. At least, a place to start. He replaced the cover on the silver box and slid it aside. Opening the laptop lid, he waited for the security facial scan to give him access to the desktop. He launched the browser and then typed in "triangle" and "symbolism" as the key words and hit the Enter key. Thousands of results. A long list of links popped onto the browser screen. Selecting one which looked promising, he scanned the content, then started over slowly. Pay dirt.

As he thought, a triangle pointing down suggested the feminine; pointing up, masculine. The ability to mean opposites depending on the position of the shape made the triangle popular as a magical symbol. Mystic teachings referred to the power of three, the joining of the "one" and "two" to create the child of "three." A trinity able to embody many historical and cultural concepts, such as the religious one of the Father, Son, and Holy Ghost. But also more generic triads of past, present, future, or creation, destruction, sustenance, and even mind, body, spirit.

Then he spotted what he searched for, the five symbols used by Aristotle to represent the five natural elements of air, earth, fire, water, and unity. The triangle drawn in the journal was what the great philosopher used to represent earth. But what did that mean to the mysterious and mystical Starling?

He searched on "owl" and "symbolism" and found tons of unhelpful information. In several ancient cultures, the owl served as guardian of the underworlds and a protector of the dead. Essentially, the keeper of spirits who passed from one plane to another. Native Americans revered it as the keeper of sacred and secret knowledge. He chuckled when he read that in medieval times owls were thought to be witches and wizards in disguise.

He added "triangle" to his key words and hit Enter. Another long list of links filled the screen. Intrigued, he skimmed them, searching for the likeliest candidate to contain the information he sought. He needed to narrow down the search. He added "image" to his search criteria and hit Enter again. He blinked and stared incredulously at one of the many images including owls on the screen. The very symbol in the book, or nearly the same since it didn't include the bar inside the triangle, stared back at him. He clicked the image, taking him to the website of the Golden Owl Books and Brews. What chance existed that the two symbols were unrelated and yet so closely aligned? Coincidence? He shook his head. No such thing in his experience. He'd bet on a connection.

He searched for the contact information and discovered the store was located in some Podunk town in Tennessee. Roseville. Curious. Maybe the history of the store would include an explanation for the symbol. Selecting the link, he waited for the site to appear on the screen.

Behind him, hissing reached his ears, distracting him from his search. He turned to investigate the sound but ended up thrown from his chair when the beaker of solution exploded.

Chapter Two

The next morning, Paulette was determined to create in fabric the basic wedding dress she'd designed on paper. Then she'd play with the finishing touches to adorn the satin. Each step up the stairs to the attic made Paulette's lower back ache. Yet the dress dummy resided in the dusty room. They should have moved it into the sewing room sooner. She wanted to use it to create Meredith's wedding dress, but neither Max nor Meg's husband Sean were available to do the lifting. Thankfully, the wire dummy wasn't very heavy. She and Meredith had sorted through most of the trunks and boxes, arranging them so the women could more easily reach their contents. And such strange contents they held. Besides the expected books and clothes, they found candles and feathers, even rocks. Deciding which items to keep and which to dispose of would take a lot of time, but at least the containers were accessible. Unlike the dress dummy which she hadn't realized she'd need quite so soon.

She reached the landing, pausing outside the closed door. Two long breaths slowed her heart rate and helped prepare her for the journey back in time which waited among the plethora of books, journals, letters, and newspapers in the various trunks and boxes. She had discovered her old diaries tucked in the closet of the bedroom on the second floor she and Meredith once shared. Reading decades old entries rekindled a need to capture her thoughts on paper. As a result, she had started journaling again. So much to wrestle with and untangle about her situation. In particular, she'd scratched page after page coming to terms with the depressing realization of Johnny leaving her to pursue his own dreams, ones she apparently couldn't help him achieve. Not that she wanted to live in the cold of Alaska, truth be told. She'd loved him, but apparently the love she thought they shared proved inadequate. Still, she carried their child. Meredith had been reluctant, to put it mildly, about Paulette moving in. But ultimately she had encouraged her to stay and raise the little one amidst the love and family embodied in the historic plantation. An offer only a fool would refuse.

The soft thump of cat paws announced Grizabella's arrival. The feline monitored all activity in the house, nosing her way into everybody's business. Even the guests loved the colorful cat. She scritched the cat's neck, using the backs of her fingers to rub in all the right places, a quiet purr her reward. Straightening, she peered down at Griz. "You coming in with me?"

Griz flicked her tail and meowed once.

"Here we go then." Turning the door knob, she pushed into the room. She flipped the switch and soft light glowed from the lone ceiling fixture. Daylight shone through the dirty windows at the far side of the space. She longed to wash them, to enable a clear view of the vista beyond, but more pressing matters snared her time and attention. Griz preceded her into the room, aiming for the dust bunnies snuggled up to the baseboard. She inhaled, smelled moth balls and dust, and then sneezed. She rubbed the back of her hand across her nose and sneezed yet again. She shook her head to stop the trend. Enough. She sniffed and scanned the room.

During childhood summers, she and Meredith had played among the trunks and toys hidden away from day to day usage. The old hobby horse on its springy frame, its brown plastic body faded and scuffed from little girl heels, the once black plastic mane showing gray. She'd spent hours riding the little horse, pretending to be a jockey in the Kentucky Derby, or a princess riding to a clandestine rendezvous with her prince. In her imagination she wore beautiful, flowing gowns and hats with gossamer veils trailing behind her galloping palomino. She'd never owned a horse or found a prince after she grew up, but she had worn the beautiful gowns and pretty hats.

Meredith's dreams had become reality, her desire to build beautiful buildings reaching back to her childhood. Their dad had helped her replicate Twin Oaks as an immense dollhouse. Paulette spied the gorgeous miniature plantation house situated against the far wall. Meredith had taken the time to clean it properly since they rediscovered it, removing the layer of dust and grime gathered during decades of neglect. Tiny window panes gleamed in the shadows of the front porch with its four white columns. An echo of jealousy stemming from Meredith consuming all of their dad's time one long ago summer reverberated in her mind. She couldn't change the past and erase the hurt brought about by being left alone and lonely, but she could begin to forge a stronger sisterly bond. The lyrics to "Love Can Build a Bridge" echoed in her mind although the tune eluded her.

Paulette's attention fixed upon a black, flat-topped trunk with silver hinges and hasp. It hunkered in front of the mannequin as though daring her to approach. She straightened her back, one hand automatically shielding her baby, and made her way across the room until she stopped before the ebony container. She shook off her reluctance to touch it, since she needed to move it to reach the dummy.

Grasping the handles, she pulled, but it didn't budge. She tugged again but barely succeeded in shifting it an inch. What weighed so much in such a small trunk? Leaning down, she slowly raised the hasp and then the lid until the meager illumination in the room enabled her to peek inside.

She lifted a packet of newspapers tied together with a satin ribbon. Peering closer, she determined they dated from the 1940s. Not ancient, after all. Not like the letters and journals from the mid-1800s found in other trunks. Still, old enough. Beneath the papers, a large maroon leather book nestled among men's suits and trousers. She spotted an aged white cravat and matching formal shirt, fingering the silky material with delight. Silks and satins speared delight through her soul. Their textures and sounds blended into a symphony of pleasure. She grabbed the heavy book and hauled it from its nesting place, intent on reaching the luxurious fabrics.

The leather warmed in her hands as she focused on the decadent silk cravat. Searching for a safe place to deposit the book among the dusty boxes and trunks, her fingers tingled then began to burn as though touching a flame. *Ouch.* She jerked her hands apart then tried to catch the book before it dropped from her hands. When it collided with the hardwood floor, it fell open, its pages fluttering before settling on an illuminated text. The ornate drawing of a great horned owl poised to strike, beak open, talons ready to snare its prey, curled around fancy script words. She peered at the sheet, reluctant to touch the page after the previous singeing of her fingers, but curious as to the mysterious message. She read the poem silently, and then sounded it out loud, pondering the meaning.

"Before the father came the father.

"Return the one gone before.

"To recall the forgotten

"Bring home the forlorn.

"Restore the bygone to the present.

"This I ask and nothing more."

"How strange." She gingerly reached to retrieve the book and restore it to its proper place.

With a roar of wind, the door banged shut behind her, startling a gasp from her compressed lips. The pages fluttered and whipped. The packet of newspapers soared into the air, its ribbon loosening before falling off in the chaos, allowing the sheets to fly around like crazed paper airplanes. Her jaw dropped open, a gasp followed by a woman keening in fear. Her voice. *Stop it. Get a grip*. She swallowed the growing terror. She whirled around, practically spinning like a ceiling fan on high as she tried to determine what caused the wind careening about the room. An eerie whine preceded what sounded like a wolf howling to the moon. She gulped, alarm sizzling down her spine. Grizabella arched her back, and hissed at the commotion, ears flat, tail pointed to the ceiling. Paulette exhaled, her breath visible in the chilled room. She crossed her arms both to warm them and to protect her child.

Quiet fell along with the papers settling like oversized snowflakes. She blinked three times, trying to erase the sight before her. But blinking didn't work. She gaped at the tall, gray-bearded man in his impeccable suit and angled fedora. Gray highlighted his close-cropped black hair and matched his friendly eyes. He seemed vaguely familiar, yet she had never met him. Of that, she was certain. She'd remember him.

"What a surprise." He reached toward her, palms up. "How can I help you, my dear?"

"Stay there." She held out a hand, palm facing him, and backed up until her legs bumped against the open trunk.

Trapped, she had no escape but to move past the man. Or apparition. Or whatever. She swallowed the fear threatening to make itself known. Perhaps she should yell for Meredith. She would know what to do with this specter. So much for the ghosts of Twin Oaks resting peacefully. If only she'd never realized she could interact with spirits.

"Paulette, my precious, you needn't fear your own grandfather." He moved toward her, reaching for her.

"No." Shaking her head, she held up both hands indicating for him to stay back. Then motioned for him to leave, shooing him as if he could fly away. Or dissolve into thin air. Which, of course, he probably could. "Whoever you are, you don't belong here. Go away."

Grizabella growled and hissed from her spot near the wall. Hairs along her spine stood straight, revealing the depth of her dislike of the man's presence.

"I was content where I was."

"Then why did you come here? Wh-what do you want?" Paulette shivered and wrapped her arms about her waist to still their trembling. The move left her feeling more vulnerable by removing the sense of a barrier between her and the apparition.

He tilted his head and smiled, dropping one hand to his side. "More to the point, what do you want? *You* summoned *me*."

"If I did, it was an accident." He must understand she had not meant to bring him from wherever he'd come from. Why did crap like this happen to her? Nothing in her life ever transpired as she intended. "Please, you must leave. You don't belong here."

"Now, that's not true. I belong here more than you do. So let's get acquainted, shall we? Then you can tell me why you called for me."

When he started toward her, she screamed, her hands shielding her baby.

Meredith opened the back door as Meg crossed the yard

from the caretaker's cottage. Cool air, scented with dried leaves, wove into the room behind her. The elder woman's muscular physique bespoke of the many years of domestic labor she'd engaged in. Her salt-and-pepper hair lay in curls around her heart-shaped face. Meredith leaned in the frame, noting a slight limp as the housekeeper approached. "You okay?"

She nodded twice. "I'm gettin' by." She passed Meredith and walked inside the kitchen. "Old age, is all."

Meredith snicked the door closed, its easy operation a significant improvement over the old broken one. After all the damage caused by the low-grade tornado—if a tornado of any kind could be classified as such—Max had finally replaced the ancient screened door as promised. She'd helped him install the new one, after ensuring the design complemented the exterior elevation of the back of the building. The style also fit with the overall atmosphere of the historic house. Max's appreciation for the subtleties of the architecture made her love him all the more.

Other work remained, such as repairing the rotten boards along the stone foundation, refinishing the front hall floor where tree limbs gouged into the old wood, and replacing the missing bricks in the front steps. She might even arrange to straighten the headstones in the family cemetery. She strode to the coffee pot and poured the fragrant liquid into a mug and then turned to lean against the counter. "I have news."

"Oh?" Meg didn't pause but buckled down to her chores, swiping dirty dishes into the washer with an efficiency born of long practice.

"We're having a Halloween party in a couple weeks." The thought sent apprehension wiggling in her veins. All the friends and family. Maybe even some strangers. Would they ask questions about the rumors of a haunting? Or would she be forced to endure conversations about the weather or small town happenings? Either way, the idea made her uncomfortable. But Paulette thrived on people and fun, and Meredith didn't want to prevent her from enjoying either. After the baby came, who knew how long it would be before Paulette ventured out and about again. No matter how personally difficult entertaining may be, her sister's desires counted. She wrapped her long fingers around the mug, its warmth easing the chill in her hands.

She'd invite Max, of course. The thought cheered her. She hadn't seen him in days. She longed for his return, missing him more than she'd imagined. But he'd succeeded in wiggling past her defenses in the spring, and by Christmas they'd be married. An event she procrastinated planning for so far. Paulette planned to design a wedding dress, but she hadn't spoken to her about it yet. She'd have to choose something to wear and probably soon. She and Max would have to decide on costumes for the party, too. Maybe Antony and Cleopatra? Or George and Martha Washington? Or perhaps they'd go the reenactor route.

Meg grinned as she ran a soapy cloth across the countertops. "Wonderful. Twin Oaks needs some spirit to liven up the place. What can I do?"

As long as the *spirit* remained figurative and not reality. "Paulette is planning a huge affair, thus most every room will be involved. It'll be a special weekend and we'll offer a special getaway package, so I imagine we'll be full up. I'll help you shine the house for the occasion. Since our decision to throw a party came about only last evening, I'm not sure what refreshments we'll serve." Another decision to make. Great.

"You focus on the food, and I'll handle the cleaning. I may tap my daughter to lend a hand, make the work speed by, if you don't mind."

Meredith nodded, opened her mouth to reply, but a

scream reverberated through the house, replacing her thoughts about the party with one other. "Paulette!"

Meredith raced through the kitchen door, down the hall, up two flights of stairs, and skidded to a stop inside the attic. The sight before her froze her blood and stole her breath. Meg pounded up the stairs behind her, shoving into her when she flew through the doorway. Meredith regained her balance and darted a glance first at Paulette, then to the strange man occupying the darker corner of the room.

"Are you okay?" Meredith asked, stepping farther into the room.

Paulette nodded, her hands guarding her unborn child. Her eyes grew wider. "I appear to have called our grandfather. Accidentally."

The tall man turned to smile at Meredith. "Little Meredith, it's wonderful to finally meet you after all these years."

Damn. Not again. Meredith crossed her arms, erecting a defensive wall surrounding her emotions. She wished Max stood beside her instead of Meg, but he had urgent business in Atlanta and wouldn't return for days. Unless she called him, but she wouldn't do anything to interfere with his work. And honestly, his talents didn't include ghost hunting.

She studied the man. Although his hair was touched with gray, he bore no wrinkles. He appeared to be much younger than she first thought. "If you're our grandfather, you must realize you died long before either of us were born. So what brings you here?"

"Your sister called for me." He glanced at Paulette and then back to Meredith. "Ask her why I'm here."

Meredith addressed Paulette. "Any ideas?"

Paulette pointed to the maroon book lying on the floor in front of the open trunk. "I simply read a poem."

"What?" Meg emerged from behind Meredith, though she clutched Meredith's arm in one icy hand. "Or, rather, *who* are you talking to?"

Meredith noted the woman's expression, terror held at bay for the moment. Fear thrilled down Meredith's arms and into her core. The ability to not only see but also interact with ghosts required some adjustments in her expectations. Indeed, she thought Grace and Joe would be a one-time experience. But apparently that idea proved a fallacy. The current situation confirmed that she, as well as Paulette, could also converse with them. "You don't see him?"

Meg shook her head. Her hand trembled, knuckles pale, on Meredith's arm. The woman risked a heart attack merely standing in the same room with the specter.

She covered Meg's fingers with one hand. "It's okay. Why don't you go make some fresh coffee?" She pried Meg's grip loose and gently shooed her through the door, closing it firmly behind her. Turning back to assess the situation, she studied her grandfather.

"I assume you're our grandfather who died in some scientific experiment accident back in the nineteen-forties. Grandma Mary made a note of your death in her research but nothing more about your death." Meredith strode to Paulette, standing by her physically and emotionally.

"Patrick O'Connell, at your service." He folded his arms, watching the two women with eyes the color of a battleship. "A failed experiment to be sure caused my death. Too soon. I missed so much."

Meredith shifted her weight to her left hip and stared at the man. No matter what else, they had to find a way to send him back to wherever he came from. They didn't need another ghost in the house to confirm the rumors swirling about Roseville. "Why are you here?"

"Good question." Patrick shoved his hands into his

trouser pockets. "There I was minding my own business, enjoying a leisurely chat with my lovely Mary, and suddenly my granddaughter summons me, apparently because she needs something from me." He pulled his hands from their hiding places and splayed them in a questioning gesture. "You tell me why."

"I didn't do it on purpose." Paulette pointed to the book. "I merely read a line or two, or maybe six, from a page."

"I see you found my book of secrets. You must have read one of my spells, which explains the how, but not the why." Patrick grinned, revealing a gold-capped tooth.

"Spells?" Paulette shuddered. "But it rhymed like a verse in a song. I didn't know. Oh God, what do we do now?"

Meredith gaped at her. Leave it to her to cause more trouble. "You conjured him. You'll have to send him back. He doesn't belong here."

"How do I do that?" Paulette shot a worried glance at Patrick.

Meredith rocked her head side to side. "No idea. But you'll need to figure it out."

"In the meantime," Patrick said, shrugging, "I think I'll take a stroll about the place to see how you've been caring for my house." Patrick headed toward the door, but paused when Meredith raised a hand to stop him.

"Keep in mind it's our house now." Meredith fixed him with a challenging glare. No way would she let him assume control of her property. She'd fought too hard to claim it as hers. "Don't be thinking you still own Twin Oaks."

"Granted. But Twin Oaks still owns a part of me." He walked, or rather floated, to the door and passed through it.

"Great. Just great." Meredith peered at Paulette's white face. "What have you gotten us into?"

"I have no freakin' idea, but we have to go after him." Paulette strode to the door and yanked it open. "Coming?"

"Yes, if only to save Meg from heart failure."

A high-pitched scream floated up the staircase.

"Too late. You better skedaddle." Paulette waved Meredith through the door.

Meredith raced back down the stairs, sliding to a stop at the wide doorway to the double parlor. Meg blocked her entrance, one hand at her throat trying to quell her evident panic as she pointed to where Patrick reclined in the overstuffed chair by the fireplace. He held a pipe as though enjoying an after-dinner smoke, sans tobacco in the pipe's bowl.

"He's there, isn't he?" Meg whispered as though she didn't want him to hear her. "There, where the seat of the chair is depressed? With that old curved pipe floating in midair?"

"Yes, Meg. It's okay." Meredith grasped her arm and pulled her around to look at her. "He won't hurt you, or us. I promise."

Meg shook her head, concern evident in her pinched mouth. "You can't know that."

"Paulette apparently read a…a poem out loud without realizing what might happen." Meredith studied Meg's expression for a moment. "Did you know our grandpa, perchance? Mary's husband? Patrick O'Connell?"

Meg's curls bounced about her ears as she vigorously shook her head. "No, he died long before I started working for Mary."

"He's said he won't hurt us, but you're right." She contemplated Patrick as he in turn listened to their discussion. "As long as he's in the house, we must remain vigilant."

Paulette joined them, easing down the last step and peeking into the parlor. Patrick waved at her, smirking around the pipe stem. "And keep him away from our guests."

"Right. We can't let anyone know Twin Oaks is haunted. They'll think we're crazy."

"And end any chance of furthering my business." Paulette wrapped her arms around her waist. "Now what do we do?"

Meredith snorted a sigh. "That's a *damn* good question."

Chapter Three

*P*aulette eased behind the steering wheel of her little white Ford Focus. If her belly grew any bigger, she'd have to trade in her favorite vehicle because she wouldn't fit. Or be stuck at home, waiting for Meredith to take her places. She shifted into drive and jammed down on the accelerator until the tires spun on gravel. Flinching at the sound, she eased off the gas, drove down the driveway and out onto the highway, heading for Roseville. The tune to Bob Dylan's "On the Road Again" echoed in her mind. First, she must explore ways to reverse a conjuring spell. If Grandpa wouldn't cooperate, then she'd have to take matters into her own hands. Poor Meg refused to enter the parlor without either Meredith or Paulette to escort her, which of course meant a disruption to their day. At least their guests had no clue Patrick had arrived, and she planned to keep it that way.

The Golden Owl Books and Brews boasted an impressive collection of tomes on witchcraft and wizardry. She'd noticed the section when searching for the local history books earlier in the year. Surely the three sisters who ran the place could help her find answers. Although, the last time she'd shopped there with Meredith, they'd hesitated to wait on them. It had been odd, really. The three women had looked askance at them, wary and watchful.

She parked the car and pried herself out of it. Locking the door, she crossed the sidewalk. The baby elbowed her, and she briefly rested a hand on her belly. Less than two months until her child would be in her arms and the seeming volleyball she wore under her maternity top began deflating. Then, serious weight training could be incorporated into her routine again. Maybe she'd try Zumba or kickboxing. Sounded like a good plan. After she had her baby and cleared the house of ghosts. Or no, reverse that. First, the ghost.

The little bell jangled above the door to announce her arrival. She spotted the sisters working in different parts of the store. While not quite triplets, they bore a strong resemblance to one another. Slender with two sporting varying shades of brunette hair and the other a tawny blonde, no one would accuse them of being strangers. Three pairs of eyes noted her entrance and then turned away. Why? What made them so reticent toward her? Still, she needed answers.

She strode through the store, mindful of her balance, and slowly climbed the spiral staircase to the second floor where the books on mysticism and magic waited. It was bad enough she could see ghosts, now she sought a way to use magic to rid the plantation of her grandfather's presence. Life sure had taken some strange twists.

The nape of her neck tingled. She shrugged the sensation away and kept moving. Glancing over her shoulder, she noticed the tallest of the sisters watching her. She gave her a smile and was heartened by its return. Maybe with some time the suspicion between them would dissolve.

She moved on through the stacks, scanning the titles on the spines of hundreds of books. *Ghost Busting for Beginners. A*

Historiography of Spirits and Ghosts. Spectral Contacts and Solutions Through the Ages. She'd never realized how many volumes existed on ghosts and spirits. Such a variety of approaches, ways to analyze or apply techniques and the belief systems behind all of it.

Slipping a candidate from a shelf, she perused its table of contents, and then put it back. She chose another, then another. Lots of information had been written about the history of hauntings and ghosts. Very little apparently on how to help them find peace. Or more specifically, how to reverse a spell's results.

"Need some help?"

Paulette looked up from the book in her hands to see the tall brunette sister; the one who had smiled at her earlier. The younger woman regarded her with curious hazel eyes beneath pencil brows. Up close, Paulette detected blonde strands mixed with the luxurious milk chocolate hair pulled up in a banana clip. Her black polo sported the store's owl emblem embroidered over the left breast. She wore creamy slacks and comfortable shoes. Very practical attire for working in a bookstore. Paulette considered her own decadent flowery maternity blouse over stretchy black corduroys and matching pumps. By comparison, she was overdressed. Her fun, dangly earrings seemed like overkill.

"I can't find what I need."

"Maybe I can help. I'm Roxie." The woman stuck out a hand, and they shook.

"Paulette. Glad to finally meet you." She motioned to the rows of colorfully bound books, a rainbow of covers. Faced with having to state her mission, she cringed. What would Roxie think of her desire to learn magic? If the townspeople learned of her need, she'd be ostracized, shunned. Nothing more than the spinster sister. Johnny had once meant the world to her, but he left her with nothing but a broken heart. A kick reminded her of the other thing Johnny had given her. She laid a hand on her belly. She'd always have her child. But apparently it fell to her to rid Twin Oaks of a certain ghost for everyone's peace of mind. "I'm not sure how to explain what I'm even searching for."

"Start with the general topic and we'll take it from there." Roxie shrugged. "You know that much, right?"

"Sort of." Paulette read the signs posted on top of the many rows of books. History. Self-help. Mysticism. None suggested instruction on how to use spells effectively. She peered at Roxie. "I need to know everything about magic. Um…and spells and stuff. For…a, um, a party we're throwing at Twin Oaks."

Roxie grinned and pointed at the Mysticism section. "You're in the right place. See?"

Paulette moved closer to the shelf Roxie indicated. "Well, my problem is these all discuss the history and beliefs. I need—or rather my, uh, *friend* needs to figure out how to reverse a spell—"

"A friend?" Roxie folded her arms across her chest and lifted one brow. "Does your *friend* realize how dangerous incantations can be?"

Indeed, Paulette understood firsthand the dangers of tinkering with magic. She had a ghostly grandfather hanging around to prove it too.

"Yes. It's necessary though." She glanced around the large room, relieved no one lingered in the vicinity who could eavesdrop on their conversation. "Can you help?"

Roxie studied her for the span of two deep breaths. "Can I trust you?"

That wasn't what she expected to hear. Surprised, she chuckled then sobered. "I need a book. Or a witch, if you know one."

Roxie raised both brows, her gaze intensifying. "I do."

Again, not what she expected to hear. Paulette blinked

twice and smiled, a chill inching through her. She swallowed and drew a long breath. "In Roseville?"

"Of course. Where did you think?" Roxie laughed, her smile wide and teeth reflecting the overhead lights.

She hadn't known a witch lived in such a quiet town. How could she? She'd been too busy with the ghosts. But she supposed they kinda went together. Given she had summoned her grandfather using a spell, after all. And why she came looking for guidance on how to clear the house of the specter. He needed to rest in peace, or at least go away. She'd rather he be content, given he was her grandpa. Maybe he'd go back and be with grandma, happy and peaceful for all eternity. A good thought.

Paulette glanced around the room, spotted an elderly woman wending her way through the stacks and rows of books. She peered at Roxie and whispered, "Can you tell me who the witch is?"

"The kind you need would depend." Roxie marched to a different aisle of books, one closer to the balcony railing. "Let me show you something that might give you the answers you seek."

Paulette trailed after the woman, aware customers below could see but not hear them. Why bring up the subject, then refuse to answer the question? Roxie stopped in front of books on witchcraft. She glided a finger over the spines, landing on a small, black book with script lettering. She slipped the tiny volume from its home and handed it to Paulette with a little flourish.

Basic Witchcraft by Peggy Golden. On the cover, the familiar owl, featured on the sign hanging outside, perched on an open book with a single lit candle next to it. She opened the cover and looked up at Roxie. "What's this?"

"A beginner's manual, of sorts."

She opened it to the table of contents, several intriguing chapters beckoning her. She definitely qualified as a newbie when it came to spells and spirits. She spotted a chapter titled "Spellcrafting" and flipped to it. Pleased to find sections for writing, preparing, and casting spells. Yes, the book would help. "Thanks. You knew right where to find what I need. Do you have the inventory memorized?"

Roxie chuckled. "No. But that book is special to me and my sisters since our mother wrote it."

Paulette looked at the author's name again. "So that's why the store's called the Golden Owl? Your last name?"

Nodding, Roxie started toward the staircase. "I have to get back to work. Feel free to look around."

"Right." Several other titles had piqued her curiosity. "I'll linger here a bit and see what I find."

"Great." Roxie turned back and smiled at Paulette. "You're not as bad as we thought. I hope you'll come back again."

"I'm sure I will. Thanks." Wonderful. Paulette looked over the railing, half expecting the other two sisters to have gathered below as an audience. She'd developed a reputation as the bad sister. Figured. All her life she'd been misunderstood, left to her own devices to struggle through as best she could. Somehow her personality made others uncomfortable. She'd have to work on being nicer.

The little bell jangled, drawing her attention to the entrance. *Oh. My. Goodness.* She heard in her mind The Weather Girls singing "It's Raining Men" as she stared from her place at the railing. A tall, dark-haired, gorgeous man in black jeans and a tan pullover sweater that accentuated his skin coloring strode into the store, paused to allow another strikingly handsome man to pass through, and closed the door. Her pulse tattooed a rhythm in her ears as she sharply inhaled. What a hunk. Both of them, for that matter. Hunk number one scanned the first floor in one blazing pass, and then lifted his gaze to spear Paulette's appreciative stare. She'd never seen a man with such an arresting appearance, despite the bruise on his forehead. Striking gray eyes met hers, high strong cheekbones and a jaw framed by black hair. Wide muscular shoulders tapered to an abdomen she'd bet good money boasted a washer board of muscles. His heavy brows raised as he did the guy-onceover and then turned to his buddy.

Her earlier buoyancy deflated a smidge, but she smiled at Roxie. "Looks like you have customers."

"Cool." Roxie glanced at the men, curiosity infusing her expression, and started toward the first floor. "Very handsome customers too. I'll talk to you later."

"Right. I see you have your priorities." Paulette's chuckle died away as she tracked Roxie's progress down the steps. She kept one hand resting on the rail, leaning over so she could follow the woman until Roxie reached the two strangers. After a brief exchange, she led the men toward the back of the store. The dreamy one who'd so blatantly assessed her earlier appeared to be about her own age. If she weren't about to have a baby, she'd try to make his acquaintance. As things stood, however, she wouldn't burden any man with another man's child. Doing so seemed too desperate to contemplate. Because she couldn't allow herself to be involved with anyone. At least, not under the current circumstances.

When the threesome passed the base of the spiral staircase, dreamy glanced up and winked at her. Startled, she jerked back and spun away, heart racing. *Damn.*

Trying to focus on the task at hand, Zak shrugged off the startled lioness gaze of the woman who'd been staring at him from the upper floor. He couldn't help but appreciate her beauty accentuated by blonde hair draped about her shoulders. She could be Jennifer Anniston's twin except for those memorable golden eyes. If he and Grant stayed in town long enough, perhaps he'd have a chance to become acquainted with her. Really well. But he'd taken a leave of absence from teaching so he could try to help his brother. The first step involved figuring out how the symbol in the alchemist's journal correlated to the sign outside of the store. What did it mean?

Maybe the staff might know. What was her name? Ronnie? No. Rhonda? Shit. Roxie? Yes, that's it. "I'm curious, Roxie. Why is the store called the Golden Owl?" Zak trailed after the vivacious, yet cautious, young woman leading them through the aisles to the rear of the store.

"Thank my mother, who opened the store twenty years ago." She stopped in front of a section on local geology and nature conservation. "Our last name is Golden, and she loved owls. Seemed like a good name."

"It's an interesting symbol, the owl and crossed branches." He studied her lack of reaction. Was she clueless or evasive? Only one way to find out. "Do you know its significance?"

She shook her head. "Mom never mentioned it."

"And is she around? Could we ask her?"

Roxie pursed her lips and shook her head. "Not unless you're a medium."

He frowned as he considered the mysterious smile she directed his way. "Why?"

"She died three years ago, so that's the only way to contact her."

Damn. He glanced at Grant, who frowned back at him. Reminding him about his brother's disbelief in all mystical aspects of their adventure. He really hadn't wanted to accompany him, protesting at every juncture, but Zak had insisted. After all, Grant had suggested he make the road trip. Not that Zak fought the idea very long or hard. He needed his brother's expertise in geology and soil composition to understand what was going on and how to capitalize on it. The trip also provided a chance to spend more time with him, in case… No, he wouldn't think about what would happen if the doctors' drugs or Zak's admittedly desperate Hail Mary failed. He scanned the titles of the books nearby but didn't have a clue where to start.

He raised a brow at his brother and pointed to the shelf. "So?"

Grant shook his head, then rubbed his temple with two fingers, before he finally considered the array of spines in front of them. "This is absurd."

"I'll leave you to it," Roxie said as she sashayed away. "Yell if you need anything."

Her departure entertained him for a moment before he turned back to address his brother. "What are you looking for?"

Grant ran a blunt nailed finger across the row of books, finally grabbing one then another. He shoved them at Zak. "Buy these. They'll get us started so we can go home. God, I can't believe you."

"What can't you believe?" Zak perused the books in his hands. *Analysis of the Soils of Tennessee* and *Mineral Analysis Techniques*. Although a chemist, Zak detested reading such dry materials. "I can't believe you'd volunteer to read this stuff."

"I'm not. You are." Grant crossed his arms over his weight-lifter chest.

"I don't think so. Why do you think you're here, bro? To act as my bodyguard?" The two of them had egged each other on for years to develop their strength. No weak scientists permitted in their family.

"Why, what'll you be doing?" Grant cocked his head and frowned at him when Zak glanced back to the staircase. "Don't even think about it."

"About what?" Was the beautiful blonde still upstairs?

Maybe he should go investigate whether she had any interest in him. It had been too long since he'd found a woman who intrigued him. He'd focused on his students and his research for months without taking up any of the many offers thrown his way by fellow female professors or even the occasional flirtatious student. He scanned the upper floor, what he could see of it, then dropped his attention back to his brother's annoyed countenance. Zak waited for his brother's response, anticipating what would spew from his mouth.

He didn't have to wait long.

"You son-of-a-bitch." Grant propped massive fists on his hips, leaned forward and stared at Zak. "You're not going to chase some skirt while I do your dirty work. I don't even believe in this alchemy crap and you want me to waste my vacation digging into some mystical bullshit."

Zak guffawed and slapped his brother on the shoulder. "Come on, bro, I wouldn't do that to you. I need your help or I wouldn't have dragged you along."

Grant relaxed his stance, his fists opening. "You wouldn't come here without my insistence. You would have stayed home and researched on the web instead. I just didn't expect you'd make me ride shotgun."

Zak shrugged. "If I had a home to work in, sure. But with the extent of the renovations needed to rebuild after I blew it up, your suggestion to come investigate and let the contractors do their jobs seemed logical. Dad's in his element, overseeing their work. And it was long past time for us to go on a road trip."

Grant exhaled, a long heartfelt sigh, as he raked a hand through his hair then pressed his temple. "You're right. Let's go buy these and find a place to stay. Besides, my head hurts and I'm tired and hungry." Grant trudged toward the front.

"And grumpy." Zak followed him, finally plopping the

books on the counter as Roxie approached from a back room. "We'll take these."

"Right." She lifted a book and perused the title. "A little light reading, I see. You're new in town, aren't you?"

Zak nodded and indicated the man beside him. "I'm Zak Markel, and this is my brother, Grant."

They shook hands and eyed each other. Roxie kept strangers at a distance, apparently. Her scrutiny, though friendly, still reflected distrust.

"We just got into town," Grant said. "Can you recommend a good place to stay for a few days?"

"Or weeks?" Zak added. Grant's quick glance made him chuckle.

Roxie scanned the books and totaled their cost. Zak handed her a plastic card and she swiped it, completing the sale without speaking. Finally, she looked at Grant and smiled. "There's no hotel, if that's what you're asking. But we do have a couple of B&Bs."

"Which would you recommend?" Zak asked. "We're not picky."

"Speak for yourself." Grant shifted his weight and thumped a hand onto the counter. "If we're going to be here awhile, we should at least be comfortable."

"The one here in town is nice, but a bit old and rundown." Roxie considered him for a heartbeat. She snapped her fingers and grinned at him. "But if you have discerning tastes, I'd suggest you try the new one, the Twin Oaks Plantation. I hear it's lovely and very interesting."

"Is it a real plantation?" Zak didn't usually go for antique-laden historic homes, preferring newer amenities and cleaner lines to the furniture. The older styles seemed too frilly and effeminate for his tastes. All the gingerbread decorations and curlicues carved onto the legs seemed a waste of effort to his mind.

She reached for a pamphlet tucked into a Lucite box on

the counter. She handed him the glossy paper, pointing out the map on the back. "The lady I was helping when you came in is one of the owners."

"The blonde?" Zak glanced up to where he'd last seen the woman, but she'd vanished. Disappointment swept through him. He shifted his attention back to Roxie, startled by the laughter in her eyes.

"Yes, the very *unmarried* blonde, from what I'm told." Roxie grinned and quirked her brows.

"Are you kidding me?" Grant huffed.

Hope sparked at her revelation. Zak grinned at his brother's disgust. "Sounds perfect. Let's go."

Roseville exemplified small towns across the country. Sturdy brick courthouse on the square, surrounded by ancient buildings housing clothing and antiques stores. A rundown theater long past its glory days. Ubiquitous flowering pear trees, notorious for their shallow roots and pungent scent, dotted the sidewalks to provide shade for the people hurrying by. Typical small town atmosphere, but for the first time ever, Zak didn't feel out of place, an alien among friends. Almost as though he'd returned home after a long journey. Strange.

Zak slid a key into the lock on his Prius and opened the door. Grant tapped his fist on the roof from the passenger side, impatient with Zak's insistence on not using a remote control. Tough. No way would he risk having someone swipe the code and use it to access his property. His research and equipment provided tempting targets for thieves. Why make it easier for them? He pushed the unlock button on the armrest inside the door then swung into the seat.

Grant flopped down beside him and slammed the passenger door. "You're unbelievable."

Starting the engine gave Zak time to formulate a response. One he hoped would not antagonize further. He understood why his brother acted uncharacteristically short-tempered. The prospect of losing his sight loomed like a dark cloud on the horizon ready to take away the light of day. How could he continue in his career if he couldn't see to analyze the strata or rocks or whatever? Grim determination to do all in his power steeled Zak. His mission was to find a cure for his brother. After he located one, no matter how or what, then he'd go back to his normal routine and not a single second before. He pulled out of the parking space and drove through town. They passed a hardware store, several law offices, and the local bank before Zak tossed a glance at Grant.

"Relax. It's a nice enough town to spend some time in." Zak studied the map while waiting for the traffic light to change from red to green.

"It's not the town I'm worried about." Grant dragged a hand through his hair. "First you want to recreate some ancient formula for the Fountain of Youth or some such rot. Next you rope me into this fool's journey because you say you need my expertise. Then you try to push the project onto me so you can chase some blonde."

"Elixir of Life. I have to try, right? And I'm not chasing anyone." Zak stared through the windshield at the changing scenery as he left the town behind. Immense fields of corn stalk stubble reaching to the distance. Towering silos guarded the cropland, probably filled to the brim with the harvest corn. Other fields sported cutoff soy bean stems or cotton stalks, small wisps of white littering the rows of short sticks.

"Right. That's why we're driving way out of town to find a room when we want to be in town." Grant shook his head and stared out the window.

"I thought you liked history and old homes and stuff."

He turned onto the highway and sped up. The sooner they reached Twin Oaks the better. Many questions circled in his mind, most centering on details of the beautiful woman. While Grant did his thing, Zak planned to explore other avenues of interest.

"Where'd you get that idea?" Grant cut him a look, his frown revealing his annoyance.

"I don't know. Maybe I dreamed it. But it could be interesting to stay in an historic property."

Grant shook his head. "Maybe if I didn't have this sinking feeling you really want to slip into a certain woman's pants."

"No, that's not it." Zak steered with one hand, resting his left arm on the door. "She's intriguing. I wouldn't mind getting to know her."

"I hear you. I also know you." Grant tapped the fingers of his right hand on the armrest.

"So, why do you think we need a soil sample from around here somewhere?" Maybe changing the subject would ease the tension in the vehicle. Hopefully.

Grant studied him for a long moment. "Nice try."

"Come on, Grant. You know more about what's in the ground and how it relates to what I'm trying to do than anybody else. Talk to me."

His brother had been studying dirt and rocks since he was two. Combining and separating everything he came across. He'd excelled in school and in 4-H with his projects on sedimentary, igneous, and siliceous rocks and their uses. When he reached college, the practical applications for his research soon became apparent. As a result, he'd been recognized internationally, receiving a variety of awards and honors. Zak needed his input or else he'd be forced to rely solely upon disinterested specialists, scientists who would scoff at his attempt to help his brother's chances of beating the odds.

Grant released a long sigh. "I'm thinking it has to do with the acidity levels, which I hear are higher around these parts."

"It must be more than that though." In the distance, he spotted two stone pillars with lamps affixed at the top. An iron sign arched above, sporting the words Twin Oaks.

"We'll see." Grant gripped the armrest. "Just don't go all dewy eyed when we get there, okay?"

"Sure." He turned onto the long winding gravel lane edging a huge lake, rocks pinging against the undercarriage of his car. He cringed at the sound. Easing off the accelerator, he scanned the huge house as the car neared where the plantation home commanded attention. Massive trees surrounded the building, most with colorful leaves still clinging to branches reaching for the sky while some stood broken off with jagged trunks.

"Wow, looks like a tornado struck recently," Grant murmured.

"How can you tell?" Zak squinted at him as he slowed the vehicle.

"I thought you were a scientist? The twisted and broken trees are a classic indicator."

"I'm not a weatherman."

"Good thing."

Zak stopped the car at the end of the sidewalk and stepped out. He paused at the hood of the car to appreciate the architecture. A brick sidewalk led up to three matching steps. Someone obviously loved the upcoming holiday as an immense jack-o-lantern grinned at them, nestled among corn stalks and a huge spider in its web. The front porch boasted massive white columns guarding a double front door. Matching windows flanked the doorway. Georgian style architecture, if he recalled correctly. The upper floor sported a balcony over the front entrance with a row of white eight-paned windows reaching to each side. The height of the building impressed him. His own house, a brick rancher, was small and nondescript by comparison. What must it be like to live in such a place? Knowing its history and grandeur reflected a bygone era of the country he so loved?

"Get a move on." Grant motioned impatiently from where he waited beside the huge pumpkin at the top of the steps.

Happy to if it meant seeing the lovely blonde again. Zak trotted up to the wide porch, dodging several smaller pumpkins, as Grant rapped on the door and then turned to Zak.

"Behave yourself, bro." Grant shook a finger at him. "I mean it."

The door swung open and a hefty man with denim blue eyes and salt-and-pepper hair greeted them. In one hand, he held a ballpeen hammer. For defense or construction? "Can I help you?"

"We're hoping you have room for us for a few weeks."

"Ahem, make that days," Grant interjected.

"We'll see." Zak offered a hand to the man. "I'm Zak Markel and this is my brother, Grant."

"Sean Williams. I'm the caretaker of Twin Oaks." He opened the door wider, and waved them inside. "We're usually only open on weekends, but let me find Meredith. She'll be able to tell you what's available."

Sean disappeared down the hallway, leaving Zak and Grant to wait in the huge foyer. Hardwood floors and oriental carpets interspersed throughout the space. The room to the right appeared to be a small parlor. A door farther down the hall opened into another room, sunshine illuminating its interior. To their left, a large archway led into a much larger parlor complete with overstuffed wingback chairs and settees. An oversized fireplace hunkered on the far wall, flames licking an impressive pile of logs. Oil portraits, one of two young women and the other of a man in a Confederate uniform, occupied elaborate frames flanking the chimney. A large painting of a World War Two soldier hung over the mantel.

"This is some place." Grant strode to the base of the stairs leading to the upper floors.

Zak craned his neck to determine where the brown and white steps led. He could make out a second floor with doors to what he assumed would be bedrooms. He squinted and could barely make out the outlines of another staircase leading up into darkness. An attic? He laid a hand on the newel.

"What are you doing?" Grant pulled on his arm as he placed a foot on the brown tread. "You can't go up there."

Zak shrugged and removed his foot from the tread. "I think there's an attic up there. I love attics. They're so full of interesting stuff."

Footsteps interrupted their conversation. Coming down the hall was a pretty strawberry-blonde, but it wasn't the woman he sought. Behind her, a calico cat minced, tail up and twitching. The woman started talking before she reached them.

"Good afternoon. I'm Meredith Reed. I understand you're interested in a long-term stay?"

"Yes, possibly a couple weeks, depending on how my research advances. Do you have a room with two beds?"

"I do—"

"Hold on there, bro." Grant crossed his arms and shook his head. "I want my own room."

"Why? We've shared before."

"No way. I'm not staring at that mug everyday while we're here. I want my own space so I can shut you out when you annoy me."

Meredith chuckled. "In that case, I have two smaller rooms available. Naturally, you'll have to share a bathroom, since this old place can't handle very many due to the age of the septic system. Do you want to register?" She strode to a long, narrow table holding an open guest book and fancy pen in an elaborate inkwell type of holder.

"Before we do," Zak said, following her, "can you tell me if there's another lady who lives here? A blonde?"

Meredith contemplated him with arched brows. "My sister."

She waited for him to say something more but his tongue tied. He swallowed. "Is she here?"

Meredith nodded. "Do you know her?"

He shook his head. "I saw her at the bookstore earlier. The clerk, Roxie, told me she's one of the owners, but I-I didn't catch her name."

"That's because I didn't offer it."

Startled, Zak darted a glance down the hallway toward a door swinging shut. He caught a glimpse of the kitchen before focusing on the gorgeous woman sashaying toward him despite her apparent condition. He hadn't realized she carried a child. But damn she was beautiful. Typical of his luck, actually. Probably in love with the town jock from high school, and having her first baby. Roxie said she was single, but she neglected to mention the pregnancy. He inspected her left hand where she held fast to a heavy shopping bag from the Golden Owl. Not even an engagement ring, but there must be a father somewhere.

"Hi." *Idiot.* Words failed him for a moment when she stopped beside Meredith. He continued to drink in her presence like a man dying in the desert.

She grinned in return, an I've-got-your-number smile. "Hello."

The younger man shook hands with the blonde, again startling Zak into action. "You'll have to excuse my older brother. I'm Grant Markel, and this oaf is Zak."

"You found some new books, I see." Zak shook hands

with her, holding on longer than socially acceptable. But he didn't want to relinquish their connection. The jolt of something both unexpected and necessary. Not so soon. He searched her twinkling eyes. "And you are?"

"Paulette O'Connell." She shook one last time and slipped her hand free. "Yes, I noticed you two at the bookstore. What are you doing here?"

"I'll tell you what we're doing here…" Grant inhaled to continue, but Zak glared at him until he closed his mouth.

Zak peered at Paulette. "Roxie told us this was the best place to stay while we're in the area. So here we are."

"Roxie has never been out here, but it's nice to know she's helping promote our new venture." Meredith offered the pen to Grant. "Perhaps you'll do the honors while these two chat."

Grant rolled his eyes and set to work, still shaking his head while he wrote in the guest book. Zak turned his attention back to Paulette, memorizing every detail of her face. He'd never met someone so alluring and intriguing that he stopped thinking straight. Stopped breathing for long moments while he appreciated her. Stopped worrying about what to say and merely focused on her.

"What happened to your head?" Paulette asked.

"Sorry?" Zak stopped fantasizing about the taste of her kiss to focus on the words coming from her mouth.

"How did you bruise your forehead?"

"He blew up his house." Grant laughed in the background.

"Really?" Paulette blinked twice, as if gauging the validity of his statement.

"An experiment gone south." Zak shrugged, willing to say anything to keep her near.

"At least you only suffered a bruise." Paulette shifted the bag to her other hand. "If you'll excuse me, I have to pee and then have calls to make."

Meredith squinted at her, lips tensing. "Who're you calling?"

"You'll find out soon enough." Laughter danced in Paulette's eyes as she regarded Zak. "You're in luck. We're throwing a Halloween bash during your stay, so start thinking of a costume."

"We won't be here that long, right?" Grant pinned Zak with a glare. "Pay the deposit and let's settle in. The sooner we start the sooner I can go home."

Zak shrugged, distracted by Paulette's deflating glee. "You never know, we might hang around long enough to attend the party."

"It'll be fun if you do." Her lips eased upward, as though sharing a secret with him. "Welcome to Twin Oaks, gentlemen. I'll leave you in Meredith's capable hands."

With that, she hurried up the stairs and disappeared down the hallway. A door closed somewhere in the recesses, shutting him out, leaving him behind. *Damn.* He had his work cut out for him.

Chapter Four

"He's at it again." Meg stopped inside the door to the attic and glared at Meredith. "You've got to do something, or I'll never get my work done."

Meredith scanned the black trunk's contents she'd spread on the floor around it and sighed. Why had her grandfather stored a long feather, several round and smooth stones, and what looked like a rodent skeleton? All wrapped in soft cloths amid old clothing. No time to figure out the mystery with Meg's entire posture screaming for her attention. She pushed to her feet, brushing off her jeans as she considered the housekeeper's attitude. At least she no longer panicked when she spotted signs of Patrick's presence. Still, he must understand that frightening folks simply couldn't continue. Zak and Grant had retired to their rooms immediately after arriving. They'd been holed up for the past several hours. With any luck, they wouldn't even notice Patrick's activities.

"Where is he?" She'd tried to convince him before to stay out of the guest rooms, but did he listen to her? She huffed lightly at her own question. Why would he?

"The kitchen." Meg peeked over her shoulder and hugged her waist. "I can't work like this. Please, do something."

"I've tried, but until either Paulette figures out how to send him on his way or he's ready to leave, there's nothing I can do." She tugged on her ponytail, splitting the long tresses between her fingers.

"Can't you vanquish him?" Meg waved a hand in the air. "I have to finish cleaning the oven and the fridge, but I can't while he's around. Especially with all the chaos he's causing."

"Can you see him?"

"No, but the phone receiver lifts off the cradle, or the pepper is shaken onto the table. The flower vase ended up on its side, water and Sean's beautiful chrysanthemums all across the table and floor. He's making a mess, one I have to clean up. If he'd let me."

"I can't vanquish him, nonetheless. He's my grandpa, not a demon." Meredith hugged Meg, sensing the tension rigid within her. She pulled back and studied her expression. With a rueful smile, she shrugged. "I'll see what I can do."

She trudged to the first floor where Grizabella greeted her as the calico emerged from the sewing room. Meredith continued down the hallway and into the kitchen. Letting the door swing closed behind her, she surveyed the room. How could he do this? Meg had nailed it. Her grandpa had indeed left a mess behind. In addition to the pepper and flower mess, he'd apparently been practicing moving heavier objects. One chair lay on its back, the table pulled out from its normal position tucked into the alcove created by the bay window. The aerial photo of Twin Oaks hung askew.

Patrick materialized in front of the sink, leaning against the counter nonchalantly. She flinched but didn't jump at his sudden appearance. Progress, anyway.

"Grandpa, what are you doing? We talked about this." She moved into the center of the room, drawing his attention to the debris scattered across the floor. "You're scaring Meg."

"Nobody should fear my presence." He shrugged and re-crossed his ankles as he propped himself against the counter. "I'm perfectly harmless. I promise."

"Meg needs to work, and you're making her job more difficult with your shenanigans." He appeared so casual and carefree, but lines about his mouth and eyes revealed a tension he tried to hide.

He shrugged again and winked. "She's a housekeeper, so think of it as job security."

"It doesn't work that way." Meg belonged much more than her long-dead grandfather. She had worked for Grandma Mary for decades after Grandpa Patrick died, keeping the house clean and orderly as well as befriending the lonely widow. Over time, the two women had formed a deep bond, one rivaling the bond between close sisters. "While you're here, you have to play by my rules. Understood?"

"That depends on your rules, sweetheart."

All attitude. Now she understood where Paulette's came from. "Rule number one: you can't do anything to let our guests know you're here. Rule number two: you can't scare Meg and Sean away. We need them to keep this place operational."

A twinkle appeared in Patrick's eyes. "But it's fun. You wouldn't deprive me of a little fun after all these years, now would you?"

Meredith propped both fists on her hips. "If it means our guests run screaming from the house and any chance of Paulette's new business folding as a result, then yes."

Patrick chuckled. "You do have an imagination, don't you?"

"Grandpa, please. Just stay out of sight and stop making a mess. That's all I ask."

"Not to change the subject, but who's the dad to Paulette's baby?"

Startled, Meredith blinked at her grandfather. "It doesn't matter. He skedaddled when she told him."

"Gentlemen would never behave so."

"Exactly."

"Her child will be like us, you know. Uniquely talented." He smiled and crossed his arms. "Are you prepared for all that is about to happen?"

Of course not. Who could be when you have no idea what the future holds? "I'm as prepared as possible. What do you expect to occur?"

"Since you and Paulette have embraced your abilities to converse with spirits, you've opened a channel. Others may want to tap into your talents."

"Others? Like who?" Did he mean the ghosts of other relatives? A shudder wracked her spine. She crossed her arms to quell the tremor. What would they want from her? The vision of a line of sad and needy people stretching through the house, maybe even out on the lawn, floated in her mind. Nobody would want to stay in a haunted plantation house. Nobody.

"Friends, family, strangers too." He shrugged and drifted to the cellar door. "Anyone who lost someone they need to reach."

"I'm not a medium though," Meredith said.

"Are you so sure?" Patrick glanced at her and at the mess he'd made. He grimaced and took several steps toward her. "Sorry. I keep forgetting I'm dead. It all seems so real to be back home again after all the years away. But honestly, I must remember material goods don't mean as much as they used to."

His expression revealed the truth of his statement. After he died, all his belongings, his treasures, became someone else's. Did he miss owning things? Would she? After she died, could she care? Her tools eventually would be discarded, donated, or employed by other hands. Her possessions, so full of practical use or sentimental value, would end up judged by her surviving family to determine their worth and thus their future. Such a random thought.

Meredith cocked her head and grinned at him. "You're quite the philosopher, aren't you? I wish we'd had a chance to know each other while you were still alive."

He returned the smile. "Me, too. You seem to be a lot like me in many ways."

"Paulette is even more like you. And she's working on figuring out a way to send you back from whence you came. We won't have much time to share."

His grin grew into a smile. "I'll be here longer than you think. Paulette is the only one who can send me home, since she summoned me. Until she determines what need of hers cried out to me, she'll have no idea of what to do. I'm not ready to reveal the required step until she admits to herself what is missing in her life." He folded his arms and rocked on his heels. "Solving that little mystery should take a while, so we should have lots of time."

"You know how she could send you back?" Meredith's jaw dropped open. If he'd only go away so she could focus on the Bancroft project, prepare for the baby's arrival, and the party. Oh, and maybe even her wedding. With him smirking at her and pulling pranks, chaos ruled the day. "Why won't you tell her?"

"Because, sweetheart, she needs me."

"Then talk to her." She marched toward him, shaking her forefinger at him. "You can't stay here forever causing mischief."

"My dear, that's no way to speak to me." His expression revealed his mirth. "I'll just leave you to tidy up while I take a nap." He winked. "Or something."

"Oh, no you don't!" She grabbed for him automatically,

but he vanished. His laugh echoed around her for several moments before dying away. "Damn! Not even a goodbye." Meredith surveyed the empty, abused kitchen. At least now the cleanup could begin. "Meg! The coast is clear!"

The hall door swung open and Meg hesitantly stepped into the room followed by Grizabella. Meg paused and gauged the minor destruction Patrick had left behind. "He's gone?"

"For the moment. You're right about him making a disaster here." Anger and confusion warred inside with a hint of worry. Who knew what he'd do next. All her hopes and plans put at risk because of Paulette's stupidity. Maybe she shouldn't have let her move in, not that her sister gave her much choice. The old animosity flashed through her core and then thankfully fled. They'd put the past behind them. Going forward, she hoped they could restore the friendship they had once shared. With the baby due soon, no way could Meredith have pushed her away. Family first. She crossed to shove the table back into its nook, righted the chair, and returned it to its place at the table.

"I hope he stays away. If he knows I'm in here, he'll probably pop back in for the joy of watching me jump." Meg tiptoed to the sink, wetted the dishcloth, and then, with furtive glances around the room, crossed to the table. She wiped off the surface, returned to the sink to rinse out the cloth, and then went back to kneel down to wipe up the floor.

"I've asked him to avoid scaring anyone, but I can't control him either." Honestly, she wished she could. It was one thing to scare Meg and Sean, and even Paulette, but quite another for him to threaten Paulette's livelihood by frightening their business away. As he grew more capable of moving inanimate objects, the risk increased of him scaring others. "Good thing only Paulette and I can see him.

Otherwise, this whole situation could spin badly out of control."

A fire crackled in the immense marble fireplace, the aromas of pine and hickory filling Zak's nostrils until he thought he'd gag. Wood smoke irritated him in ways he couldn't even define. His aversion stemmed from forced camping trips with his overbearing father. Sleeping out of doors made his skin crawl. Sure, he liked being outside, but not the discomfort and inconvenience of sleeping there. A sneaking suspicion formed in his mind, one involving the great outdoors and the formula's unique ingredients. Whistling the first refrain of "It's a Small World" repeatedly between his teeth, he glared at the page. What wasn't he seeing?

"Quit that incessant noise. I could hear it all the way upstairs." Grant strode into the large parlor, pausing to scan the room. He sank onto the love seat facing the fireplace. "What's wrong?"

Frowning, Zak looked at his brother. Grant appeared so healthy and normal aside from the slight frown signaling a headache. But the tumor clock ticked on, incessant and unstoppable, unless he solved the puzzle before him. "This mysterious symbol must be the clue to the correct ingredient I need for that damn elixir."

Grant relaxed against the flowered fabric, stretching his legs out, ankles crossed. "Clue? Is this a murder mystery?"

Zak huffed a laugh. "I wish. At least then there'd be a body to prove the final result is possible."

"Maybe you should start at the beginning and step through it systematically, layer by layer as it were." Grant drummed his fingers on his leg. "You know, like Dad taught us. One step at a time."

"Layers?" He ignored the dad reference and all the

subtext it implied only because Grant might be on to a lead. Zak shot back in his chair and then snatched the box containing Starling's journal off of the end table. He removed the lid and pulled the book from its bed. Lifting pages as quickly as he could without damaging the fragile sheets, he searched for the specific entry.

"Now what?" Grant crossed an ankle over his knee.

"Layers." Zak scanned the handwriting, turned the page, searching for where Starling's notes mentioned stratification.

On a sigh, Grant folded his arms and closed his eyes. "Let me know when you want to hear my news."

"Give me a minute." Poring over the spidery writing, Zak studied each stroke of the ancient pen. The old alchemist used precise swipes of the nib to detail each ingredient, each step of the procedure. The more he delved into the words and symbols—so very many symbols—the more certain he became he didn't know what any of it actually meant.

The symbols. They must be the key. But how? He'd figured out the easy ones. A circle with a dot in the center signified the sun. A crescent represented the moon. Three stacked wavy lines meant water. The downward pointing triangle with inner bar along the hypotenuse stood for earth, as Aristotle had designated centuries before.

But then there were the mysterious ones. Like the owl on the crossed bars or sticks or whatever the hell they were. What did a bird have to do with earth? His forehead grew tight as he stared at the faint drawing of the curious owl symbol. Tension bloomed in his head and he rubbed his fingertips on his temple, trying to erase the burgeoning pain. Why did the bookstore utilize the same stupid owl as its logo? A connection even the Golden sisters didn't realize existed. Their mother must have come across the symbol in one of the many books she carried in the store over the years she owned it. Perhaps one of those books held the secret key to decipher the code in the journal.

"She knew." Zak stared at the fireplace, seeking confirmation of his theory in the flickering flames. "She must have."

Grant sat up and leaned his elbows on his knees, regarding Zak. "Stop talking in riddles."

Zak chuckled. "Mrs. Golden must have known about the owl and earth symbol. Otherwise, she wouldn't have hung it out front of the bookstore as a beacon."

"That's pretty far-fetched. I mean, the journal must be close to 320 years old."

Zak rose to his feet, squeezed the nape of his neck to ease the building pressure there, and paced to the mantel. He turned to Grant, snaring him with a probing stare. "But that's my exact point. She must have used the owl on purpose, not merely by coincidence or chance. She knew one day somebody, like me, would come looking for the soil necessary to successfully create the Philosopher's Stone." He ended his little speech with a flourish of both hands.

"You could be onto something, at that." Grant put both palms on his knees and studied Zak for a long moment. "Maybe you're not crazy. Perhaps you're right, and there really is something in the soil around Roseville unique enough to enable a different chemical reaction."

"Such as?" Tobacco smoke mingled with the wood smoke, making Zak cough and glance around the room. Cross-stitched NO SMOKING signs hung throughout the house, so who dared defy the rules? He scrubbed a hand over his nose to obliterate the scent.

Grant shrugged and smiled. "Could be any of a number of things, honestly. Could be more iron, or acid, or even the presence of certain quartz crystals."

Zak coughed again. The odor of tobacco burning grew stronger though still hard to detect beneath the aroma of the smoke from the fireplace. He scanned the room, trying to locate the source. He hadn't seen anyone with cigarettes or a pipe, even, but the aroma continued to intensify. Almost like somebody stood next to him with a lit pipe. Impossible. He shook his head to clear it. "How do we know what to look for then?"

"From what you've told me, we don't, and that is the way the old alchemist wanted it. He knew what he needed. Those directions were more for his benefit than anyone else's."

"You've got a point. Damn." Zak paced the room, moving farther from the fireplace and its mingling smoky odors. "Since he wrote the ingredients using code, he likely didn't intend for anyone else to be able to duplicate his process. That would keep his secret safe."

"Right. But at least now you know you're in the right part of the world." Grant stood and considered Zak. "Ready to hear my news?"

A noise in the hallway made Zak glance to the doorway. Paulette approached the opening, paused with wide eyes and raised brows, and put one hand to her distended belly. The calico started to follow Paulette into the parlor, paused in midstride and bolted down the hallway, out of sight. Paulette frowned in the direction of the matching overstuffed chairs, shook her head, and then realized Zak was staring at her puzzling actions. "Don't mind me, boys. Simply passing through." With a last glance at the chair and a wave of her pretty hand, she hurried up the stairs.

Zak focused on Grant again. Grant's eyes sparkled with suppressed mirth. Zak found himself smiling in anticipation. "Shoot."

"Those books we bought at the Golden Owl? They turned out to be a great investment."

Zak nodded, anxious to hear what Grant had discovered. "Go on."

"The soil tests conducted over the last two decades reveal pockets of high concentrations of manganese and iron, in some instances coupled with very high acidity levels. Including areas with nitric and hydrochloric acid detected." His grin revealed his awareness that he'd solved a major part of the riddle.

"The acids used to make the *aqua regia* that dissolves gold. We must be getting close. Nice work, bro." Zak bopped him on the shoulder with a fist. "Now we need to figure out which pocket holds the key."

The squeal of the attic door shuddered through Paulette as she eased into the shadowy space, searching for any sign of Patrick. Newspapers, books, and magazines lay strewn among the many boxes, trunks, the faded rocking horse, and the huge dollhouse. All because she read a spell and caused the windstorm that carried her grandfather home. What a mess. She propped the doorstop, a cloth-covered brick, in place to keep the door open so she could flee if necessary. Spying the red book lying beside the open trunk, she squared her shoulders. What specifically had she been thinking when she grabbed the heavy tome? When she read the poem? If she could recall her thoughts, perhaps she'd solve the puzzle of her mysterious need.

Stepping into the dimly lit room, she flipped on the light and then hurried to the trunk with its contents arrayed on the floor. Meredith had told her she had started to sort through the items, but had been interrupted by Patrick's shenanigans. She'd handed the task over to Paulette while she attended to business making Paulette promise not to read any of the spells out of the book. Like she'd be stupid twice.

Her mission remained to find a way to make Patrick go away. The tune of "I'm Gonna Wash That Man Right Out of My Hair" wormed its way through her mind, the image of the woman washing her hair on the beach in the musical *South Pacific* in tandem. She hadn't seen the movie in ages, but the song sure fit her mood. Anything to make him move along, out of her life and mind.

Drawing closer to the trunk, she glanced into its interior and spotted the silk shirt. The temptation to remove the article proved too much. Lifting the luxurious fabric reverently from its bed, the fabric flowed like melted white chocolate. She shimmied the shirt side to side, delighting in the sparkling sheen and gentle swishing sound. Draping the silk over her arm, she peered at a rectangular black box now revealed to the light. Perhaps whatever lay within the box had prevented her from moving the trunk. She folded the shirt carefully and laid it in the lid as she bent over and searched for a means to open the container.

Trailing a finger along the top edge, she located a small silver button but hesitated to press it. What might leap out? Or ooze? What if it contained something scary, noxious or, worse, poisonous? Shuddering at the images flashing behind her eyes, she sighed. As she studied the black box, a noise filtered through the doorway. She straightened, homing in on the source.

Footsteps echoed on the stairs, announcing the arrival of Zak who paused in the doorway. Damn, the man took her breath and sent sparks skittering across her skin merely by smiling in her direction. She returned the smile, aware of him on a cellular level even from across the room.

"I hoped to find you in here. What are you doing?" He sauntered toward her, his stride fluid and rhythmic. And sexy as hell.

Focus. She shrugged and turned back to the trunk. Anything to keep from imagining the feel of his hair between her fingers, or his lips on hers. "Nothing much."

"I love old attics like this, filled with hidden treasures."

Glancing about, he made his way through the debris. He finally reached her side and leaned closer, resting one large hand on her shoulder while peering into the interior of the trunk. "What's in the case?"

"Beats me. Shall we find out?" Paulette glanced at him where he stood way too close for comfort, then back at the mysterious container.

"Absolutely." He reached around her and lifted the case into the open. "Do you mind?"

She shook her head, too mesmerized by the light dancing in his eyes, the curve of his full and inviting lips, to form a coherent sentence. Better to keep her mouth closed. The tendency to say the wrong thing and end up in trouble haunted her as much as her grandfather's ghost.

Supporting the good-sized box on his left arm, he pressed the little silver button. A soft click preceded the lid popping open. She held her breath as he slipped a finger under the edge and lifted. Inside, a beautiful golden saxophone nestled among black satin.

"Whose is this?" Zak pulled the instrument from its bed as Paulette took the case from him and laid it on the floor.

"My grandfather's, I'd imagine." She waved at the open trunk. "All of this stuff belonged to him."

Zak angled the wind instrument, checked the fingering keys, and shot her a teasing look. "Shall we see if it still plays?"

"You know how?" The man never ceased to surprise her. The combination of alluring male along with his intense interest in her proved dangerous to not only her peace of mind but also her heart. Add in his apparent interest in music, and her very soul reached out to his. Not good.

"Some. Grant's more proficient, though." He grinned. "Here goes nothing."

Wrapping his lips around the mouthpiece, he blew and the sax screeched in response.

"Stop!" Paulette covered her ears with both hands, the noise a welcome interruption to her wayward thoughts. "What an awful noise."

Zak chuckled. "I told you Grant's better, but it does at least have some sound. With some tuning up—you know, replacing the fingering key pads, and the reed, that sort of thing—I bet it's still useable."

"I don't know whether my grandpa would approve of us using his instrument." She gazed down on the dull surface. It really did need some tender loving care to restore it to its former beauty.

Zak replaced the sax into the case, and clicked the lid closed. In the process, his hip bumped hers as she reached to put the silk shirt in on top of the case again. She jerked to one side, putting distance between them and putting the quash on the sparks shooting along her nerve endings.

"Sorry." Zak looked anything but sorry when he winked her way.

"Right." She continued putting the various items back into the trunk, his presence at her side a constant thrill held at bay by the slight separation of their bodies.

Zak picked up the book of secrets and opened the cover. He flipped through several pages while Paulette frantically tried to think of a polite way to remove the book from his hands. Then he paused and stared at the very spell she'd read. Her heart thrummed in her throat, blocking her voice.

He laid a finger on the owl with its beak open as though ready to snare a rodent from tall grass, then pierced her with his eyes. "What's this mean?"

The intensity in his expression broke the logjam in her throat. "No idea. It's just a picture." Paulette snatched the book and plopped it into the trunk before swatting the lid closed. Zak raised his brows, waiting for an explanation.

"Grandpa collected illustrated poems." Would he believe her fabrication? "Nothing exciting."

"Does the owl remind you of the book store sign?" Zak eased a slow grin onto his lips and winked again. "I wonder if there's a connection. At least we know he was a very creative person. A poet, musician, and well dressed."

"I suppose." She wished he'd stop winking at her, like they shared a juicy secret. What connection might exist between Patrick and the book store? None came to mind. "What brought you up here?"

"Meredith told me you were working in here, and I wanted to see you. I was curious as to what antiques and stuff might be in here as well, so it was a win-win for me."

"I see." Dang. His expression brightened as if she'd told him she loved him. Whoa, Nelly. Do not even go there. No way would she consider pursuing a relationship with him or any man. "Well, the show's over since I've done what I came to do." Partly at least. She couldn't help glancing at the remaining mess left by the whirlwind, but honestly a nap sounded like a very good idea.

"After you, m'lady." He swept one arm down and across his waist, indicating his desire for her to lead the way from the room.

"Thank you, kind sir." She half-curtseyed, going along with the charade, and then strode to the door. She leaned down to remove the brick propping the door open, realizing too late what she'd done.

"Nice view." Zak came up behind her, resting both hands at her waist as she straightened abruptly.

"What are you doing?" Holding her frame rigid, she allowed him to turn her to face him, pulse thudding in her ears. He stood so close she could detect flecks around his irises, the tiny crow's feet shooting rays from the corners of his eyes, the edge of the scar running down his cheek to his jaw, and even the varying shades of the healing bruise on his forehead. Mostly, she found the curve of his lips fascinating, tempting.

"Have you ever met someone and felt compelled to touch them? Like this?" He squeezed her waist before raising one hand to trail a finger down her cheek to the point of her jaw. "Know what I mean?"

Yes. With him. "You shouldn't do that."

"Why?" He matched the action with his other hand and then slid both hands down to clasp her hands, holding them up between them.

I want to kiss you, that's why. "I'm not interested in having an affair with someone who is planning to leave in a few days."

He kissed her fingers then studied her for several seconds. "You're lying."

He could tell? She shook her head. "No, I'm really not interested." She tugged on her hands, and he reluctantly allowed them to slip away from his grasp. "Shall we go?"

He smiled and shrugged. "If you insist, but don't think we are over."

"You're wrong." She breezed past him, her chest painful from the thumping of her heart.

"Want to bet?" The door closed behind him as he followed her down the stairs, his footsteps in time with her own.

"I don't gamble."

"Afraid of losing?" His deep chuckle echoed in the stairwell.

"Think what you will, but it doesn't change the reality that you'll be sorely disappointed." As long as her heart didn't command her head, everything would be just fine.

Cookbooks surrounded Meredith. She'd consulted every one, searching for the best ideas for party food. So many possibilities, but which combination would create an appropriate theme for the festivities? She'd contemplated simple fare such as a cheese ball and crackers and a cookie tray, but dismissed the concept as boring. On the other hand, the higher end appetizers of crab dip and stuffed mushroom caps seemed extravagant. She needed help.

Leaving the stacks of books, she rose and gathered her purse and jacket. The short drive into town on such a gorgeous fall day flew by and soon she strolled into the Golden Owl. As usual, she paused beneath the jangling bell to inhale the heavenly blend of cinnamon and coffee. The aromas tempted her toward the coffee bar, but first she needed to complete her task. Then she'd reward herself with a treat.

A brunette woman, whose nametag identified her as Tara, greeted her, a small smile hesitantly sliding on and off her lips. Meredith nodded and continued scanning the large room. Behind the counter, Roxie, the one who had befriended Paulette, watched her as she perused the shop. The two women definitely looked like sisters, both with long chestnut brown hair and hazel eyes, similar cheek bones, and slim figures. Meredith envied their trim build; no matter how much she exercised and watched her caloric intake, she never felt slender. She exchanged smiles with Roxie before the other woman turned back to continue stacking tiny volumes of gift books, the impulse buys of a book store, neatly on the counter.

She started toward the circular stairs, intent on locating books on party themes and thus suggestions for refreshments. Looking up as she reached for the handrail, she paused. The third sister came down the steps, a polite smile greeting her. Although she resembled her sisters, her hair created a warm golden mane about her shoulders and her eyes were a pale green.

"Hi. You're Meredith Reed, right?" The tawny blonde stopped at the bottom and extended a hand.

Meredith shook her hand and nodded. "You're Beth.

Nice to finally meet you. I've been in and out several times, but never had chance to talk with you."

Beth grinned. "I'm usually busy in back. I'm not much for interacting with the customers."

"I feel honored you've taken the time to greet me." Meredith gripped the handrail, preparing to head upstairs, and then peered at Beth. "What do you know about party food?"

Beth giggled. "I love a good party. What do you need? Perhaps I can help you find it."

"God, I hope so! We're throwing a party and I have no idea what I want to fix. Can you point me in the right direction?"

"Better yet, I'll show you." Beth turned and led Meredith upstairs to the section featuring books on party planning. "I'm sure you'll find what you need, but let me know if you want more help."

"Thanks, I will." As Beth made her way back downstairs, Meredith scanned the titles. *Parties for Little Ones*. Nope, too young for the mostly adult crowd they'd invited. *Be a Party Planning Ninja*. What? *Planning the Perfect Wedding*. Oops. She stared at the title for a long moment, and then slowly drew it off the shelf. Flipping through the pages, she cringed inwardly.

She and Max planned to marry the day after Christmas. But she hadn't started planning for it yet. She really should talk to Paulette about the dress, order some invitations, hell, even figure out exactly where the event would take place. What held her back? Why did she delay making the necessary arrangements to marry the man she loved? What the hell was wrong with her? Still, another party loomed first.

She put the book back and pulled out *Planning the Perfect Party* which looked promising. She scanned the table of contents.

"Hey, beautiful."

She smiled at the rich chocolate voice and raised her gaze to Max's smile. "Hey handsome. I didn't know you'd gotten back in town."

"I just drove in, saw your car outside, and came to find you." He kissed her, pressing warm lips to her hungry mouth. She inhaled his special scent, earthy and spicy combined, and held her breath for a long moment. Love for him ballooned in her heart. Exhaling, she smiled at him.

Max took her hand, drew her closer to him. "I've missed you." He glanced at the book in her hands.

"I've missed you more than I can put into words." She searched his expression and detected the question lurking in the depths of his eyes. She clutched the book to her chest. "You won't believe what's happened."

"What?" He studied her, his grin drooping. "What have you done?"

She glanced around to make sure no one could hear their conversation. "Not me. Paulette."

"I can only imagine. Tell me." He waited, his expression guarded yet intrigued.

"She summoned our grandfather, the one who died before we were born." She waited for his reaction.

"You're right. I don't believe you." He rubbed a hand over his jaw, eyes intent on her. "Why do you keep pretending that Twin Oaks is haunted?"

"I'm not." Meredith hugged the book tighter, wishing for inspiration on many fronts. Max believed in flesh and blood beings but had yet to actually come face to face with a ghost. If she had her way, he wouldn't ever meet a real spook. But he should know the facts of the situation. "And the best part is, he won't leave."

"You have to make him leave." Max stared at her. "Don't you? Isn't that part of the act?"

She shrugged. His aversion to admitting even to himself

the existence of the ghosts would not change the reality. Perhaps it was better for him to keep the illusion that she and Paulette pretended and let it go. "I can't. He says only Paulette can send him home, and he's not revealing how, and she doesn't know. It's a mess."

"So why are you planning a party?" He motioned to the book in her hand. "Is that related to our wedding?"

She took a deep breath to delay her response, but that would only work for a very short span of time. She let it out and shrugged. "We've decided to throw a Halloween party in a couple weeks."

He frowned. "What about our wedding? You insisted on doing it all yourself, but tell me what you want me to do and I'll help. What have you done so far?"

"I, um, made a list of people to invite. And, um, thought about where it might take place." Sort of. She'd tried to figure out where at the plantation they could wed, but in December the options were limited. If they had chosen any other season, they might have been able to hold the ceremony in the gazebo, but not in the dead of winter. Not even in southern Tennessee would it be decent weather for an outdoor wedding. She wanted someplace unique and memorable. But where? Maybe if she could settle on a place the remaining details would follow. She could hope anyway.

His frown deepened. "It's only a couple months away. Shouldn't you have done more about a dress, and invitations, and the cake? We are going to have a cake, right?"

"Of course. I know you love cake." If she had to bake it herself, which probably wasn't a great plan, come to think of it. No vision arose when she contemplated their wedding. A vague idea for a long flowing dress with a veil, but what color? She wasn't a virginal bride, but a widow, so white probably wasn't the right choice. Stymied described her perfectly. "But we're only planning a small gathering, so it's okay. It'll all come together as it's supposed to. You'll see."

"I'm here to help if you'll let me." He searched her face, glanced away, then back. Sighing, he kissed her hand and held onto it. "Or are you having second thoughts about being my wife?"

"No, not that." She hoped. She hadn't really given herself time to think about it one way or the other. She peered into his vibrant blue eyes, drawn into their sincerity and depth of love. He'd come to represent the future for her. His love saved her from imploding into the grief consuming her after the death of her first love and their child. "I love you."

"I love you, Meredith. Never doubt me on that point." Pulling her against him, he kissed her, long and deep.

He'd been away from town far too long. She pressed against him, reaching to deepen the contact of their tongues, the twining and playing. Despite the public setting, the stacks of books surrounding them created the illusion of privacy and made their actions part risk and part daring. She chose to ignore the murmur of voices of other patrons from below. The distant jangle of the bell. All she cared about lay beneath her palms, the taste of him, the smell of him. She pressed against him for one last kiss. Although part of her would always hold Willy near and dear, he would've wanted her to move on, to be happy. Max made her smile, laugh, and feel safe. What more did she have the right to ask for?

"I'll start our wedding plans in earnest after the Halloween party. Promise."

He considered her for a long moment, and then kissed her again, a quick peck. "Okay. I'll see you later. I need to check in with Sue and see what's been happening at the office."

"Let me pay for this, and I'll go with you." She wasn't ready to let him out of her sight after he'd been gone a week. Especially after his kiss ignited sparks in her veins. Meredith tugged his hand, noted the familiar zing from skin touching skin, and they started for the steps. "I haven't talked to her in weeks. It'll be good to catch up with her."

At the bottom of the steps, Max placed a hand at the small of Meredith's back and guided her to the checkout line. "I'm glad you two became friends. She's pleased to be in the wedding too."

"I see you found help with your party planning," Beth said, emerging from the back room. She wiped her hands on a rag she kept tucked in her back pocket.

"Something like that." Meredith handed over the book.

"I'm sure whatever you decide for party foods, your guests will enjoy." She scanned the book's label and then slid it into a bag. "After all, parties are about coming together to celebrate, not the particulars."

"That's true to a point," Meredith said. "But people love to eat, and that's what they'll most remember about the occasion. How tasty the food was."

Beth chuckled and Meredith finished paying for her purchase. She waved good-bye and they emerged onto the street. The October sunshine warmed her face and arms, dried leaves eddying on the sidewalk. She strolled beside Max down the street to his office, situated in a charming bungalow off the town square. The sign swinging lazily in the breeze included Max's name second on the list of partners at the firm which specialized in historical preservation law. She grinned at the visible notice of his recent promotion within the firm.

Inside the cozy office, Meredith spotted Sue hurrying toward her. The older woman's short brown hair came from a bottle, but her energy exceeded Meredith's by far. Grandmother and legal secretary, she kept busy in the office and throughout the community. Calling her a friend seemed very natural.

"Meredith, how are you?" Sue reached her and enveloped her in a hug.

"It's been too long, my friend," Meredith said. "I ran into Max, and thought I'd come with him."

"I'm glad." Sue pointed to the small shopping bag boasting the Golden Owl logo. "What's that?"

Meredith withdrew the book. "Getting ready for a Halloween party. I expect you to come in costume too."

"I don't go in for costumes very much." Sue shook her head. "But I bet it will be a fab party."

"You should dress up like a legal secretary, that would fool everybody," Max said, striding past the two women and into his office.

"Ha. Leave it to him to be so creative." Sue chuckled.

"Want to help me with the party menu?" Distant memories of previous failed parties fought to unnerve her current efforts. What if nobody came? Or if they labeled her the worst hostess ever because she didn't serve great food? She wiped sweaty palms on her jeans. "I'm struggling with what to serve. You wouldn't think throwing a party could cause so much stress. But this party means so much to Paulette, I'd hate to let her down by having lame hors d'oeuvres."

"Sure. I'd be happy to. But it's your party also." Sue flipped through the book and then looked at Meredith.

"Yes and no. As Max reminded me, my party will be in December when we get married."

"How are those plans coming along? Have you chosen your gown?" She handed back the book and snapped her fingers. "Before I forget again, what kind of bridesmaid's dress have you picked out for me? I really hope it's not some hideous thing I'll be embarrassed to wear. I've worn too many of those in my life. So which gown did you choose?"

"Good question. I haven't decided. But I will. I'll start working on wedding plans as soon as this party is over."

Sue gaped at her, eyes mirroring those of the owl on the bag. "Little more than two months away and you haven't even decided on a dress?"

The shock in her friend's expression made her swallow and blink several times. Perhaps she had procrastinated too long. Meredith held up a finger and then all five. "Don't worry. It's all under control."

Chapter Five

A little more than a week before the party, Paulette hurried into the sewing room and strode to the writing desk. She sank onto the desk chair, humming snippets of "Good Morning" from the old musical *Singing in the Rain* under her breath, and shuffled through the stack of papers. Letters and notecards mingled with costume designs and party plans. Finally locating what she searched for, she examined several pages of invitees. Pleased at the positive response, she counted forty folks planning to attend. Not including the B&B guests. She smiled to herself. They would be full up, attracting the most lodgers in one weekend since they opened their doors in July. Her efforts to spruce up the interior had paid off handsomely over the past months, more than breaking even on the balance sheet. For each paying guest, she'd provide information about her costume business and interior decorating skills. The prospect of providing for her baby and herself without relying solely on Meredith's goodwill made her heart sing.

Pounding on the back door roused her from hope-filled thoughts. Gaining her feet, she hurried to answer the summons. She pushed into the kitchen, greeted by her parents' faces peering through the back door. The difference in their height made her mom appear childlike next to the bulk of her dad. Brock O'Connell exhibited gray hair and a new mustache, still working on thickening. Meredith had inherited his green eyes. Paulette obviously took after her mom, sharing both faded brown eyes and blonde hair, though her mom's included a few wisps of gray. Moving here made it possible to reconnect with her parents too. She loved them to death, but was something wrong?

"What a surprise!" Paulette twisted the little knob and pulled the door open, ushering them inside. "I wasn't expecting you until next week."

"I had a job in the area so thought we'd come sooner." Brock hugged her, followed by Dina. "You don't mind, do you?"

"No, of course not…" Good thing she'd set aside a room for them already. Another trip to Edna's Grocery loomed as a result of the early arrival. "We'll have fun."

Dina relaxed. "Perhaps I can be of some use while your dad is off doing his thing."

"Perfect. We can definitely use your talents." She hugged her mom again, for good measure. "Meredith should be home any moment. Have you had lunch yet?"

"No, but I'd appreciate a beer if you've got one." Brock slapped the door shut.

Paulette indicated the refrigerator, surprised at the early indulgence. In a jiff, Brock swigged from a dark brown bottle and swallowed. "Where'd she take herself off to?"

"She's presenting her elevations, you know, the drawings of what the place will look like after the renovations, to clients across town. She'll be back by noon to meet Sue." She rummaged in the cabinet under the island counter, finally locating a medium-sized plastic platter adorned with poppies. Placing the platter on the counter, she glanced at her mom and dad. They exchanged a look, making her wonder why they really showed up a week early.

"Sue Grimwood?" Dina removed her straw hat and hung it on the ladder-back chair pushed under the small table by the bay window.

"Yep. They've become great friends." Crossing to the fridge, Paulette retrieved several packages of cold cuts and sliced cheese, bread, mayo, and pickles. Resting the items on her belly, she hugged the menagerie as she moved to drop everything onto the countertop with a muted thud. The jar of dill slices bounced harder than the rest of the pile. It banged onto the hard surface, then flopped onto its side, and promptly made a dash over the edge. She grabbed for it but missed, the jar crashing onto the floor, splattering pickles, juice, and shattered glass across the kitchen and her bare toes. "Oh!"

"Stay there, I'll get a broom." Dina raced through the doorway toward the cleaning closet in the back hallway.

"We need to mop this up." Brock gazed at the spreading puddle and then at Paulette, as though not quite sure how to proceed. He lowered the beer bottle to the counter.

"Grab some paper towels, Dad, and stop the flood." Paulette retreated behind the island counter while her dad acted on her instructions. She wiggled her bare feet, annoyed with herself for not wearing at least her slippers. She stayed put, not wanting to risk glass in her soles.

Dina returned with the broom and gathered the shards, sweeping them into a dust pan and dumping the mess into the trash can. Paulette used some wet paper towels to mop up the remainder of the glass bits and pickles and plopped them in the can. "I'm such a klutz."

"No problem, we'll survive." Dina grinned at her daughter. "I'm glad you're not hurt."

"I'm fine." Why did tears threaten if so? Get a grip, woman. Paulette sniffed and reached into a cupboard for a stack of sandwich plates. "How about you two take your bags up to your usual room, and I'll throw together some sandwiches sans pickles."

After her parents left her alone, Paulette paused in spreading mayo on bread to take a deep breath. Her emotions boomeranged all over the place. She didn't want to cry over spilt pickles, but tears leaked down her cheeks anyway. She swiped them dry and slathered mayo on another slice of wheat. Silly woman, get over it. They're pickles. Nobody died. Stop the fool waterworks. But the waterworks continued until the crunch of tires on gravel forced her gaze out the window over the sink. Meredith's Camaro pulled into its space. Paulette dashed a hand across her cheeks, sniffed, and then swallowed.

Meredith hurried through the rear door carrying a briefcase in one hand and a purse on her shoulder. Her keen gaze landed on Paulette's face and then shot to her damp eyes. Despite Paulette's best attempts, she apparently showed her distress over the tragic death of the poor dill pickles. She sniffed again and cleared her throat.

"What did I miss?" Meredith set the briefcase beside the island and studied Paulette's expression. "You've been crying."

"It's so nothing." Shaking her head at the foolishness of the situation, Paulette grinned. "Mom and Dad are here."

"I saw their truck outside. What gives?"

"I invited them for the party, but they came early. Dad has a job nearby so decided to extend their visit." She slapped a slice of wheat on top of the pile of sliced pastrami and provolone. A quick movement of the knife and she'd separated the sandwich into halves and then laid it on top of the red poppies. "They're upstairs. I'm surprised they arrived so early."

Dropping her purse on the little table by the door, Meredith paused by the island counter to peer at Paulette.

She held still under her sister's scrutiny, but it was all Paulette could do not to flinch backward.

"Do they know about Grandpa?" Meredith leaned toward Paulette, intent on her response.

"Not yet. We can ask them about how he died when they come back down." She sliced another sandwich, smoked turkey and Swiss, arranged it on the platter, and started on the next. Pastrami and turkey with cheddar for her dad.

"That and why Dad didn't let us know the man possessed certain abilities all his own." Meredith stalked to the cupboard and nabbed a glass. "I really want to hear the answer to that particular question."

"Yeah, me too." She added the sandwich to the pile then started on one with turkey and no cheese for herself. "Would you pour me some tea? It's probably safer for me to not handle glass for a while."

Meredith pulled another tumbler from the cupboard and filled them both from the pitcher by the sink. Depositing a glass near Paulette, she sipped from the other. "So why the tears?"

A chuckle forced from her throat. "I killed the pickles. All over the floor. They've been buried in the trashcan." She bobbed her head slowly up and down, a rueful smirk curving her lips.

Meredith grinned. "Tragic, just tragic."

"What's tragic?" Brock asked as he led Dina into the kitchen.

"The poor pickle disaster." Meredith hugged her parents in turn. "Such a sad occasion."

"It was an accident." Paulette arranged the last halves on the stack of sandwiches. "Being pregnant apparently has made me prone to them."

Dina regarded her with a raised brow. "What else have you done?"

The sisters exchanged a glance. Meredith nodded. Taking a deep breath, Paulette shrugged and exhaled. "Invited Grandpa Patrick to visit."

Brock crossed his arms but said nothing for a few moments. His jaw slowly dropped as her meaning sank in. He continued to stare at her for three slow breaths. "Say that again…"

Meredith lifted the platter with both hands. "Let's move into the dining room and we'll explain."

Dina snared the pitcher of tea and hurried after Meredith and her dumbfounded husband. Grabbing the plates and more glasses, Paulette followed everyone into the other room. She skirted the stack of plastic tubs placed inside the wide doorway. Sean had lugged them down for her, each filled with an assortment of fall and Halloween decorations. While performing an inventory, Meredith had stumbled upon a walk-in closet dedicated to seasonal decorations. Tubs and shelves crammed full of goodies. Paulette literally squealed when she explored their contents. Grandma Mary had really been into dressing up Twin Oaks in style. Paulette planned to start decorating the interior of the house right after lunch.

She placed the platter in the center of the long banquet-sized table and then scanned the rest of the room. The antique silver tea service gleamed on the sideboard, its home ever since being recovered from its hiding place back in April. The manner of Grace's death during the Civil War still shot tremors of horror through Paulette. At least by locating her remains and burying them she rested in peace beside her beloved brother in the family cemetery. Unlike Grandpa Patrick.

Which apparently came about due to her being stupid and reading aloud a strange poem. Why didn't she realize the rhyme was a spell? Blame it on the hormones. Surely her idiocy stemmed from her pregnancy. She clung to the hope that intelligence would return along with her baby. In the meantime, resolving the Grandpa issue held pride of place as a top priority. What need did she have only he could help with? Such a puzzle.

After everyone took their seats and selected a sandwich, Paulette cleared her throat to attract their attention. All eyes turned her direction. "Dad, what do you know about how Grandpa died?"

"Not much." Brock chewed and swallowed, watching her. "When I was five, Dad died in some experiment he tried. Mom didn't talk about it."

More secrets in the family history. Grandma loved them, based on recent discoveries. What other surprises waited in the stuffed attic?

"You never asked?" Meredith angled her head, studying his reaction.

"No, I never thought about it much." He bit into the sandwich, his gaze drifting to fixate on his plate.

Dina lazily stirred sugar into her tea. "Your mom told me a long time ago he died in an explosion, but she didn't know the cause. He'd gone to some friend's lab to work and she never saw him alive again. What a horrible way to die."

"At least it was quick." Brock laid his hands on either side of his plate, glancing between the others at the table. "Explain what you meant about Dad being invited here."

"Well, it's like this. I went into the attic and tried to move a trunk—"

"A trunk? Which one?" Brock's hands fisted then relaxed.

"A black and silver one, which was heavier than it looked." Her dad's tension became palpable, pulsing in the air around Paulette. She tasted fear in the back of her throat. "So when I opened it to find out why, I found a book—"

Brock fisted his hands again. "Don't tell me...a dark red one?"

She nodded and continued despite the growing tension. "And dropped it trying to get to the clothes beneath it. When it fell open to a certain page, I made the mistake—"

"Of reading the so-called spell." Brock sighed heavily. "I can't believe Mom kept such crap. I thought she'd made up the warlock story."

Meredith's eyes popped wide. "You knew?"

"Why didn't you tell us?" Paulette shook her head. "Why the secrecy?"

Brock chuckled humorlessly. "Why would I want anyone to think my dad practiced witchcraft? I realize Wicca is a religion, but magic? I don't think so."

"Still, it would have been nice to know about the possibility." Meredith shook her head. "I can't believe it, but I suppose I really shouldn't be surprised."

"Right, we can talk to ghosts, after all." Paulette folded her napkin and laid it by her plate. "Of course, now I need to learn about witchcraft too."

"Wait a minute." Dina glanced from one to the other, finally peering at Brock. "Are you telling me all of you have supernatural abilities?"

"Meredith and I do." Paulette drummed her fingers on the table as they contemplated each other silently. "Do you, Dad?"

Brock shook his head vehemently. "No, I do not. I refuse to believe in such crap." He pushed back from the table and stood, a vein pulsing erratically in his neck.

"Where are you going?" Paulette also rose to her feet, albeit slower than her father. "We have more questions in need of answers."

"They'll have to wait because I need air." He whirled around and stomped from the room, his booted steps echoing down the hall.

She listened as her dad stormed into the kitchen, followed by the slam of the back door. So much for answers.

Sitting back down, she pursed her lips and regarded her mother. "Does he possess special abilities he doesn't want to admit?"

"I'm not sure." Dina sat back in her chair and fingered the edge of the plate on the table. "Not that he's mentioned to me."

"Have unusual things happened when he's around?" Meredith asked.

"Odd events of any kind?" Paulette racked her memories, searching for any hints.

Dina stared at Paulette, brows drawn together. "Perhaps. I-I don't know what to make of all this. I should go after him." Dina rose and gripped the back of her chair, obviously debating her next move.

"Leave him alone, Mom. He'll be back." Meredith motioned for her to sit back down.

Paulette shot a glance at Meredith and then back to her mother. "I think he knows more than he's letting on, or wants to admit. But one thing is certain, he's hiding something."

Later that afternoon, Paulette settled in the sewing room to explore the books she'd purchased on witchcraft. Opening the one dealing with the basics, she perused the contents before turning to the first page. Her father had eventually returned from his walk and gone to his room. To rest or because he didn't want to interact, she had no way of knowing. Somewhere in his memories perhaps resided a hint as to what she must do to send Grandpa into the light. With or without his help, his dad must depart. Hopefully, the answer awaited discovery within the volume cradled in her hands.

She focused on the words, learning about will and intent and the risks inherent in both. Especially risky when a beginning witch tried to work her will before she was properly trained. Becoming a witch required more time than she had. Years of instruction and practice went into the effort. No way did she want Grandpa around for years while she worked on developing witchcraft skills. Wait. Perhaps she should talk to Roxie about locating a witch to help her with the—what was it called?—oh, right, the banishment spell.

A noise at the door interrupted her study. Filling the doorway, Zak grinned at her. Damn, he snatched her breath and made her palms itch to touch him. Self-conscious of the book in her lap, she closed it and turned the title toward her belly. "Can I help you?"

Zak strode into the room, electrifying the space with his presence. "I don't mean to bother you, but you looked so beautiful I couldn't tear myself away. Mind if I join you?" He motioned to the matching goose-necked rocking chair.

Oh, baby, could he join her. But he didn't mean in the biblical sense. Good, because at this stage of pregnancy, no joining permitted. Doctor's orders. Given her advanced age and the advanced stage of her pregnancy, she had listened carefully to every word the woman had intoned. But if she weren't pregnant… After her reaction to him in the attic, she must be on guard to protect herself. She quashed the direction of her errant thoughts. "Of course, if you have nothing better to do than sit inside on a lovely fall afternoon."

He sank into the upholstered chair and rocked lazily. "Not a thing. My brother is doing the dry reading, so I'm left to while away the day. Without knowing the specific locales for what I'm searching for, I can't move forward with my own efforts."

"Oh? What is he researching?" She clutched the book closer. A tiny foot pushed back, stretching her skin in resistance to the increased pressure.

"Dirt and what's in it." His rocking sped up.

"What's he hoping to find?"

"The key ingredient I need for an…let's just say, an experiment." He regarded her for the span of two heartbeats. "A potentially career-saving experiment."

"I wish you both success then." Goodness, what was he talking about? "Anything I can help with?"

"Thanks for the offer, but no. Grant may lose his eyesight. We're investigating an alternative therapy."

"How terrible for him. What kind of therapy are you hoping to use?"

"We're not sure what we're searching for even exists let alone whether it will help, but I have to try. I'll do anything to find a cure." Zak dragged curved fingers through his hair and then noticed the black book in her lap. "What are you reading?"

"Nothing important." The baby's foot pushed harder as she squeezed the volume against her belly.

He tilted his head so he could read the spine. "*Basic Witchcraft*. Thinking about becoming a witch?" He laughed as he regarded her, rocking steadily.

"No, just curious." His reaction indicated his lack of belief in witches and spells. What would he say if he knew Twin Oaks had a spectral visitor? Or that Roxie knew a witch in sleepy Roseville?

He peered closer at the book, then searched her expression. "Golden? Like the bookstore?"

"Roxie's mother, actually." Interesting that the three sisters' mother had written a book on magic. Why? What connection extended between the women and witchcraft? Hmmm. Maybe she answered her own question.

Stopping the rocking chair's motion, Zak tapped a finger on the arched neck of the wooden goose forming one armrest. "Roxie seemed a bit cautious when Grant and I were there. I wonder…"

"She was with me too at first."

"When you bought that book?" He pointed to where she still clutched the tome to her belly, despite the fact he already knew the title.

"I suppose witchcraft brought us together. I haven't lived in these parts very long, so am just getting to know the sisters."

"They're sisters? I hadn't realized. How many are there?"

"Roxie, Beth, and Tara. They inherited the store from their mother when she passed three years ago." Zak leaned forward at her words, as though fascinated by her revelation. The intensity in his gray eyes sparked equal measures of desire and caution. "What?"

"The triangle on the sign. Three sisters. Three years. That's a lot of threes."

"It's a universal, isn't it? Lots of things come in threes, including bad luck."

He relaxed and set the chair to rocking again, his expression distant and thoughtful. "I guess."

The baby punched her tummy, sending the book sliding from her grasp. She reached out at the same moment Zak grabbed for the escaping book, which tumbled to the floor as his hand caught her wrist. Her gaze zeroed in on his face. The jolt of awareness rushing through her also reflected on his features as he searched her expression. If she weren't big with child, oh how she'd love on him. Flashes of positions and sounds flitted through her mind. She swallowed, willing her heart to settle and her rapid breaths to steady.

He loosened his grip on her arm but didn't free her. She met his gaze, intensely aware of the warmth of his hand. Torn between encouraging and discouraging his attentions. "Now what?"

He blinked, released her with a flash of a smile, and

retrieved the errant book. "Here you go." He held the book in midair, staring at the cover with the owl and candle. "Another owl? Like the one on the book upstairs."

"So?" The tension in him radiated across the space separating them. "What's the matter?"

"Don't you find it rather too coincidental to find owls in so many associated places? This book, the store sign, and the book upstairs? The same owl?"

"Owls have been associated with magic forever. I wouldn't put too much weight on the matter." She slipped the book from his fingers and laid it on the round table between the two chairs.

"Still, it seems to be a sign, a connection, but I can't discern the meaning." He reclined and rocked the chair once more. "One day I hope to solve the story behind the mystical owl. By the way, it's your fault Grant is barely speaking to me."

"How so?" He didn't really mean that. Did he?

"He thinks I'm more interested in you than our mission." He cut her a look, a smile on his face.

His sideways glance suggested the brother had the truth of the matter. "And?"

"Which of course is true." He grinned, laughing. "I'm glad to finally spend time with you, to discover you're more woman than I imagined."

If he were sane, he'd be running for the hills, not looking at her with desire and interest. He moistened his lips, the tip of his tongue flashing into view and then gone. She swallowed, hard. "For Grant's sake, it's probably a good thing you'll only stay a short while then."

"I want to spend more time with you, Paulette." He leaned forward, stilling the chair as he propped elbows on knees and studied her. "I'm serious. We should explore where this might lead."

A chill swept through her. If only it were possible. She

rested her hands on her belly, protecting the wee one inside. "I'm sorry if I've given you the wrong impression."

He tensed, glanced at her hands and then gripped his hands together between his knees. "You do like me?"

"You're a nice man, Zak Markel." She rubbed her tummy, caressing her baby. If her life had unfolded differently, perhaps she'd pursue the course he wanted. "As you can see, though, I'm expecting in a few weeks. It wouldn't be fair to lead you on when I have no business starting a relationship with anyone."

His smile froze and then dissolved into a flat line. He chewed on his lower lip for a second and then stared at his hands for two beats. When he looked at her again, the smile glimmered back into existence. "And yet we share a connection, the beginning of a relationship, whether it's 'fair' or not. You felt it. I know you did."

"Yes, I did. I admit I'm attracted to you." Damn straight. She held herself still with an effort, the longing to touch him nearly overwhelming.

His quick glance at her, gauging her sincerity, thrilled her soul. She couldn't put him through raising another man's child. She found it a daunting prospect, and she had once loved Johnny. Inflicting such a burden on him or any man simply wasn't in her.

"I'm sorry, but we can't act on those feelings no matter how much we'd like to."

"I disagree." He pushed to his feet and regarded her, relaxed and confident. "Maybe it wouldn't work out in the long run, but if we don't give it a try, how will we ever know?"

Pressuring her only made her resist more. It always had. Whether a friend insisted she go to a Friday night school dance, or a party, as a pseudo chaperone. Or her mom pushing her to do her homework. Or even Johnny begging for her to go out with him. The resulting reflex remained to resist, to pause and consider more deeply her true desires. Zak's riveting eyes shone with self-assurance. Well, not this time, bucko.

"The babe is my responsibility. He comes first, before my own happiness and desires. Including any desire for you."

"Your child at least needs a dad, if not his biological father." Zak shoved his hands into his jeans pockets. "What happened to him, anyway?"

His tone suggested he was actually thinking "what did you do to him to make him run away." Cute or not, enough was enough. She shifted forward in the chair and then stood. Zak held out a hand, but she ignored it. She could stand on her own. Although tall for a woman, she still had to angle her head up to meet his eyes. Fists on her hips, she glared at him.

"Let's get one thing straight, Mr. Markel. You have no business poking your pointed nose into my affairs." She shook a finger in his face, anger bubbling and rolling inside until she felt ill. The abrupt switch from wanting him to wanting him to leave made her unsteady. "If you think you can waltz in here and tell me how to live my life and with whom, then you best stop the music, because I won't have it. Do you hear me? I'll say it again to be sure. I won't have you trying to run my life."

Zak pulled his hands free and flung them in the air as if to stop a runaway horse. "Whoa, slow down. You don't need to shout."

"I'm not. Yet. But I'll start if I don't see your cute little backside heading out of this room in the next two seconds." She pointed to the door, hoping he didn't notice her trembling. He'd be vain enough to think he intimidated her when in truth anger rocketed across every nerve ending, leaving her breathless and in awe of the depth and intensity of the emotion searing inside. Hormones. Had to be.

"Cute, huh?" He winked at her then chuckled. "I think the lady doth protest too much."

"Don't you dare quote Shakespeare at me. Get out!" Heat flooded her neck as she pointed to the door and prayed he'd do as she demanded before she collapsed from mortification. Why had she called his butt cute of all things? Despite the obvious reason, of course. She fought back a wry grin at her own contradictory emotions. Had to be the hormones.

"Fine. But I'm not leaving Twin Oaks." He chuckled again then strutted to the doorway, where he paused and glanced over his shoulder. "See you later."

If there'd been anything within reach, she would have hurled it after his retreating back.

Chapter Six

The sun hung low in the sky, strips of shadows stretching across the immense meadow. Paulette spotted Meredith near the old hawthorn standing sentinel in the center of the expanse. The fairy tree had been planted by some distant ancestor upon arriving in America from Ireland. Although true fairy trees existed only in Ireland, family tradition continued to regard the hawthorn as their protector. She needed all the help she could reasonably expect, even from a tree. She strolled toward her sister, intent on insisting the two brothers be sent packing. Zak Markel had no business meddling in her life. Striding faster, she neared the fairy tree.

Meredith turned to nod at her. "How are you feeling?"

"Damn hormones will have me breaking something important yet." Maybe Zak's neck. "I need a favor."

Meredith exhaled a long sigh. "Now what?"

"Don't give me attitude, I've had my fill of it from Zak Markel."

"What happened?" Meredith plucked a blade of grass and twirled it in her long fingers, one brow raised as a smile grew on her lips. "Did he try to make mad, passionate love to you?"

"Worse." Paulette related the conversation and then crossed her arms. "Make him leave."

"I can't. He's done nothing but make you upset. That's not an evictable offense."

"Huh? Is that even a word?" She shook her head. "Never mind. You're taking his side. Fine. Be that way."

Meredith laughed. "I'm staying out of it, not taking sides. There's a difference."

"He's so freaking exasperating." She stomped a foot, pleased by the solid thud of her shoe on the ground.

"Don't let him rile you. All that fussing can't be good for junior." She shredded the grass into squares, letting them drift away. "I've been thinking…"

The sudden switch in Meredith's voice to a contemplative tone sharpened Paulette's attention. "About?"

"You know how I wanted to turn Twin Oaks into a memorial garden, a place where folks could come to feel closer to their loved ones?"

"I'll never forget. Don't tell me you've changed your mind about preserving the old place?"

"No. But what if we built the garden part out here around the fairy tree?" She mapped out with her hands a circuitous trail beginning at the break in the wall and wrapping slowly around the outer edge of the meadow. "A winding path with flowering trees and shrubs, a few benches here and there."

Paulette imagined the setting easily. "Perhaps some statuary and a fountain or two to add ambiance. I like it."

"It's important to me to never forget Willy and our little unborn son." She scanned the field around them, coming to rest on the squat gnarly hawthorn. "Every time I see this little guy I think of our ancestors and their dreams and hopes for Twin Oaks. I think of my first husband and how much he would have enjoyed living here with the beautiful gardens and landscaping."

"What about Max? Do you think of him too?"

"Max? Of course." Meredith studied the toes of her boots. "That's my future."

"Soon to be your present in a couple months." She searched the frown clouding Meredith's eyes. "Or are you having doubts?"

"Not doubts. I love Max. I do." She sighed and shook her head. "He's wonderful and a perfect fit for me, even though I didn't believe such a thing possible at first."

"Then what's troubling you?"

"I'll never be able to have his children and he desperately wants several." Crossing her arms, she hugged herself. "He deserves to be a father, to be a dad."

"Unlike Johnny?" Paulette shifted her weight, the baby moving against her hands where they rested on her belly. "He walked away from being a dad."

"Have you told him where you are?"

"Why would I? He doesn't care about me."

Meredith regarded her, fingers beating a cadence on one arm. "The baby is still his child. He should be kept informed."

"Ha. He walked out on me, on us." Shaking her head, she gripped her belly with both hands. "No, he's out of the picture, and I'm not letting him back in."

"I think you're making a terrible mistake." She reached out and gripped Paulette's hands. "Even so, I'll back you up no matter what you decide."

"Thanks. Johnny is out like I wish Zak were. I guess I'm stuck with him for now, but I'll do my best to avoid him while he's a guest."

They strolled back toward the house. How could she totally escape from running into the man when he'd inferred he would look for ways to connect?

"I'll talk to Sean about our thoughts on the garden." Meredith paused at the gate to the cemetery, scanning the tilted headstones and ancient graves. She glanced at Paulette. "And about sprucing up the graveyard."

"I'll go make sure things are on track for dinner tonight." She spread her hands wide and grinned. "We'll have a full table for a change."

"Yes. Will you be okay with the guys there?" Meredith quirked a brow. "No throwing things or heated debates?"

"I'm good." She bobbed her head and smirked. Many years of fielding questions and dodging unwanted advances taught her how to handle men. The words of Gloria Gaynor's declaration of "I Will Survive" chanted through her mind. Zak wouldn't best her. "Promise."

"Okay. Talk to you later." With a nod, Meredith turned and hurried toward the caretaker's cottage.

Paulette lingered in the yard. She faced the west and soaked up the last rays of the October sunshine, its gentle warmth bathing her closed eyes and cheeks. Breathing deeply, she remained motionless for several minutes letting her mind calm before reentering the house. Before daring to face her eager suitor however unwanted. Centered emotionally once more, she squared her shoulders and strode toward the back door. She was tougher than he gave her credit for and she'd prove it.

Touching the lighter to the last of ten vanilla votive candles lined up down the center of the dining room table, Paulette found herself humming. She moved back to assess the effect. A childhood ditty vibrated her lips as she scrutinized the room. Pale green walls provided a backdrop to the vermillion drapes and cherry furniture. She sniffed, pleased to detect the final whiffs of the freshly painted walls. A fire flickered in the oversized fireplace, the mantel bedecked with gilded pine cones, yellow pillar candles, and a silk fall foliage garland. Her gaze drifted back to the votive candles as she hummed "You Are My Sunshine." The fully extended table wore a heavy bronze tablecloth. Small, orange pumpkins and ropes of bright red and gold berries snuggled around the candle holders. Simple yet elegant décor. Perfect.

Before long everyone would converge on the lovely table where they would eat and chat. Dinner would bring together the sisters and their parents, also Meg and Sean, and even Max. And, unfortunately, Zak and his brother. That situation had to change for her peace of mind.

Altogether nine folks to enjoy Meg's famous Westphalia— boiled veggies and fragrant smoked pork butt—and tossed salad with cranberries and almonds. Maybe her hot rolls as well, with cinnamon butter melted on the golden crusts. Her tummy growled as her mouth watered. Dinner seemed too long from the moment. Another guttural noise sounded as she scanned the room for one last check and strode out of the dining room, heading for the kitchen and a light snack.

She pushed through the swinging door and stopped abruptly. "Dad, what are you doing?"

Brock sat at the table, a bowl of popcorn at hand. An open bottle of beer stood ready. "What's it look like?"

She crossed to occupy the other chair and grabbed a handful. Popping several kernels into her mouth, she nearly moaned with pleasure as the caramel flavor hit her tongue. "Where've you been?"

"I told you. I have a job nearby." He munched on more popcorn and then drank from the bottle.

She peered at him. Her dad acted different, tense. Clipped sentences with little content. Time to get to the bottom. "Where?"

He glanced at the door and then back to meet her steady gaze. "Nearby."

More caramel joy hit her tongue as she considered his evasion. "Tell me why you really came here a week early?"

"Do I need a reason to see my beautiful daughters?" He drew another swallow of beer.

"When you're being this cagey, yes, you do." She smiled at him to soften her challenge. "Talk to me, Dad. What's up?"

"I don't know exactly. Call it a hunch that my girls needed me." He swigged the beer and squinted at her. "Haven't you ever had a feeling about something and acted on it?"

She nodded and tossed another kernel onto her tongue. She chewed and swallowed, opened her mouth to reply, but as the first sound emerged the back door jerked open behind her. She swiveled in her chair to see Meg and Sean carrying in a large covered pot, a baking sheet of browned dinner rolls, and an immense container of salad. A pulse of annoyance rippled down her back. Such foolishness, really. She pushed to her feet and hurried to help them navigate through the door and place the items on the island countertop.

"You should use this kitchen to cook, Meg." Paulette shook her head at her. "Grandma would have wanted you to."

"I know, I know. She used to grumble about it too. But I prefer my own little stove. It feels right." Meg turned on the burner under the aluminum pot and then swung back to Paulette. Then she spotted the bowl and bottle before Brock and frowned. "Quit that. You'll ruin your appetite."

Sean heaved an exaggerated sigh, a smile sliding into place as he patted his rounded belly. "She'll skin you alive if you don't do justice to her feast. I know I intend to enjoy her fine cooking."

Meg swatted Sean's arm but grinned. "Let me slip the rolls into the oven to keep warm and then I'll help you with setting the table." Meg shoved the pan inside and eased the door closed with a muffled thump.

"Sure smells good, Meg." A low rumble in her belly filled the silence. She puffed a laugh. "See, I'm anxious."

Meg chuckled. "I hear more so than see, but I'll take it as a compliment."

The distant sound of tires on gravel drew Paulette's gaze to the window. Max's green pickup pulled into view, stopping under the ancient magnolias near the cemetery. He emerged, tall and dark haired with a bit of gray frosting at the temples, and sauntered across the expanse. As if on cue, Meredith strode into the kitchen in time to meet Max as he entered the back door. Damn but he had the most beautiful blue eyes she'd ever seen on a man. He kissed Meredith, a quick peck of greeting with a lingering secret smile. When she turned around, her cheeks boasted bright pink swipes and her eyes sparkled. Those two belonged together no matter what else happened.

Meg and Paulette made short work of laying plates and flatware on the dining room table. Dina arrived in time to fold and arrange burnt-orange napkins, providing a splash of color. The three ladies paused to take stock of the results of their efforts. Footsteps in the hall alerted Paulette to the arrival of Zak and Grant. Her heart skipped, but she ordered it to behave. She stared at the weave of the millions of bronze threads covering the table. She stared at the scroll on the knife handle. She even stared at the swirl of color imbued in the artificial fruit as she tucked a stray berry back into place. Anywhere but the doorway.

"Something smells good enough to eat." Zak marched into the room, Grant on his heels.

His deep voice reverberated in her chest, but his flippant tone grated on her last nerve, sending tiny shocks of irritation down her back. Or was the sensation more of an utterly intense awareness picking at her, insisting she look at him. The urge to flee settled in her stomach. She swallowed the sharp retort forming on her tongue. Forced her gaze to lift and find his.

They'd dressed for the occasion. Zak debonair in black slacks and tan sports coat, both cut exquisitely to emphasize the muscular body beneath. A dark green shirt collar and cuffs provided contrasting points. He smiled at her and winked, setting her pulse on fire. *Damn.*

Beside him, Grant stopped and scanned the room. He appeared handsome in his khaki slacks and midnight blue jacket relieved by a crisp, white, buttoned-down shirt. But he couldn't hold a candle to Zak. *Stop it. Focus.* His eyes were a lighter shade of gray than Zak's, like the underbelly of a mourning dove. She hoped they succeeded in discovering a way to prevent him from losing his sight. She motioned to the row of empty chairs on the side of the table facing the door. "Please."

"Anything we can do to help?" Grant moved to his place, resting his hands on the back of the chair.

Zak sidled around the table to his seat and sat down, his attention never wavering from Paulette's face. *Look away, damn it.* Still his attention weighed upon her like those lead aprons the dentist made her wear for a mouth x-ray. God, how she hated going to the dentist. The thought steeled her. She could do this. Be in the same room without melting down. Ignoring him, she addressed Grant.

"Just have a seat." The younger man's sincere offer helped soothe the tumult inside. Zak's thoughtful gaze pressed upon her, but she focused on Grant's open expression instead. "It's under contról."

"You two can sit there and be patient." Meredith moved around the table, making tiny adjustments to the silverware to align them to her satisfaction. "You're guests, after all."

Unfortunately for her. Paulette took her seat at the opposite end of the table rather than heed the temptation to escape this most uncomfortable situation and take dinner in her room with a good book. Despite her near constant need to reach out and touch the man, she kept her hands in check and her butt firmly in her seat. She suppressed a sigh and squared her shoulders. Zak wouldn't scare her away in her own home.

Meg returned, carrying a serving bowl piled with the fragrant boiled dinner and placed it in a large space at the foot of the table. "Take your places, everyone. Dinner is served."

"Anyone want wine with dinner?" Brock hefted two bottles of wine, one merlot and one chardonnay. He slipped the white wine into the ice bucket on the sideboard, placed the red beside it, and then took his seat at the head of the table. "I'll play wine steward."

Paulette's view of her father included the tea service over his shoulder, gleaming in the light from the crystal chandelier hanging above the table. The muted lighting enabled the row of candles to create the intended atmosphere. The silver set evoked chills each time she gazed upon it. Better to look at Zak than stare at the tea service. She shifted in her chair and cleared a place for the salad.

"Just don't drink all of it yourself." Dina added the glass bowl with its tongs to the table and sat down at her husband's right, beside Grant.

"Beautiful salad, Meg." Paulette reached for the tongs and pinched the mixed greens, tomatoes, cranberries and other toppings into the bowl by her plate. She passed the large salad bowl to Meredith on her left.

Brock chuckled but made no reply to the jab. Paulette understood her mom's reminder though. Her father had a tendency to imbibe too much at a time, leaving him very merry but forgetful of what transpired. At least he didn't become angry or violent as a result. Unlike other men in her life.

Meredith cleared her throat. "I'd like to formally

welcome Zak and Grant to Twin Oaks. We hope you enjoy your stay with us."

"Thank you. We plan to." Zak nodded at Meredith and then Paulette. "With such wonderful hostesses we can't fail."

"We need a toast." Brock retrieved the wine and poured some into the glasses around the table, though he skipped Paulette's glass with a wink. Returning to stand at his place, he hoisted his wine.

She raised her water glass when everyone followed her dad's lead. She could only hope whatever spilled out of his mouth wouldn't embarrass her or commit them to anything. She watched her father as a slow smile etched onto his lips. Now what?

"To new friends."

Friends? The men could barely be termed acquaintances. If the situation were different, she could imagine Zak as her lover. *Whoa. Hold up. Not that.* She couldn't permit even the thought. She glanced at her dad, then to Grant, and finally Zak. Zak regarded her, bemused, so yummy to look at she could lose herself in him without any qualms. His fathomless eyes, his sultry lips, and his deep rich voice, summed up to a perfect man. If only…

"Hear, hear!" Meredith chimed in and then sipped her wine.

Paulette hesitated and then drank from her glass.

Zak cleared his throat and stood up, lifting his glass in salute toward her. "And to discovering new possibilities."

"He's sweet on you." Patrick materialized at her elbow.

The glass in her tense hand trembled as she glanced up to where her grandpa stood. "Don't do that."

Zak frowned at her from across the table. "Why not?"

"Not you." She shook her head, remembering too late only she and Meredith could actually see the ghost beside her. She noted her sister's face had paled. "I thought I saw…the cat, but I was wrong."

"Oh. Well. I'll say it again. To new possibilities." He lifted his glass along with everyone else except Paulette. He hesitated before drinking, intent on her still trembling glass. "You didn't drink."

"You should have gone along with it." Patrick moved around the table, stopping behind each person to inspect their plate of untouched food.

She shared a horrified look with Meredith as their grandfather reached their dad. Patrick laid both hands on his shoulders and leaned around to put his face up to Brock's. Paulette braced her hands on the table edge, waiting and preparing for her dad's reaction.

She didn't have long to wait.

"What the hell?" Brock jumped up, pushing into Patrick's space, sending him flying backward.

"It's okay, Dad." Meredith reached him where he stood by the sideboard, his massive frame shivering as though he'd stepped into a walk-in freezer.

Zak rose to his feet and dropped his napkin on the table. "Are you all right?"

Paulette glared at her smirking grandfather. "You need to leave. Now."

Patrick grinned. "Not until you're satisfied with why you summoned me, my dear."

"I'm not going anywhere." Zak speared her with his stare. "Something odd is going on here, and I want to know what it is."

"Nothing is going on." She couldn't reveal the truth. Zak's horrified expression as well as her father's discouraged her from revealing any more about what they couldn't perceive. "You may as well leave."

Patrick sidled up to Paulette. "You alone have the power to send me home."

"She does?" Meredith laid her hand on Brock's arm, a calming gesture, even as she stared at Patrick.

"All she has to do is delve deep inside." Patrick patted his chest. "Where it counts the most."

"What are you staring at?" Zak crossed his arms and addressed Paulette and Meredith in turn. "I don't see anything out of the ordinary, but obviously you two do."

Meredith shook her head, though she kept focused on Patrick. "It's nothing. Really. Dad is having a moment, that's all."

"Ha!" Patrick barked out a laugh. "I'll give him a moment. He owes me that much, at least."

Paulette considered Zak's suspicious expression. He knew more than he realized. Patrick had to vanish before their guests learned the truth about the plantation. If they believed the house actually played host to ghosts, they'd leave and take their money with them. Money Paulette counted upon to provide for herself and her baby. A chill inched through her at the scenarios cascading through her mind.

"Dad, why don't you sit back down and finish your dinner." Paulette waved toward the abandoned chair. "Come on, your food is going to be cold."

"I lost my appetite." Brock didn't shiver as violently after Patrick had retreated to the other side of the table from where he stood with Meredith. "You all go ahead without me."

"He owes me!" Patrick shoved a chair aside, causing it to crash to the floor. "If only Brock had told me of his vision, then I'd be alive and none of this would have happened."

Grant jumped to his feet, his chair falling backward. "What was that?"

Dina gripped the table, eyes wide and unblinking.

"Calm down, everything's fine." Paulette glared at Patrick, who ignored her. "Sit down and let's finish our meal."

Beside her, Dina looked up, fear evident in her

countenance. She slowly shook her head and pushed back from the table. Without a word, she left the room at a trot.

"I have some work to do." Grant headed for the door, pausing at the entrance to do a quick scan of the room and then regard Paulette and Meredith. "Thanks for dinner. It was unusual, to say the least."

Zak pinned Paulette with a steady assessment. "One day, you'll tell me what's going on here."

Not if she could help it. "Nothing is going on."

"I'm not stupid. I will find out." He headed to the door, stopping at her side to peer into her eyes. "There really is more to you than I first thought.

"I'll go check on your mother." Brock hurried past Zak, practically running from the room.

After the room had cleared, Paulette marched to where Patrick stood chuckling. "That was uncalled for. And…childish. And…and…bad manners."

"Dad couldn't have known your future, for goodness sake." Meredith crossed her arms and glared at the ghost. "We'd know if he had such an ability."

Patrick disappeared in a huff.

"Come back here and explain yourself, damn it!" Paulette spun around, searching for some sign. "You can't just come and go as you please."

"Of course I can." Patrick slowly materialized sitting in Brock's chair. "He does have a gift, one he used to enjoy playing with. Until…"

"Something bad happened, didn't it?" His brow wrinkled and he nodded. She waited, but he remained mute. Her dad always hid his true feelings, downplayed his talents, and apparently allowed something awful to occur. "I knew it. Tell me."

"I died."

"Because of his gift? How?" Meredith sank onto a chair by Patrick.

"What did he do?" Paulette stayed on her feet.

Patrick blinked at each of them in turn. Steepling his fingers, he nodded. "Fine, I'll tell you. But you won't like it."

"Go on." Meredith glanced at Paulette and then at Patrick. "Spill."

"My son can foresee the future." Patrick leaned back in his chair, laying his palms flat beside the remains of Brock's dinner.

"I don't understand." Paulette shifted her weight from one foot to the other. "How did that kill you?"

"Simple. He didn't tell me about the explosion."

"So you couldn't change the future." Meredith leaned her elbows on the table and propped her hands together.

"He's never even hinted at his talent." Paulette didn't blame him, if he truly believed his actions caused Patrick's death. "I wonder if his vision can at least tell me about my mysterious need."

Chapter Seven

The toaster popped up, flinging wheat toast onto the counter. Quickly, Paulette nipped the hot bread onto her plate, blowing on her fingers to cool them. Twisting open the apple butter, she dabbed a knife into the jar. The mix of cinnamon, spices, and apples proved intoxicating. Drawing in a long breath, she savored the scent that was chockfull of childhood memories of baking and canning with her mother and grandmother. She spread the rich brown topping onto the warm toast, swirling patterns as she did so.

She poured a cup of coffee and carried her breakfast to the table. Meredith had already left the house, off to put out yet another fire on her frustrating redesign job. Meg would be busily preparing the guests' morning meal: something fabulous. More than a piece of toast and coffee, no doubt. Outside, the sun struggled to rouse itself above the line of clouds at the horizon. A front was moving in, bringing heavy rain.

After the events at dinner the night before, she planned to visit the Golden Owl and Roxie. She needed to talk to someone outside of the situation to get a different view of the startling revelations all around her.

The kitchen door swung open and Zak hesitated in the doorway for a split second before continuing. "Morning, beautiful."

"Don't call me that." She sipped her decaf coffee, trying to convey with her eyes the distaste his comment caused within her. From his twinkling orbs though, she'd failed in her mission. "You have no right."

"I call it like I see it." The smile grew until his white teeth flashed. He pointed to her cup. "Any more of that?"

She nodded toward the coffee maker. "Help yourself. Mugs are in the cupboard to the right."

He nabbed a mug and filled it with the steaming liquid. Propping himself against the counter, he regarded her between sips. "What's on your agenda for today?"

She bit into her toast, chewed, and debated how scathing of a reply to give him. How dare he? Her business was just that. Hers. She took another bite.

She focused on her toast, savoring the taste in her mouth, while she ignored the man beside her. It didn't matter, though, as his mere presence ignited tiny thrills along her arms. She had to force herself to not look askance at him or drink in his manly beauty. His aftershave wafted to her nose and she inhaled, exhaled. Commanded her pulse to slow and breathing to return to normal.

"Ignoring me doesn't make me go away, you know." He walked to the chair facing her and scraped it out from its home under the table. Turning it backward, he straddled the seat and then settled on the hard surface, putting the mug on the table. As she continued to eat, he leaned his arms along the chair back and rested his chin on them, contemplating her silence. "I see. You don't think it's any of my concern what you do."

She blinked, took a sip of coffee. Swallowed. *Go away.* Sitting right in front of her made it impossible to not look at him, not wish to run her fingers through his luxurious hair.

Trail a hand along his strong, stubborn jaw. She had to protect her heart from him. She took another bite.

"I thought so." He pushed up, grabbed his mug. Swallowing the hot brew, he smiled. "Why don't you tell me what really happened last night at dinner? We can start there."

He would ask about that right off the bat. "I already told you. Nothing happened." Nothing he needed to know about anyway.

"See, I don't believe you. Why did your dad jump up and start shivering? And how did the chair fall over all by itself?" He shook his head, waggled a forefinger at her. "And don't tell me it was nothing."

She shrugged. "You won't let it rest, will you?"

"No way, sweetheart."

"Okay. Fine. Dad has what we call 'moments' when his imagination runs away with him and he reacts. Weird, I know." She hoped he'd buy that.

He stared at her, blinked, smirked. "You almost had me. But not quite. Try again, this time with the truth."

"You didn't believe the truth when you heard it." The lie rested uneasily on her conscience, but she had to divert this line of inquiry. "Nothing happened."

"You know, you're reminding me of that Roxie woman at the bookstore. Your new friend, right?"

She angled her head, raised a brow. "What about her?"

"You said her mom wrote the book on witchcraft." He studied her, toying with the mug between his hands. "Does that make those women witches?"

Not a chance. Where did he come up with that idea? "No. It doesn't."

He shook his head at her. "I think it does. And I think you're in on their secret."

"You're way off base here, Zak. Roxie's not a witch."

"I also think the store logo points to them as involved in

the secret elixir. The owl as a guardian of the witches. And the branches the owl holds represent Twin Oaks and you and Meredith."

She leaned back in her chair and laughed. "I'll give you one thing, you sure have a creative imagination."

"I'm serious." He rested his arms on the chair. "Not that I have any hope of actually settling the issue one way or another."

She nodded, relief a sweet visitor. "Anyone who could answer your question died a long time ago."

"You know, the more I look at you, the more I realize you do resemble them, quite a lot."

"You're crazy. I'm not like them, nor do I bear any resemblance to them."

"They could be your sisters."

A smile eased onto her lips at the absurd notion. "I only have one sister."

"Cousins then." He waggled a hand at her, skimmed his gaze over her body. "You do have the same eyes and similar frame as they have."

"Hazel eyes are very common. I know how hard this is for you." Her smile widened even as she fidgeted from the intensity of his inspection. She'd seen how much he counted on being right, in everything. "You're wrong, on all counts, and you'll just have to live with that fact."

"I don't think so." He lifted the mug to his lips and replaced it on the table. "But suit yourself."

So smug, so righteous. So *wrong*. "We're friends, nothing more."

"Have it your way." Zak rose and pivoted the chair back into place, leaning on the back as he regarded her. "You're a very special woman. I have one favor to ask. Please allow me to spend time with you."

His sincerity shocked her senses. While the prospect proved enticing, she had to stick to the plan. Her heart pleaded to go to him, but her brain shackled the irresponsible organ in its place. "That's not a good idea."

"You keep saying that, but I don't believe you." Zak pulled the chair back out and sat down. Leaning across the table, he reached for her hand, waiting for her to move to touch him.

Despite her resolve, her fingertips finally touched his warmth. He wrapped his long fingers around her slender hand, as gentle as if he held an injured bird. Such a tender gesture from a powerful man sent tremors through her. Rocked her inner determination. She raised her eyes to search his face, detected his desire in the set of his mouth and darkened irises. Damn, but she wanted him too.

He lowered his gaze until she felt him want to kiss her. Literally could feel the pressure of his gaze upon her mouth. She flicked her tongue across dry lips. He watched the movement with the expression of a starving man at a forbidden banquet. She swallowed, trying to force moisture onto her tongue.

"Paulette, I'm going to kiss you." He focused on her mouth, then her eyes, and back to her lips.

"I don't—"

Her words died as he stood and drew her up with him until they faced each other beside the table, mere inches separating them. His intense desire sparked an answering need in her, one she should ignore but which tempted her to the point of intrigue. He engulfed her hands in his, resting them against his broad chest. A gentle lift to the corners of his mouth preceded Zak pulling her closer, until only the baby wedged distance between them. His eyes fixed on her lips and slowly he lowered his head to press his mouth to hers.

At the first taste of him, the scent of him, she lost herself in the sensations rocketing through her. When Zak parted her lips and slid inside her mouth, she moaned as little thrills shot across her tongue. Heaven's joy. Too soon, he withdrew, lightly pecking her lips as a coda to their passionate kiss.

"Thank you, sweetheart." He squeezed her hands and then released them. "You've started my day off perfectly."

She wanted to deny her desperate response to the man, but she hated to lie. Bopping her head to the side, she offered a wry grin. "I'm glad I didn't disappoint after all of your insistence."

"And it will only improve with practice." He smiled back at her, touched an invisible hat, as he moved toward the back door. "I'm afraid I have some errands to run, so I must leave you for now."

Keep it light and easy. Can't get attached to this gorgeous hunk of a man or risk my sanity as well as my heart. She tried to grin, but the idea of the promised future practice quailed her insides. "And as they say, 'parting is such sweet sorrow.'"

In two long strides, he reached her side and ducked in to kiss her soundly. She gasped against his mouth, resistance a reflex. But the man could kiss. She'd give him that. She relaxed into his embrace, certain she'd chastise herself later for her weakness but determined to enjoy the experience.

He pulled back and scanned her face with a Cheshire Cat smile. "You're addicting." He kissed her again before she could formulate a reply. "I'll see you later."

"Thanks for the warning." She returned his wave as he disappeared out the door. Oh man, what had she gotten herself into this time?

The little bell jangled as Paulette entered the Golden Owl. She scanned the store, searching for Roxie. Her friend would laugh at Zak's foolish notions. Sisters? Cousins? No way.

Spotting a dark head in the cookbook section, she darted

through the shelves and stacks of books. She caught up to Roxie, skirting a table loaded down with various book lights, stands, and beaded bookmarks. The brunette straightened up from where she hunched over a stack of books, one splayed open on top. On one page a photo depicted a tiered stand holding a dozen cupcakes with Halloween themed decorations.

"Hey friend, what're you looking at?" She folded her arms and smiled at Roxie. Zak's words echoed in her memory when she noticed the blonde strands intermingled among the chocolate brown tresses.

"Great timing. I was hoping you'd stop in." Roxie pointed to the photo, then closed the book and picked it up. "This is what Meredith needs for your party."

"Hopefully it'll help her finally settle on the menu." Paulette accepted the book. "You and your sisters are coming, right?"

"We wouldn't miss it." Roxie grinned. "Guess what our costumes are going to be?"

Don't say witches. Please. Don't. Dare she ask? "I have no clue."

"Guess." She turned to shelve one of the dozen cookbooks.

"Must I?" Guessing games annoyed her six ways to Sunday. Most of all the delay in reaching the point of the discussion. Her out of whack hormones didn't help her hide the impatience zinging inside, either.

"Yes."

"Fine." On a sigh, Paulette shook her head as she racked her brain for threesomes. "The Three Little Pigs?"

"Nope. Guess again."

What else came in threes? "The Billy Goats Gruff?"

"Come on, be serious and guess." Roxie slipped two more books efficiently into their homes.

Okay, but she sure hoped she was wrong. "Witches?"

"Yes. We've found the perfect costumes to be sexy vixen type witches."

Really? Zak would have a field day with their choice. "No green faces and pointed hats?"

Roxie tossed her head with a laugh, her wavy locks rippling down her back. "We're not in Oz. But wait until you see the adorable short skirts and flowing black capes we picked up for a song. You'll love them."

"Are you sure you want to dress like witches?"

"Sure, we thought it would be fun." Roxie frowned and then arched one brow. "Wait, were you planning to be a witch too?"

"No, it's not that." Truth be told she hadn't chosen her own costume as of yet.

Roxie snapped her fingers. "If you did, then we'd make our own coven for the evening. Would Meredith want to join us?"

Great idea, a pregnant witch. Just great. "I think she and Max are planning something together."

"Oh, right." Roxie finished placing the last book into place. "What's your costume? I bet it'll be fabulous."

"I'm still debating." As if she'd really thought about it. How does one dress up when big with child?

"Have you considered coming as the belle of the ball, in one of those marvelous hoop skirt type of gowns?"

"Don't expect me to wear the corset." Paulette shook her head, ponytail bopping tense shoulders. She laid a hand on her belly. "I don't think I'd fit into one of those this year."

"You could always paint your baby bump like a basketball or something, dress like an NBA player."

Paulette chuckled as the image bloomed in her mind. "Paint it?"

"Sure. At the costume contest we held here last year, one lady even made hers look like a watermelon and shared slices of real melon with other contestants."

Paulette laughed as she folded her arms. "I wouldn't be comfortable exposing myself like that. I'd rather wear something flowing."

"You only have a week to be creative, but I bet you'll come up with something fabulous." Roxie led the way toward the front of the store. "What brought you in today? I wasn't expecting you so soon after our last chat."

"I wanted to share the silly notions one of our guests told me this morning." She laid the book on the counter, pulling out her wallet to pay for it. Tara and Beth worked in the coffee bar, preparing a variety of hot beverages for the line of customers. "He's so off-base, it's hysterical."

"Which guest? Do I know him?" Roxie slipped behind the counter and scanned the book with the device.

"Yes, one of the guys who came in here a few days ago. Zak Markel."

"Right, I remember." Roxie indicated for Paulette to swipe her card. "What did he say?"

"He asked if we're related, sisters or cousins." She put her credit card back in her wallet. "I told him we're friends, nothing more."

"Good friends." Roxie slipped the book into a bag without meeting her eyes.

"Hey Paulette, I have a question for you." Beth approached from the coffee bar, wiping her hands on the bib apron protecting her red polo and khaki jeans.

"Hey, yourself. It looks like business is good." Paulette motioned to the queue of customers and smiled at the younger woman. "What's your question?"

"Have you chosen your costume yet?" She braced her hands on the counter. "We usually go as witches, but I thought I might do something different this year."

Beth's dark blonde hair and green eyes distinguished her from the other two sisters. She was the same height as Paulette and similar in build. As the woman neared, her eyes caught the light and revealed gold flecks against the bright green irises. Just like Meredith's. She stilled, swallowed the lump of disbelief forming in her throat. It couldn't be.

She studied Roxie's face, her golden eyes and blonde highlights, her similar height and build to Beth. Could Zak have been right?

"What do you mean, something different?" Roxie gaped at Beth. "We always dress as witches."

Tension hummed between the sisters. "I haven't decided yet." She couldn't stop staring at the two women. Comparing their features to her own and her sister's.

Beth stayed focused on Paulette, avoiding the surprise on her sister's face. She sighed, a heartfelt release of tension. "I suppose it's easier to go with the flow rather than buck tradition."

"I'm glad that's settled, Beth. Paulette, do you have time for lunch?" Roxie glanced at Beth, who nodded. "If you give me a few minutes to finish one little task, we could go down the street to the café for a sandwich and discuss the options."

"Sounds good. I'll text Meredith to let her know."

The bell jangled again and Zak and Grant filled the doorway. Those two certainly had incredible timing.

"Lookee there, Grant." Zak strode across the store to stand next to Paulette. "Ladies."

The closer he came, the more she trembled. His eyes fixed on her face, a mysterious smile lifting his lips ever so slightly. He made her feel on edge, anticipating, like the air before the arrival of a thunderstorm on the horizon. Their earlier meeting of mouths added to the tension between them.

"Hey Zak, Grant." Roxie emerged from behind the counter, stopping beside Paulette. "Nice to see you again."

"What are you doing here?" She glanced at Roxie,

grateful for her silent support. Had he followed her? She didn't recall telling him where she intended to go. "I thought you had some errands to run."

"It's a free country." He lifted a brow as he explored her expression, his gaze drifting to her lips. "Maybe I wanted a good cup of coffee. What I had this morning didn't have any kick."

"It was decaf, silly." Paulette grinned at him, suddenly realizing she'd forgotten to warn him. "I'm not supposed to have caffeine."

He flicked a glance to her belly and back to meet her eyes. He nodded twice as his mouth performed a widening grin. "That explains it. I need real coffee."

"You've come to the right place." Beth acknowledged the men with a nod. "I can help you over there."

"At least one addiction can be satisfied this morning." He reached out and tucked a stray hair behind her ear, sending bolts of lightning through her.

She retreated a step, putting enough distance between them to break his contact. "Then get in line."

"I'm buying, so I'll stand in line." Grant looked at her, then Zak. "You two behave yourselves while I'm gone, okay?"

"Oh, we will." Zak smiled at Paulette. "Can we talk? In private?"

Paulette glanced at Roxie, willing her to stay by her. Roxie examined her expression then grinned at Zak. "I'll be right over there in case either of you need me."

She strode away, leaving Paulette alone with the man she least wanted to be alone with. After this morning's adventure, she couldn't trust herself to resist him. Maybe if she hid behind her hormones she could survive the challenge.

Paulette crossed her arms and glared at Zak. Maybe that would put him off and he'd leave her be. "What now?"

Without replying, he caressed her elbow and escorted

her to the little nook where a writing table waited for a customer to sit and address a note or postcard. The cozy corner featured a charming faux distressed table with matching chairs. After they were seated, he regarded her for a long moment. While he silently studied her with serious gray eyes, she returned the favor.

Thick wavy black hair framed a strong jaw and straight nose. He sported a black-and-blue welt from the explosion in his lab he'd told her about, but it didn't change the fact that he was strikingly handsome. His full lips enticed her when he pressed them together and then relaxed into a smile. The cords on his neck stood out in stark relief, leading down to broad shoulders and muscular arms. His chest rose and fell in a steady rhythm, the beat of his heart apparent in the pulse at his throat exposed by the unbuttoned collar. She inhaled and caught the scent of his after shave, pleased at the spicy blend.

"I wish you would let me take you to dinner one night, Paulette." He leaned toward her, closing the distance between them.

"You tempt me, Zak, but I can't." She prepared to stand, and he reached out to lay a hand on her arm. "I told you why. Please, remove your hand."

"Please sit back down. I want to talk." He kept his hand on her arm until she reluctantly resumed her seat. "Thanks."

"We don't have anything to say." Folding her hands, she propped them on her belly, a silent reminder of why she wouldn't agree to see him.

"I know you don't believe me that the sisters are witches, but hear me out."

"Why should I?" His perceptions may be more on target than she cared to admit, but she wouldn't let him spread harmful rumors about her friends. "Give me one good reason."

"Do you know why I came to Roseville?"

"You said research."

He nodded, keeping his eyes on hers. "Into the specifics of an ingredient for an experiment, one that apparently can only be found around here. The symbol on the sign out front was sketched into an alchemist's journal."

"So?"

"The journal is dated more than three hundred years ago."

Her brows shot up of their own volition. "How is that possible?"

"My question too. So I came here figuring the store must be related to the ingredient, or perhaps holds the clue to solve the mystery."

"What do Roxie, Tara, and Beth have to do with your puzzle?"

"If I'm right, and they are witches, then they should know what the symbol represents, and thus how to find what I'm looking for."

"But they're not witches." Or were they? Why had they chosen to dress up like sexy witches?

"I think they are, and I think they know about the dark arts and black magic."

She gasped. She couldn't help it. "How dare you. My friends are not into evil sorcery."

"I didn't say they were into anything evil, just magic." His gaze remained steady in the face of her vehemence. "I'm right again. I can prove it."

"No, you can't, because you're wrong again."

"Those three women know about magic and they can lead me to the answers I seek. Believe me."

She pushed to her feet as quickly as she could manage. "Get out of here. I won't listen to your accusations and you won't mention your false beliefs to anyone." She poked a finger at him. "Stop spreading lies and vicious rumors about my friends."

"But, sweetheart…" He stood up and shook his head at her. "You don't have any control over what I do. And definitely not over what I believe."

"Maybe not, but I can insist you leave me alone." She bristled when he laughed. "Get out of here before I forget I'm a pregnant woman and show you just how angry you've made me."

Chapter Eight

*H*alf an hour later, Paulette followed Roxie to their seats at the little sidewalk café. Amber's buzzed with customers sampling the new fare, unaccustomed to a menu smacking of California health foods. Word had it Amber had recently moved from San Diego, but nobody knew why she had chosen Roseville. Sure wasn't the sightseeing. A parade of pickups and SUVs flowed by on the street. Sparrows hopped among dried leaves on the concrete sidewalk, pecking in search of dropped bits of food. The light breeze brushed wisps of hair into the corner of her eye. She pulled them free and tucked them behind one ear. Perusing the menu, she debated between a grilled tuna salad and a pulled pork BBQ sandwich. Healthy or indulgent?

Roxie laid her menu down. "What did Zak want to talk to you about?"

Her friend's expression revealed her curiosity. "He insists he wants to take me out, that's all."

An elderly waiter interrupted their conversation, took their order, and hurried away. Interesting that Amber had hired such an old guy to wait on customers. With so many folks scrambling to make ends meet, she shouldn't be surprised at the variety in age. She understood the need to find a way to provide adequately for loved ones. She'd pinned her dreams of success on her costume business as well as her attempts to restart her interior decorating venture, but this time following her own designs and not the demands of an uninspired boss.

"What's wrong with him dating you?" Roxie quirked an eyebrow, a he's-too-yummy-to-ignore grin curving her lips. "He's a hunk."

Paulette patted her baby bump and shook her head. "It doesn't seem fair to saddle anyone with being a dad to another man's baby."

Roxie sat back and blinked twice. "He knows you're pregnant and still he wants to see you. Give him some credit."

"I know, but…" She glanced down the street, the shade trees cooling the fall air even more. High thin clouds cluttered the sky. Another week and the temperatures would drop enough to dissuade anyone from sitting outside. "I'll deliver this babe in a little more than a month, and I don't know Zak at all." She sipped her water.

"That's not quite true, since he's living in the same house as you." Roxie placed the clear plastic straw between her lips and sipped her sweet tea. "Have you seen him without a shirt yet?"

Paulette guffawed, nearly spraying her swallow of water across the table. "No, and I don't wish to. Behave."

"You should date him. He's smart and has a good job." She fiddled with the sugar packets, riffling through the white, pink, and yellow packages. "Both good qualities in a dad."

Paulette flung a shut-your-mouth glance at her new friend. "I want more from a man, or a dad, than that. He has to like my friends too."

"Why? He's not marrying your friends." Roxie selected a

yellow one and fanned the sweetener, flopping it back and forth against her fingertips, then tore it open and dumped the white powder into her tea.

Paulette grimaced but said nothing about the amount of sweet in the glass of already-sweet tea. "This particular man seems to like to accuse my friends of outrageous things."

Roxie stilled her hand from swirling a long-handled spoon in the glass. "What friends are we discussing?"

The waiter returned carrying a large brown tray. He deposited Paulette's salad, the tuna steak perched on top of a mass of bean sprouts, grape tomatoes, cucumbers, and shredded cheese before her, and a turkey club sandwich on ciabatta and sweet potato fries in front of Roxie. After checking that their order was correct, he moved on to the next table.

"It's nothing." She shook her head and mixed the poppy seed dressing into the greens. Zak's words flitted through her memory, stirring a defensive anger in her stomach. "It's silly, really."

"I can tell he's upset you with whatever he said." Roxie tapped the spoon on the rim and laid it on a napkin. She picked up a fry and searched Paulette's face, then she smiled. "It's me, isn't it?"

Reluctantly, Paulette nodded. "And Tara. And Beth."

Roxie leaned on her elbows, one hand around her tea and the other laying on the cold metal, and peered across the table. "What did he accuse us of exactly?"

Could she say it? Did she believe it, even a tiny bit? "I'll tell you, but he has no way to prove what he believes."

"I'm dying here. Tell me." Roxie bit delicately into her sandwich, chewed, waiting for a response.

Paulette dragged in a long breath and let it out slowly. She half shrugged, forcing her shoulders down into place as she glanced around. The other diners chatted and laughed, deep into their own conversations. No one sat alone, able to overhear what she prepared to say. Leaning forward, she lowered her voice. "He thinks you're all witches."

Roxie chuckled. "Oh. That."

Flummoxed by the casual acceptance of the outlandish accusation, Paulette could only blink slowly at Roxie, fork hovering halfway between the bowl and her mouth. "What do you mean, 'oh that'?"

Roxie laughed outright. "I wish you could see your face."

"Answer my question." It couldn't be true. Could it? She rested the fork among the bite-sized pieces of romaine.

"It's not something we talk about, but he's right." She popped a fry into her mouth.

"Why didn't you tell me?"

Roxie relaxed against the white metal chair back shaped like a stylized open heart. "We've only been friends for a short while, so we didn't want to spring it on you."

"Is this why you three are coming as witches to our party?"

Laughter echoed in her eyes. "Of course. It's the one time of year when we can openly dress as we like." She bit into her sandwich, a drop of mayonnaise lingering in the corner of her mouth. With a swipe of a finger, she wiped it away.

"Sexy vixen witches? Isn't that what you said?" Her new friend admitted to being a witch. How should she react? Casual like her? Curious? Hickory mingled with tuna on her tongue as she chewed.

Roxie nodded and swallowed. "We're single and available and looking to have some fun. So why not?"

"I see. Maybe *you* should date Zak. Or Grant. They're both available too. I'll set you up."

"That's not a good idea. After all, he's interested in you, not me."

"Well, Grant's available, though he does seem impatient with Zak's quest."

"That's because Grant doesn't seem to believe in magic or even alchemy." Roxie shrugged and cocked a brow. "So you see, unless either of them believes in magic, they won't make for a good match for any of us. But *you* are an entirely different matter."

"Are you forgetting about what's been happening out at Twin Oaks…" The people around her continued to murmur and eat. Cars and trucks rolled by. Sparrows searched as before. "And our special guests?"

"If you're talking about your Civil War ghosts, that was a temporary problem, not a life choice." Roxie poured ketchup on her plate, dipped a fry in the red sauce, and then pointed it at Paulette. "And you don't need to worry, nobody's listening to us." The fry disappeared between her teeth.

"Still, Meredith and I agreed to downplay a certain reality." Paulette speared a grape tomato, dragged it through the dressing, and popped it into her mouth.

"Makes sense, but don't hesitate to talk to me." Roxie lifted her sandwich. "I know something about protecting and warding properties, should the need arise."

Like her grandfather. "Actually, I may need your help convincing the spirit of my grandfather to leave."

Roxie swallowed and shook her head disbelievingly. "Another ghost is haunting your place? Must be a magnet for spirits."

"It's my fault." She cut up her tuna, mixing it into the greens and reds in the bowl. "I accidentally summoned him and now he refuses to leave. Not until whatever need I have is satisfied, but I have no idea what *need* I have."

"That's curious." Roxie started to take a bite then stopped, staring at Paulette for a long moment. "What were you doing when you summoned him?"

She relived the moments prior to Patrick's appearance. Striding into the room with Griz, humming as she tried to budge the trunk, opening it, reading the spell. "It all started because I wanted to move a heavy trunk so I could reach a dress dummy. Beyond that, nothing really."

An adventurous sparrow landed on the table and hopped toward Paulette. It chirped twice as it neared. She reached out a finger to see if he'd fly away. It cocked its brown and white striped head, aiming one eye at her as it considered its next move. Another chirp and it reached her finger. Marvin Gaye's "Sparrow" echoed in her mind, his call to the bird in the song to sing to him personally and let him know everything was as it should be. She moved her hand closer and it hopped onto her finger as if she'd trained it to do so. Startled when the tiny talons wrapped around her skin, she jerked her hand and the sparrow flew away.

"That was weird." Roxie reached for her drink and took a long pull on the straw. "Are birds usually so friendly with you?"

"No, that's never happened before." She reached in her purse, drew out her hand sanitizer. Rubbing in the gel, she gazed at Roxie while "Sparrow" flowed through her thoughts. "You were saying about my grandfather…"

"At least you have the opportunity to get to know him." A fry landed on her tongue and she chewed slowly. "My grandfather died years ago in a freak accident so none of us ever knew him."

Paulette stopped chewing. Not wanting to play "see food," she shielded her mouth with one hand. "What kind of accident?" Chewing slowly, she contemplated the woman before her, so similar and yet distinct. Was it possible?

"Mom said he'd tried to replicate an ancient potion but the spell backfired." She cocked her head, similar to the little bird moments before. "Are you all right?"

"An elixir you mean?" Her fork clattered against the ceramic bowl. "When you say potion?"

"I'm not certain. Why?"

"What was your grandfather's name?" Anticipation mingled with expectation into a tension spreading from her core.

"My mom always referred to him as Papaw Finn."

"Oh." *Dang.* A swarm of butterflies invaded her stomach. Relief? Or disappointment?

"Why? What's wrong?"

"Nothing." She studied the light brown eyes regarding her. "Just some crazy idea."

Roxie leaned closer, her hands flat on the table. "You can tell me. I promise not to laugh."

Shrugging, Paulette speared a bite of cucumber. "I will, but later, after I do some digging." She chewed the crisp veggie, plotting her strategy.

"You're killing me." Roxie relaxed against the chair and fiddled with her lunch. "What's so secret you can't share now?"

Not a secret so much as an uncertainty. "Enjoy your lunch, my friend. When I know one way or the other, I'll reveal all to you." She had some work to do first.

Afternoon sunshine highlighted dust motes in the sewing parlor. Paulette perched on a hard chair before the writing desk, her laptop displaying her favorite genealogy site. She'd located the family tree her grandmother had created over the past years before she died. As a relative included on the tree, the site enabled her to import the data into her own account. The process of copying all of the names and dates dragged by. Another five minutes until the download finished. She'd dug around for twenty minutes before she'd located what she needed. She drummed her fingers on the desk, glaring at the slow bar inching across the screen. Her buttocks ached from the wood beneath her, but she wasn't moving until she had an answer.

Sorting through the hundreds if not thousands of names included in the complete tree would take time, but she had an idea of where to poke first. Starting with the full name of her fun-loving yet errant grandfather.

She stared at the recalcitrant download progress bar on the screen, urging it to hurry up and finish. Shifting to relieve the ache, she leaned back and rested both hands on her baby bump. Before long she'd be adding a new name and set of statistics into the family tree. What name would it be? Selecting a name proved challenging and it didn't matter whether she had a boy or a girl. Names seemed to somehow determine the personality of the child. Or at least, she'd seen studies discussing how the two influenced each other in some way. She'd elected to not determine the child's sex, but keep it a mystery until the birth day arrived.

Should she name the child after Johnny's side of the family, or her own, or some combination? Did Johnny even deserve a connection to the baby, when he'd walked away from them? He may not, but the child deserved to know who its father was. His name would not be a secret. No shame existed in her heart for loving the man, after all. No shame would attach to the child resulting from such love.

A chime announced the data dump completed. Leaning forward, she sorted the list by surname, then scrolled down until the entries for O'Connell appeared. She skimmed the names, finally spotting Patrick O'Connell. And there was his middle name: Finn. *Damn.* It could be a coincidence. She'd never heard anyone refer to Patrick as Finn. She swallowed the lump clogging her throat. The mouse pointer hovered over the name as she lightly tapped a finger on the button. Although she longed to know, she also dreaded what she might learn. Tap, tap, tap. *Chicken.* She took a deep breath and then pressed the button.

The entry expanded into a diagram with rectangles linked by connecting lines depicting the descendants of her grandfather. Patrick's rectangle sat beside one showing that he had married Mary Sullivan in 1940. Below those two linked boxes, one line extended down to a rectangle for their child, Brock, born in 1950. After he'd fought in World War Two. The portrait in the double parlor confirmed he had indeed been in the army, the uniform reflecting the time period.

Beside Brock's rectangle, a line linked to another one showing he had married Dina Anderson in 1970. Below their boxes, were boxes for Paulette born in 1971 and Meredith three years later. Nothing about any other offspring appeared on the screen.

Then she spotted another tab for an additional spouse for Patrick. He was married twice? She clicked the tab and studied the boxes. On this page, Patrick Finn O'Connell had married Georgette Anne Golden. A chill washed through her. In 1954 apparently. How? He was still married to Mary. He had a four-year-old boy, her father. How could he marry someone else?

Beneath the boxes for Patrick and Georgette appeared one box for Roscoe Louis Golden, born in 1955. A year after he married his second wife. She shook her head and peered closer. Roscoe married Margaret (Peggy) Jackson in 1990. She calculated he would have been thirty-five, rather a late bloomer in the marriage category, but not unheard of by any stretch. They had three children. Spots appeared before her eyes. She blinked and took a deep breath. *Push on.*

In three identical boxes linked together beneath those for Roscoe and Peggy were Roxana in 1991, Beth in 1993, and Tara in 1995. *Holy crap.* The sisters were cousins to Paulette and Meredith?

A note box displayed on the right side of the screen. When she clicked it, Grandma Mary's words appeared. "Georgette was not his wife; only his mistress." Grandma knew of the affair. The system didn't allow one to include children if two people were not married. So Grandma had to pretend they married in order to enter the descendants resulting from this affair. Well, that didn't surprise her. Grandpa Patrick did what he pleased. How awful to keep such a discovery to herself. How long did Grandma Mary know? Did she learn of it during the affair, or after the boy was born? Or even much later after seeing the three sisters?

Only one person may know the answers to her questions. Glancing at her watch, she determined the dinner hour neared. She marched out of the room and crossed the hall to the double parlor. Brock sat in an overstuffed chair, reading what appeared to be some kind of a mystery novel. He looked up when she paused at the open doorway.

"Hey, sweetheart. What are you up to?" He closed the book and laid it on his lap, one finger marking his place.

How should she start? Blurt it or feel him out on the topic? "What are you reading?" She needed a plan. Dropping a bomb in the middle of the quiet afternoon seemed wrong.

"I'm just killing time until the cocktail hour. Come sit with me. Talk to me." He motioned to the settee and then placed the book on the table beside him.

She sat on the soft cushion, her aching buttocks grateful for the relief. She propped a pillow behind her and regarded her father. The act enabled her to formulate an approach, a new thing for her. She'd never been very good at diplomacy. More often, thoughts became words before she could stop them from tumbling out. "I've been digging into your ancestors and all of their descendants. Pretty interesting stuff too."

"Oh?" He chuckled. "Why is that?"

"It seems you have a half-brother."

She sensed the tension running through Brock at her statement. His emerald eyes widened as his bushy brows raised like scared black cats. Confirmation. He didn't know about the affair.

"I don't have any siblings." He shook his dark gray head, pursing his lips to mirror his disbelief. "I'm an only child. I thought you knew that."

"According to Grandma Mary's family tree," she said slowly, "your father had an affair with Georgette Golden."

"An affair?" He launched to his feet, staring down at her. "I never heard such nonsense before. Mom would have told me."

"Her records indicate Georgette was Patrick's mistress, and they had a son, Roscoe."

"I won't listen to this." He paced to the fireplace and turned to shake his head as she pressed on.

"Apparently, Georgette raised him on her own, because his last name is given as Golden, not O'Connell." She paused, detecting a pulse racing in her father's neck. "Roscoe then married Peggy Jackson and they had three little girls."

"I don't believe this." He raked a hand through his hair, grabbing the nape of his neck as he toured the oriental carpet. "My father was all about honor and code and duty to family and country. He wouldn't have taken a mistress. He couldn't have."

"Guess who those three little girls grew up to be?" When he turned questioning eyes to her, she smiled. "They own the Golden Owl."

Brock sank back onto the chair he'd vacated earlier. Leaning his elbows on his knees, he rubbed his face with both hands. "Are you absolutely certain?"

She nodded. "I take it you didn't know any of this? That Roxie, Beth, and Tara are more than friends, they are my cousins?"

He shot to his feet again and looked down at her. "Are you trying to cause trouble again?"

"I never try to cause trouble, Dad, it merely happens. Anyway, I was following up on observations by Zak and even Roxie."

"What do you mean? Does Roxie know you're related?"

"I don't think so. She doesn't refer to your dad as Patrick but as Papaw Finn."

"His middle name." Brock stared through her, his thoughts far away. He stood with feet braced apart, fists at his sides. After a swollen pause, he focused upon her. "What does this have to do with me, anyway?"

"Don't worry about it, Dad." She cradled her baby bump and smiled. She loved discovering family secrets and bringing them to light. Loved feeling useful and needed. Loved how her family kept growing and expanding, often in surprising ways. With new capabilities and talents she'd never imagined. It didn't matter whether her grandpa slipped and had an affair since his wife apparently had forgiven him, and she gained three beautiful, very special cousins in the bargain. "You wouldn't believe me if I told you." Even with Patrick standing right behind him, grinning at her as if he'd read her very thoughts.

Pale sunshine eased through the kitchen windows, reflecting the chilly start to a new day. The aroma of strong, decaf coffee invited Paulette to grab a mug and help herself. She added a half spoonful of sugar from the bowl and stirred it in. Apparently Meredith had already cleared the dining room table, based on the stack of breakfast dishes in the sink.

"I hadn't realized it was so late." Paulette sipped her coffee, hot and sweet. "I must have been more tired than I thought."

"After your revelations of last evening, I think we're all a bit dazed." Meredith lifted a plate, rinsed it and stuck it into the rack. "I never would have guessed we had cousins in town."

"Dad didn't even know about Grandpa's indiscretion." She swallowed a gulp of coffee, leaning against the island counter. Spying the half-empty plate of ham biscuits, she snared one and bit into the crumbly piece of heaven.

"I wonder if Grandma Mary kept the secret out of a sense of betrayal or pain." Meredith paused and looked at Paulette. "I know I'd be angry as hell if I were in her shoes."

Paulette chewed another bite and swallowed, washing it down with coffee. "It was bad enough when Johnny left me and we weren't married. But to marry a man and bear his child, and then he has a fling resulting in another child, how do you forgive that?" The sweet salty ham surrounded by the buttery bread enticed her to savor another bite.

"Grandma apparently forgave but never forgot. I suppose after he died, it no longer mattered one way or the other to her."

"The betrayal couldn't be taken back whether he lived or died." Paulette wiped her hands on a paper napkin, then balled it up and tossed it into the trash can. "We'll never know how she really felt about the matter, that's for sure. Hey, I have to go to town to talk to Roxie and our other cousins—so strange to think of them as relatives—about what I discovered. I bet they'll be flabbergasted by my news."

"Tell me all about it afterward." Meredith continued arranging bowls and plates and mugs in the washer. "I'm curious how they'll react to being related to us after all the defensive attitude they've shown toward us."

"Will do. I'll be back in a bit." Paulette retrieved her purse and car keys from the small table by the door. She turned back to address Meredith. "Do you need anything in town?"

Meredith put the last dish into the dishwasher then

grabbed the tea towel to dry her hands. "No, but I think Zak mentioned heading that way. You might offer him a ride."

"You're kidding." Paulette jangled the key ring. She couldn't think of the man without remembering their first bone-rattling kiss. He was dangerous, threatening her plans, her future, but mostly her heart. The best course of action remained to keep her distance from him. "You must be."

Tilting her head, Meredith regarded her for the span of three breaths. "Give him a chance, sis. He seems to be sincere in his desire to know you better."

"I know he is." She slipped the strap of her purse onto her shoulder. "But like I said, even if I were interested in him, junior here reminds me I shouldn't be."

"Junior has no say in the matter and you know it. You need a man in your life, if for no other reason than to be a dad for junior." She shut the dishwasher door and pressed the start button. "I think you still have a thing for Johnny and won't admit it."

"No, you're wrong on both counts. I don't need a man, and I don't have any feelings for Johnny other than sadness over what he'll miss by walking away from his own child." She shrugged and moved toward the door. "So you don't need anything?"

"No, but it looks like Zak does. Good morning."

Paulette spun around in time to catch Zak nodding a greeting to Meredith. Then he turned to her, setting her pulse flying. The tune to "Getting to Know You" sprung into her head, a song about knowing the most intimate details of another person. Her heart and soul longed to do so with the hunky man. When he smiled, his even, white teeth parting slightly, almost in invitation, her breath hitched. Those lips of his were designed for kissing, no two ways about it. Warmth spread from her chest up to her throat and then inched into her cheeks.

"Good morning, Paulette." He dipped his head in greeting. "Where are you off to so early this morning?"

The force of his charisma surrounded her like a lasso, tugging and pulling her to move toward him. Touch him. Her fingers itched with the need to reach out and make contact with him, somewhere, anywhere. She rubbed her hands together in an attempt to quell the desire, keys adding their music to her movement.

"The bookstore and probably the grocery store. Do you need a lift into town?" *Damn.* She hadn't meant to actually invite him. She darted a glance at Meredith. The smirk on her sister's face revealed her awareness of Paulette's reaction. She looked back at Zak and again the zing of desire to connect to him nearly overwhelmed her senses. She swallowed and gripped her keys tighter with one hand, the other hand looping around the strap of her purse and clinging for dear life.

"Great. I'm ready if you are." He strode toward her, so delicious in indigo jeans and a red pullover sweater she wanted to eat him.

Stop thinking of him like a piece of chocolate. Rich, creamy chocolate. What she could do with... She spun back around before he reached her, hopefully before he saw the incriminating flush in her cheeks. "We'll be back, Mer."

His proximity in her small car on the drive into Roseville did nothing to ease her inner tension or discomfiture. Life had seemed to be settling into a comfortable routine since she made the decision to keep her child and raise it with Meredith's support. And Max's too, once they married. Oh, and she couldn't forget Meg and Sean. And probably her parents from time to time. Add in three cousins to the mix. It did take a village, didn't it?

"Are you looking for anything in particular at the bookstore?" Zak glanced at her and then back out the window at the fallow fields and farmhouses whizzing by.

"I'm going to speak to my…to my friends." She gripped the steering wheel harder and then flexed her fingers to ease their tension. Her relationship change with the Golden sisters was none of his business. He'd be leaving in a few days, and she'd never see him again. The thought buoyed and weighed heavily. Why air the family's little secret to a relative stranger? "What do you need in town?"

He peeked at her, a sheepish grin promising she wouldn't like his answer. "Nothing. I wanted time with you."

A thrill of excitement lanced through her. To cover, she huffed out a sigh as if nothing could be worse. She dropped one hand to rest on her leg, forcing herself to appear relaxed and in control of the careening emotions inside. "Seems like a waste to me."

His grin widened. "Not to me, though." He covered her hand with his.

The touch of his skin on hers thrilled and danced all the way up her arm. Flicking a glimpse at his face to determine if he experienced the same shocking sensation, she slipped her fingers free and gripped the wheel. Held on for dear sanity. "I told you why I won't get involved with you."

"You did, but I don't accept your reasoning." He turned in his seat so he could look at her directly. "Many people with children find new loves in their lives. You're no different."

She stared straight ahead, wishing with all her heart for events in her life to allow her to be happy. To be able to give her heart to this man without fear he'd walk away like Johnny and all the others before him. Each one had left her a bit more afraid, defensive, and worst of all alone. Sure, she had relatives, but no man she could trust to be her companion, her soul mate, her friend. Someone interested in sharing her day, or helping her accomplish her goals. "Drop it, Zak. We're almost there."

Turning onto Main Street, she located a parking spot and brought the car to a halt. Pulling the key from the ignition, she glanced at the gorgeous man sitting a measly six inches away. The urge to touch him swelled inside until nearly irresistible, but she snatched up her purse instead and popped the driver's side door open. Without a word, she stepped out of the car and slammed the door. Zak emerged from the other side and pushed his door closed before trailing her onto the sidewalk. They strode in silence into the Golden Owl.

"Hey girl, how are you?" Beth sauntered up to greet the pair hovering inside the door, the small bell above their heads tinkling into silence. She peered closer. "Are you okay?"

"Yes, I'm fine." Paulette scanned the store, searching for Roxie. "I need to speak to Roxie. Is she here?"

Beth waved black-tipped nails in the direction of the coffee bar. "She's bringing in supplies, but I'll let her know you're here. Want some coffee while you wait?"

"Please." Zak followed Beth, her swinging ponytail a metronome for each step toward the café area.

Paulette sauntered after them, formulating what she'd say when her friend and cousin appeared. Should she come straight out and tell her? Or work through the family history lesson she uncovered? Maybe one day she'd find the nerve to ask Patrick about what happened and why, but somehow she didn't think he'd answer honestly. He didn't owe her an explanation as much as he owed one to her grandma.

Tara came out of the store room carrying a book box filled with paperbacks. Her dark curly locks shot through with golden highlights cascaded around her shoulders as she lugged her heavy load toward the stacks. As she passed she greeted Paulette with a smile.

"Need a hand?" Paulette stepped toward her, reaching out to share the burden.

"No, I'm fine. I do this all the time." She tossed her hair out of her face and continued on her way. "Enjoy your decaf."

Zak approached carrying two steaming cups. "Beth said this one's yours."

She accepted the proffered cup and peered at the lid. "Decaf with sugar. Thanks."

"Let's go over by the window while we wait for Roxie to finish." He led the way, even pulled out her chair with his free hand so she could easily sit.

"Such a gentleman." She chuckled, removed the plastic lid, and sipped from the cup. She jerked away from the lip of the cup. "That's hot."

"Careful, you don't want to burn that pretty mouth of yours." He occupied the other chair and followed suit, removing the lid and letting the steam rise between them.

She did her best imitation of a teen rolling her eyes, but he merely smiled in return. "You're insufferable."

"Among other things." He sipped and grinned. "Like persistent."

"And annoying." An array of baked goods tempted her from behind the safety of the glass display. Cupcakes with colorful icing piled high sat between chocolate éclairs and gooey cinnamon buns. The source of the sweet and spicy aromas enticing customers.

"Most people say I know what I want and how to acquire it."

His protracted silence after his declaration forced her to look at him.

"And what exactly do you want?"

He inclined his head in her direction. "That's easy. You."

Before she could respond to his audacious and not unexpected claim, Roxie appeared at her elbow.

"You wanted to see me?" Roxie smoothed her hands down the thighs of her khakis. "Hey, Zak."

"Hi, Roxie." Zak glanced from Roxie to Paulette and back again but kept mum.

"Can we talk in private?" No way would she have a confidential conversation under Zak's steely scrutiny.

"I'll just wait here."

Paulette rolled her eyes again at the sarcasm dripping from his words. "Good idea."

Roxie motioned for her to follow and soon they faced each other in the store room. Having never been in the back of the store before, Paulette indulged in a quick scan of its contents. Shelves filled with boxes and cartons lined the walls of the small room. A metal work table stood in the center toward the front, laden with sundry items needed to open and sort through the merchandise before placing it in the store. A stack of folding metal chairs leaned against the back wall. Such a work-a-day room. What the place really needed was some color and décor. Maybe she'd offer to help them decorate to improve productivity and overall job satisfaction. Another time. She pivoted to face the other woman.

"So what's on your mind?" Roxie folded her arms and raised a brow, waiting for a response.

"I don't know how to say this." She considered blurting out the truth, thought better of it. "It's hard to know what to say."

Roxie regarded her, blinking several times. "The easiest way is to simply say it, whatever *it* is."

She nodded and sighed. Let the words flow, bring the concept into sharp focus. "We're cousins."

Roxie grinned. "Took you long enough to figure it out."

"You knew?" Here she thought Roxie would be the one flabbergasted. "How?"

With a shrug, Roxie smiled. "Seems my mom discovered the affair between our mutual grandfather and my grandmother when she first started researching her family tree."

"Why didn't you say anything?"

"We talked about it when you and Meredith first came back to Roseville, but with our little secret…"

"You didn't know how we'd react." She bobbed her head. "I can understand not wanting to take the risk without knowing us better. Is that why you all acted so wary around us?"

"Yes. Since you and Meredith have discovered your own abilities, we decided we'd see if you'd figure it out on your own. If you didn't, then we would have told you at the party."

"So I guess there's only one question left."

"Oh?"

She laughed at Roxie's quizzical expression. "Yep. What other family secrets await us?"

Chapter Nine

*M*onday arrived with a cold snap that left frost tingeing the fallen leaves and dried grass in the meadows surrounding the house. Paulette checked on the jack-o-lantern, afraid the freeze would ruin it before the party. It only needed to last another five days. Standing on the front porch, a heavy robe tucked snugly around her, she quietly sang the Eagles version of "Witchy Woman" as she inspected each item of the fall décor. So far they'd held together without any breakage or deterioration. She shivered despite her warm robe and hurried back inside, shutting the ancient wooden door with a hearty thump as she ended the song.

Meredith sauntered down the stairs from the second floor, dressed in maroon jeans and a cream sweater, short black boots tapping on each wood step. Paulette wished she could wear a comfy outfit like hers, but until she delivered the babe and then regained her figure, she'd have to wait.

"Ready to go browse the antique stores and boutiques?" Meredith reached the foyer and paused to assess Paulette's attire. "Or aren't you feeling up to it today?"

She started up the stairs. "I'll be with you in a moment. I need to put on some clothes and we can go."

Within ten minutes, Paulette hurried into the kitchen dressed and ready to leave. She'd selected her favorite stretchy forest green slacks with an oversized, button-down, lemon yellow man's shirt. She'd paired it with comfy black loafers, though she would have preferred her pumps. But with all the walking they'd be doing, comfort was more important than aesthetics.

Meredith sat at the little table, a mug in one hand as she perused a newspaper lying on the surface. Paulette crossed to the cupboard to retrieve a mug.

"I appreciate you helping me by drinking decaf." Paulette lifted the carafe and watched the steam rise as she poured.

"Not a problem. I'm glad you're finally willing to do this shopping spree. You've made me nervous waiting so long to make preparations." Meredith set her mug down and folded the paper.

"I'd always said I'd wait until one month prior to the due date, but..." She sipped then lowered her mug. "Somehow I feel we should do this sooner than later."

The time was fast approaching when she'd need baby furniture and clothes. She'd put it off as long as possible, not willing to jinx the pregnancy by preparing for the little one too soon. The babe moved frequently in her distended belly, assuaging any worry about a stillbirth. So many missteps could occur up until the baby emerged into the world. She insisted on doing everything she could to safeguard the life within, trusting and depending on her.

Her doctor had increased the frequency of her appointments due to the high risks associated with childbirth at her age. Everything was progressing normally, a fact she reminded herself daily. Her only complaint was a tendency to lightheadedness, apparently due to dilated veins according to her doctor. She simply had to remember to stand slowly to prevent the dizziness.

"Six weeks, four weeks, not much difference between them." Meredith rose, grabbed the jacket off the back of the chair, and strode to the side table where she grabbed her purse. "Ready?"

"I'll drive." Paulette pulled her coat from the hook beside the door and then followed Meredith out into the cold morning.

The little car practically navigated itself into Roseville. She parked in front of the Southern Treasures antique store and maneuvered herself out of the car. Stretching, she surveyed the possible boutiques and furniture stores, debating where to begin their search.

"Let's start here, and work our way around the square." She locked the car and stepped onto the sidewalk.

"What first? A bassinet? Cradle?" Meredith joined her, adjusting her strap more securely on her shoulder.

"We'll see what we find." Paulette led the way into the dim interior of the store.

She paused to let her eyes adapt and scan the contents of the cluttered and dusty shop. Tables and cabinets and chairs, indeed every horizontal surface, held dishes, vases, and glassware of all kinds for sale. Bouquets of silk flowers provided spots of color among the clusters of place settings and collectibles. Moving through the narrow aisles meant proceeding carefully, to avoid accidentally bumping into a table and knocking the glass items. With her girth, she cautiously meandered through the store, waiting for something to call to her to buy it.

Meredith wandered in the opposite direction, slipping easily through the store, skimming the furniture as she went. Paulette sighed and continued her quest. So many items sported mars and scars, some which could be refinished, but most requiring too much time to accomplish the redo before the baby arrived. Then she spotted a dark cherry cradle tucked beside a matching dresser with changing area on top, low sides providing a measure of safety to prevent a baby from rolling off. She sidled toward the cradle, filled with a menagerie of stuffed animals and dolls, searching for any negatives even as hope swelled in her chest.

Running a finger along the top of the spindled side rail, the wood wiggled beneath her touch. While the cradle had some rubs on the finish, it still appeared practically new, as though little used. Who would have abandoned such a beautifully crafted piece? It was heirloom quality, made with care and attention to the joints and the brass fittings. Pushing gently, the bed rocked with a high-pitched squeal as the brass fittings suspending the bed over the sturdy stand protested.

"Find something?" Meredith arrived at her side.

"What do you think?" Paulette fingered the tag, surprised at the low price.

"The spindles are spaced right, so the baby can't wedge between them." Meredith moved closer and inspected the piece, peering at every side and almost dumping the menagerie onto the floor when she peered at the bottom. "I think it's a steal at that price."

"Me too. It needs some work though, right?"

"It's not too bad. A bit of refinishing, a little tightening of a screw here and over there." Meredith spied the dresser and nodded at it. "What about that?"

"It seems to be a set, don't you think?" She pictured the two pieces snugged into the corner of her own bedroom. Her baby close by her side, cared for and loved.

Meredith slipped around behind the cradle and tugged on the top drawer. At first it refused to budge, but then the reluctant wood groaned open. "It'll need some smoothing, but I can take care of that for you."

"Sold." Paulette grinned and selected a green stuffed frog and a pink teddy bear from the menagerie. "Our mission didn't take long. Almost as though it waited for me to find it."

After paying for the items, they made arrangements for

the furniture to be delivered and then emerged back outside, squinting into the late morning light. Paulette carried the two stuffed animals tucked into the crook of her arm so they could see where she walked. The weak sunshine managed to soften the hard edge of the cold air. Traffic had also picked up, a river of cars and trucks flowing slowly by. Leaves once weighted with frost now tumbled down the concrete sidewalk.

"Look who's here." Paulette pivoted to greet Tara striding toward them.

"Hey, Paulette, Meredith. What brings you to town?"

"Baby shopping. I figured it was time." She patted her belly and told her about the beautiful cradle and dresser. "Next up are the essentials."

Tara shook her head, eyes worried. "I'll check out the cradle for you. We don't want any unwanted guests tagging along."

Meredith's brows dipped into a frown. "What do you mean?"

"It's probably fine, don't worry." Tara shifted her weight and regarded Paulette. "I'll take care of it."

"Now you have to tell me what you're talking about." A chill inched across Paulette's shoulders.

Tara shrugged. "Antiques can have residual spirits attached. Not all by any means, but some do. I wouldn't want you to invite more trouble to your home."

"We don't need more uninvited guests, so thanks." Paulette hugged Tara. "I'm so glad you've got my back."

"Have you decided where you'll have the baby? Which hospital, I mean?" Tara asked.

Paulette stepped back and considered Meredith. She'd thought about this over many a sleepless night. Hospitals harbored every awful germ imaginable and no way did she want to subject her child to such an introduction to the world. She had another idea, one her doctor had supported given the ease of the pregnancy. Meredith had agreed with her in theory but they hadn't discussed it recently. She peered at Tara. "Didn't you say you're a midwife?"

"I'm a healer too." Tara angled her head, quizzical brows aimed her way. "Why?"

"Would you attend me at home?"

"The hospital is a safer place, in case something goes wrong. At your age, you're at a higher risk for complications. Are you sure you don't want to be where the doctors and nurses could assist?"

She'd researched the pros and cons of home birth and the answer to Tara's question came easily. "Positive. My doctor has already okayed the idea, and will be on stand-by in case she's needed. Please say you'll be there when the time comes."

Tara nodded. "But if complications arise, you'll need a backup plan for which hospital. Agreed?"

"Sure. But there won't be any need." Paulette hugged Tara and then glanced at Meredith standing at her side. "We've got this."

"I'll visit you tomorrow and we'll see about setting up for the big day."

"Sounds perfect." Paulette hugged the stuffed animals and glanced up the street.

"I love the animals," Tara said, rubbing the soft fur. "They're so adorable."

"Something fun to decorate the room." She looked down at the green and pink animals, and thought of Grant. How much longer would he be able to see what's around him? "I hate to think of Zak's brother going blind."

"What?" Tara peered at her, shocked. "Grant's going blind? I thought he might have some kind of illness, but I didn't think it serious."

"He didn't tell you? I suppose that's not surprising. He's probably reluctant to admit the possibility." Paulette shifted her weight and slowly shook her head. "Zak told me the doctors are trying to slow the tumors in his brain with drugs and treatments, but they don't have much hope."

"I wish I could do something." Tara glanced from Meredith to Paulette, two grooves furrowed between her brows. "He's so young and vibrant."

"Handsome too. His job depends on being able to see and analyze specimens." What would he do instead if he did lose his sight? "We can only pray the doctors figure out a way to help him."

"Or come up with an alternative therapy." Tara crossed her arms and tapped one hand on her folded elbow.

"You look like you have an idea." Meredith tilted her head, regarding the golden-headed woman with humor in her eyes.

"I'm working on it." Tara bobbed her head, lips pursed.

What exactly was the petite healer contemplating? "Should I be worried?"

"Maybe."

Great. "No 'hey y'all, watch this' type of acts, okay?" She didn't want to have to run away before someone got hurt. "Promise me."

Tara's smile hinted at deep, dark secrets. "I'll promise to give you fair warning."

Perfect. "All right, well let's move on before I regret mentioning any of this and causing more trouble."

Meredith chuckled as they started down the sidewalk. "Why stop now?"

Everything looked so normal along the street, the cars and trucks easing by, songbirds chirping in the pear trees. Yet the feeling that everything was about to change settled in her stomach like raw bread dough. "Why indeed."

Monday afternoons in Roseville meant a sleepy town. Hair salons and even some restaurants slept after the weekend rush of customers. Zak parked in front of the Golden Owl and went inside. The bell rang above him. A queue of hungry and thirsty folks waited for Beth to serve them in the coffee bar. Others browsed the shelves or relaxed with a book and a beverage in luxuriant chairs clustered in dedicated nooks around the store.

He spotted Tara arranging books on a table near the stage. Two rows of folding metal chairs faced the elevated platform, its podium and microphone front and center, providing seating for twenty. Had they been there before? He recalled the image of the space in his mind's eye. No, there'd been tables of gifty things for readers but no chairs. Maybe an open mic night neared, and she had prepared for the event. Tara regarded him with a shadow of a frown. He lifted a hand in greeting, and she acknowledged him before resuming her task. Interesting. Her guarded expression hinted at wariness about his sudden appearance. Beth had completely ignored him, though perhaps the long line prevented her from noticing yet another customer walked through the door. That left one sister.

Where was Roxie? He scanned the store but didn't see the distinctive brown pony tail or flashing green eyes. Just as well he didn't run into her. For his mission, he didn't need anyone to assist him. In fact, Grant had flatly refused to accompany him on yet another "futile" effort to find the elusive ingredient for his Elixir of Life. But damn it, if the answer existed anywhere, it must be within the walls of this shop. All the clues—the downward triangle and the owl on two branches—pointed to the Golden Owl and the three sisters. Hell, the two branches might be Paulette and her sister, or more to the point, Twin Oaks, for all he knew. Working on his unprovable assumption, coupled with the use of the Aristotelian symbol for earth, everything seemed to point to the soil in the Roseville area. Nothing was certain, but he'd bet he traveled the right track. He hadn't come all this way to give up until he'd exhausted every possible option to save his brother's sight.

He sauntered toward the science section, pausing on the way to select a title and return it to the shelf, then moving on to repeat the exercise, purposefully keeping his pace casual. Nonchalant so nobody would suspect his sweaty palms and burgeoning headache from the tension in his neck. Skimming the area, he gravitated to the books on soil analysis and local geology.

Grant's efforts had yielded little. The county soil analysis highlighted a few pockets of excessively high acidity levels in the soil. Grant postulated the higher amounts of acid could cause the necessary breakdown of the other elements to create the fluid, or elixir. Surely something more specific to this area was needed to complete the formula correctly. But what?

He chose a likely book and opened to the list of contents. He skimmed the chapter titles, then closed the book along with his eyes. He recalled the faint symbol in the journal's margin which led him to the store, and its uniquely specific section of books, to find the answer. Or at least another clue pointing to the final answer. So many possible repositories of both the information and the location made his head swim. Damn it, he must have the answer. He wasn't leaving until this hole in the wall store coughed up what he desired.

The thought raised Paulette's face into his imagination. The Golden Owl had provided his first glimpse of the woman of his dreams. If only she would agree to be his, then perhaps failing at his other mission wouldn't sting quite so much. Failing at both goals, however, couldn't happen. He wouldn't let it.

"Finding what you need?"

Startled, he opened his eyes and spun to see who had sneaked up on him. The movement shot pain into his head, making him wince.

"Sorry, I didn't mean to scare you." Roxie cradled a short stack of books in one arm, resting a hand lightly on top.

Her smirk told him otherwise. "You startled me, that's all."

"I heard about your brother. I'm sorry."

"Thanks. He's the reason I'm here, actually."

She stared pointedly at the book in his hand. "You're really into dirt, aren't you?" She hugged the stack.

"Something like that." He regarded her and the books she carried. Classics. *Adventures of Huckleberry Finn. The Turn of the Screw. Complete Works of Poe.* "You're into ghost stories?"

"Something like that. You've come here a lot since you rolled into town. What is it you expect to find here anyway?"

"I'll know when I find it." She made him tense, distrust evident in her pointed assessment. Did she suspect he knew her secret? Hell, all three of them acted mysterious. Always looking over their shoulder at him, watching him as though he meant to harm them. Had Paulette tipped her to his accusations? That would explain the caution. Perhaps a test could prove one way or the other. "The Golden Owl contains quite an eclectic mix of books. I'm surprised at the quantity on local geology and soil content. Why is that?"

"We strive to meet the needs of our patrons." She hesitated and then lifted her chin. "Let me know if you need help finding anything. I'd hate to keep you here longer than necessary. I'm sure you have more important things to do than read up on dirt." With a brief dip of her head, she turned and strode toward the front of the store.

He gripped the tome so the binding on the hard backed book in his hands creaked as she strode away. Her quick gait made her ponytail swing. Seemed his being in the store was enough to upset her. Easing his grasp on the clothbound book, he slowly opened it again to the contents.

He glanced up, feeling as though someone watched him. His gaze met Roxie's as she stood near the tall rounder of handmade beaded necklaces sparkling in the sunlight angling through the front windows. Man, he hadn't realized how deeply her mistrust went until that moment. She sported a worried frown flowing across her features. He blinked, breaking the taut silent contemplation, and she pivoted and hurried into the back room.

Nabbing a couple other volumes, he located an empty chair and sank into its plush confines. Focusing on the words in front of him, he soon lost track of time.

Generally, the dirt around Roseville appeared to contain the expected elements in the soil. A bit silt, a quantity of clay, some areas with a loamy texture. He flipped to the section on particular soil samples and how they were classified around the county. Dirt studies bored him. He'd rather be mixing elements than analyzing them. Yet understanding where a unique mix of elements in the soil might exist in the surrounding area might lead him to the mystical ingredient the owl symbol steered him toward.

Closing one book, he laid it aside and opened another. Pay dirt. He grinned at his own pun. A table provided the chemical properties of the soil, a topic more up his alley. According to the text, the chemical properties directly affected soil behavior. As in, how the dirt impacted the outcome of the alchemist's experiment.

"What a surprise to find you here. Again." Paulette sank onto the chair beside him and nodded at the open page. "How dry."

"Well, hello, beautiful." He closed the book and stacked it on top of the others. Before he left Roseville, he'd have invested a small fortune in books. But if shopping for books meant more time with the woman beside him, he'd consider it money well spent. He glanced at his watch. "It's later than

I thought. What brings you here? I thought you'd be home setting up the nursery."

She shook her head. "Meredith is working on refinishing the furniture we found this morning and replacing worn hardware. Besides, I had a call for help." Grinning, she eased back in the chair and rested her hands on the armrests. "So I came to rescue you."

"From what?" Noting the humor in her eyes, he relaxed a fraction. "Or should I say from whom?"

She folded her arms and nodded. "Roxie called. Apparently, you've outstayed your welcome." She pointed to the stack between them. "Ready to buy those and vamoose?"

He bristled. No woman would chase him from a store. Especially one he contended to be a witch. "No, I don't think so. Those three are hiding something, and I think we both know what that is. Don't we?"

She laughed, though her eyes didn't reflect humor when she flicked a glance at him. "Don't start on that again. Come on, I'll buy you an ice cream." She made to rise, inching forward in the chair.

He stopped her by circling her wrist with his fingers, drawing her attention. "Maybe that's why I've been led to this town, to reveal the truth."

Paulette turned back to search his expression. "There's nothing to *reveal*, as you say. Roxie, Beth, and Tara have lived here all their lives. Among these good people who have known them forever. You're merely a visitor."

He laughed at her attempt to dissuade his intent, changing the worry reflected in her countenance to dread. "Roseville is kinda growing on me." He rubbed a thumb on the back of her wrist. "As are you. You could convince me to stay."

She swallowed but maintained eye contact. "Why would I do such a thing? I've told you, I'm not interested."

Beneath his thumb, her pulse beat faster. He smiled. "Sweetheart, I don't believe you."

"Stop calling me that." She tugged on her hand, but he held firm. "Please, let me go."

"See, that's the thing. I can't." He squeezed her wrist, moving his fingers so they laced with hers. "You intrigue me, and I'm drawn to protect you."

A tiny gasp escaped. She inhaled and stared at him, her fingers tense in his. "You've nothing to protect me from. This place is my home now."

"You're wrong about one thing." He glanced toward the cash register, and confirmed the women in question were indeed watching the exchange. "They know I'm aware of who they really are. That's why they fear me. Why they called you. And why I can protect you."

"They will not hurt me, Zak." She squeezed his hand, drawing his attention back to her. "Suggesting they are witches would hurt not only them but me as well."

"I don't understand." How could they be connected? "You're not a witch, are you?"

"No. You were right after all." She sighed and opened her hand. He let her palm slide free from his grasp. "They're my cousins. They're family." She studied him, folding her hands and resting them on her baby bump.

The gesture drew his awareness to how soon she'd deliver the child. He didn't know who the father was, or where he was, but he did know he wanted to be a part of her life, and thus the child's. He'd never experienced such an intense desire to be with a woman. He couldn't ignore it, but he also couldn't force himself on this strong, beautiful person. He must find a way to convince her to see him, really see him. When she was near to him, he longed to make contact with her. He tried to refrain, knowing her opinion of him, of a relationship between them, but merely touching her wrist, her fingers, satisfied the tendrils of need conjured up by her presence.

"Have dinner with me and I won't say a word." Her raised brows reflected his own surprise at his words. Not a bad idea, though. "One dinner so we can get to know each other better."

"All I have to do is share one meal?"

"With an open mind." He couldn't help himself, he took her hand again. When their hands touched, a jolt of desire, deep and intense, shot through him. The same intense reaction he'd experienced in the car. When she'd removed her hand and placed it on the steering wheel, he nearly snatched it back. He needed this woman to be in his life. Nothing else mattered. Not even the blasted mystery that brought him to Roseville. He'd started the adventure as a means to spend more time with his brother, and possibly to work a miracle for him. He'd tried his damnedest to help Grant, hoping Roseville would prove to have the answer to his crazy prayers. Somehow he'd expected to find the answer to his brother's illness in the quaint locale. If nothing else, coming to the town brought him together with Paulette, so not a total failure of a road trip. "You may find you actually like me."

"Okay, but I make no promises about liking you." Freeing her hand once more, she pushed to her feet. "Let's get this over with."

"Now?" He stood and gathered up his books.

"Yes, since it's about time for dinner. I'll let Meredith know I won't be home while you pay for those." She led the way toward the register without another word.

He trailed after her, happy to watch her sashay away from him and knowing he'd catch up to her. If things went his way, despite her objections, he'd catch her too.

Chapter Ten

Toying with the knife handle gave her something to think about other than what the hell she was doing sitting next to Zak looking out over the sleepy streets of Roseville. If the young black-haired waitress boasting a score of freckles hadn't seated them at the table for four nestled in the front window, then she'd be across from him instead of so close his sleeve brushed hers. Like a second sensitive skin, each time his cotton shirt made contact with her silk blouse the sensation zinged across her nerve endings, lightning to a dead tree. He'd been such a gentleman, pulling her chair out so she could settle herself facing the window. She assumed he'd sit across from her, his back to the street. But no. Before she knew it, he'd plunked down on her left side, scraping his chair in with a harsh squeal of metal on tile.

"So what's good?" He perused the menu as if it contained the secrets of life. A quick glance and a wink indicated he sensed her tension, her discomfort with his surprising choice of seat.

Shifting right in her chair, she considered the list of options for her meal. She'd agreed to have dinner with him but not to fall head over heels. If he expected such a response, disappointment would be his dessert. "It's all good southern cooking. The chicken-fried steak is my favorite though."

He laid the menu down and angled toward her. "Done. What about you?"

"The baby doesn't much like the spices in the gravy, so I'll stick with a safer choice."

Leaning closer, he propped an arm on the back of his chair. "Safer?"

She retreated from his proximity with difficulty. How far could she lean without falling off the damn chair? "Grilled chicken and steamed veggies, no spices."

"Safe." Pulling back, his expression challenged her. "And boring."

"Yes, but I won't experience repeat performances all night."

He chuckled. "I see. We wouldn't want you to miss out on your beauty sleep."

She tilted her head at him, the cold metal handle between her fingers a sharp contrast to the warmth coursing through her as she slid it left, and then right. "No, I need all I can eke out each night."

"It's been working so far, so why mess with success?" He drummed his right hand on the back of the chair. His knee brushed her thigh, setting off a deep thrumming in her core. The wide smile softened to a grin. "You are beautiful."

A guffaw erupted from her throat before she could stifle it. "What is it they say about flattery? It gets you nowhere."

"Or everywhere." The wide smile returned. "I'm hoping for the latter."

"Good luck with that." Shaking her head, she denied his goal at the same time realizing she was leaning toward him. She forced herself to sit up straight and focused on the knife instead of the gorgeous man.

"Thanks, but I don't think I'll need luck. I mean,

really…" After a long pause, she turned to meet his steady regard. "My efforts seem to be yielding the desired results."

He sure had a way with words. His fingers stilled on the metal chair. Long digits attached to strong hands capable of yielding *her* desired results. She gasped at her wayward train of thought. What was she thinking? Focus on something other than his body parts. Heat flooded her chest, spread quickly to her neck before warming her cheeks. "What—what results did you have in mind?"

"By your blush, I think you know." He brushed the back of his fingers down her left cheek, lingering at the jaw bone before trailing down her neck to the open collar of her blouse.

Yes, she did, but they couldn't go there. Her reasons for resisting his tempting offer still sounded logical. Right? What were they again? His touch, a light brush of the pad of his thumb along her collar bone, dissolved her ability to think coherently, evoking sensations overriding reason. Provoking her body to react in invitation to his caress, angling her head away from him so he easily accessed her flaming skin. She closed her eyes, savoring the remnants of the current shooting through her.

"May I take your order?"

Startled by the high-pitched voice, she blinked open her eyes. Luxurious energy fled, leaving behind renewed tension.

Zak quickly ordered their meals and the waitress sauntered away. She met his eyes, noting the understanding reflected in their depths.

No doubt about it. She was in deep trouble. Even before they'd ordered their meals, she'd nearly succumbed to his advances. Never had she experienced such an intense reaction to the touch of a hand. Or any other appendage. Johnny included. She studied Zak, neither of them speaking, neither apparently wishing to interrupt the moment with meager words. For the span of five of her pounding heartbeats they remained mute.

Zak cleared his throat and grinned, sinking back against the chair. "I don't need an appetizer after that."

"Wait until the main course." She slapped a hand over her mouth. Where had such a flirtatious thought come from? She lowered her hand. "Did I say that out loud?"

"Yep." He reached for her left hand, engulfing it with his. "Methinks you and I have quite the chemistry between us. I should know, being a chemist."

Indeed. His smile resonated in his bass voice. He wrapped his fingers around hers. Holding hands, such a simple act, yet thrilling in its simplicity. The press of skin on skin between a man and a woman. Willing victims of the dangerous emotional journey they walked together. Lifting her gaze to his, she searched for any sign to run from him. Only expectation and hope, mingled with the assurance of a man who succeeds in his endeavors.

"Do you always accomplish your aim, achieve what you want?" She nodded at their joined hands.

He shrugged and then squeezed her fingers. "Usually, once I've selected a goal."

"What exactly is your goal?"

"I want to know you better. See if we're as compatible as I imagine."

She opened her mouth to respond, but the teen returned with their steaming plates. Placing them on the table, the girl smiled at Zak and regarded him with doe-like eyes. Really? The chit wasn't more than nineteen. "Thanks," Paulette said dismissively.

After the waitress marched away, Paulette removed her hand from Zak's grasp and picked up her knife and fork. She cut into her chicken. "I don't know that it's a smart move on your part to want to be with me."

"Let me decide who I want to be with." He tossed her a glance then sliced his steak.

She chewed slowly, savoring both the herbed poultry

and the delay in responding. "I think I have a say in the matter."

He nodded. "You're here, so you chose to be with me too."

"For dinner." She plopped a crown of buttery broccoli in her mouth.

"How about lunch tomorrow? We could go to Lynchburg and explore the stores and find some quaint diner?"

She nearly dropped her fork. "Tomorrow?"

"I told you. I want to see you, find out what makes you tick, and why I'm so attracted to you."

"You want to go shopping though?" No man in her experience volunteered to go browsing through stores.

"If that's what it takes." He sipped his tea and studied her. "Whatever you want to do is fine with me. As long as we do it together."

She slowly blinked at him, her neck growing stiff the longer she held it turned to study the sincerity evident in his expression. Meredith's words echoed in her mind. Perhaps she owed it to herself to give him a chance. A sincerely interested handsome, intelligent, passionate man sat beside her, awaiting her answer. A man who elicited an intense physical response from her. Fate had drawn him to her new hometown, so why not give it the opportunity to forge her future? "Why not? It's just a date, right?"

The drive back to Twin Oaks gave Paulette time to reconsider her rash decision. Zak followed her in his blue Jeep Wrangler, making her realize exactly how small a vehicle they'd share the next day. They had decided, at her rather panicked suggestion, to spend the day wandering through the malls in Nashville, stopping for lunch wherever they ended up when they grew hungry. The idea of folks seeing them together in the historic town of Lynchburg made her quake inside. What if they didn't get along? Or worse…what if they did? She didn't need an audience for either outcome. Not that she expected him to stick around. He had no reason to be involved in the whole labor and delivery part of the pregnancy, after all.

She parked in her usual spot and went inside. Closing the back door, she dropped her purse on the table and glanced outside as the Jeep pulled in beside her car. Zak emerged from the vehicle and strode toward her. Even with the scar running along his right jaw, the man was almost beautiful, if a man could be beautiful. Luxurious ebony hair, pewter gray eyes, and a tall, lanky build combined to create the distinct impression of confidence and capability. Even the way he walked announced to the world he knew who he was and what he wanted, and what's more, how to obtain it.

He entered the kitchen and slapped the door shut. He caught her elbow and drew her to him. A slight lift to the corners of his mouth helped the sparkle in his eyes. "I want to thank you again for a nice evening."

"I enjoyed it too." Her mouth went dry and she swiped her tongue over her lips. His gaze sharpened, focused on the movement.

Without preamble, he pressed his lips to hers. He slipped inside her mouth, igniting the embers of attraction she'd experienced earlier at the restaurant. She closed her eyes as he deepened the kiss, his tongue dancing with hers. His hands at her waist pulled her as close as possible with the baby between them. The sensations ricocheting inside left her trembling. Her nails bit into his shoulders, hanging on as though she'd drop to the floor if she let go.

Zak ended the kiss, pecked her lips once, twice, three times, and then smiled. "Good night, sweetheart. I'll see you tomorrow."

"Sweet dreams." Her tender lips tingled from his

attentions. Her own dreams stood in question, if in fact she slept at all.

"No doubt." With a wink, he turned and sauntered from the room.

After the door closed behind him, she leaned against the island counter and dragged in several deep breaths, willing her body to stop reacting. Even the baby bopped around in her belly as though it too had experienced the intense response to Zak's touch.

A cup of herbal tea always calmed her nerves, and she needed calm tonight. Filling the kettle, she put it on the stove and flipped the dial to high. She reached for a mug and dropped a tea bag into its depths. While waiting for the water to heat, she strode through the swinging door toward the sitting parlor. As she expected, Meredith sat in the goose-necked rocker reading, wearing dark blue sweatpants and a gray sweatshirt sporting an orange Tennessee Volunteers logo. Paulette paused in the doorway until her sister looked up. "Want some chamomile and mint tea?"

Meredith slipped a beaded bookmark into the page and closed the book. "What's upset you?"

The potential for mind-blowing sex? Mer didn't need to hear that, so Paulette merely shrugged. "I agreed to go out with Zak tomorrow."

Meredith laid the book on the round table between the matching rockers and then rose to her feet, an I-told-you-so grin appearing. "I thought you didn't like him."

She shrugged again, still reluctant to reveal the depth and intensity of emotion he sparked in her. "He's not so bad." She turned and led the way to the kitchen.

"This goes against everything you've been saying about dating him, or anyone for that matter." Meredith snagged a mug from the cupboard and Paulette dropped a tea bag into it.

Facing each other across the island counter, Paulette

braced her hands on the horizontal surface. "Like I said, he's not as bad as I imagined once we had dinner tonight."

A frown appeared on Meredith's face. "Yeah, about that. Was that smart? He's threatened to expose our cousins to the town."

The kettle whistled and Paulette switched off the heat. She poured steaming water into each mug. "Exactly. To keep him quiet, I had to have dinner with him."

"But it doesn't mean you need to see him again, right?" Meredith dunked the bag to emphasize her words. "I mean, if he thinks the girls are witches, what will he think when he finds out about us?"

"We'll cross that bridge before we burn it down, okay?" Paulette pulled two spoons from the drawer and handed one to Meredith.

"I'm afraid it'll be the other way around, and we'll all be burned by his accusations." She pulled the tea bag out of the hot liquid and used the string to squeeze the trapped tea back into the mug.

Paulette stared at her. "You don't want me to be happy, do you?"

Startled cat eyes blinked at her. "What? No! I want you to be happy but not at our expense. I don't think Zak has our best interests at heart."

"He has mine. You're about to marry Max. Then what happens to me? Will you kick me out?"

"Of course not. There's plenty of room here, like I promised. I'm looking forward to helping you raise your little one."

"Then why can't you be happy since I might have a man of my own?"

Meredith snorted. "You've had plenty of men over the years; they simply don't hang around very long."

Despite the fact that her sister had pegged it, Paulette bristled. "Maybe so, but my past errors in judgment don't mean I'll be stupid enough to go down that particular path again. I like to think I learn from my mistakes. Unlike you."

"What do you mean?" Meredith propped her fists on her hips.

"I think you're toying with Max." She threw away the used tea bag with a flick of her wrist, a wet smack echoing across the kitchen when it landed in the trashcan. "I don't think you're intending to marry him. If you did, you'd have plans in place for the wedding."

"Of course I am!" Meredith spluttered. "Why would you say such a thing?"

She sipped the hot liquid, burning the tip of her tongue. She wiggled it over her lower lip to cool it off. "You haven't asked me about your wedding dress I'm designing for you. You haven't even set a date or made a guest list or anything. Where are the invitations to address and mail? Who's making the cake?" She drew a breath and fixed a stern look on Meredith. "So tell me. When are you going to tell him the wedding is off?"

"It's not off. Stop saying such a thing." Meredith wrapped both hands around her mug, staring into the steam rising slowly until it disappeared. "We're planning to marry the day after Christmas. We did set the date."

Paulette shifted her weight to her right foot and studied her sister. "And the dress?"

"I was going to ask you about it. Honest." She raised worried eyes. "It's all so overwhelming. All the decisions and choices. Just make me a dress, and it can be a surprise when you're done."

Paulette shook her head so hard her vision blurred. "I'll give you options, but a bride has to select her own gown. It has to be bad luck to not, wouldn't you think?"

Meredith sighed and then lifted her mug to her lips. After she swallowed, she nodded once. "Granted. It's not that I don't want to marry Max, it's just…"

She waited, but Meredith merely gazed at her. "Just what?"

"Do you think Willy would approve?" A hitch in Meredith's voice made the last word three syllables. Her irises darkened with worry. "Would he understand?"

"Oh, sweetie, of course he would." Now she understood the problem. Paulette hurried around the island to wrap her arms about Meredith for a fierce hug. "He'd want you to be happy and share your life with someone who can love you at least as much as he did. Isn't that why he gave his life for you?"

Meredith shrugged. "I suppose but…"

Pushing Meredith to arm's length, Paulette squeezed her shoulders. "No buts about it. You have to live, not figuratively die, because your first husband died trying to protect you and your child even if he didn't know about the wee one."

Tears leaked down her sister's cheeks and Paulette wiped them away with her thumb. "We both deserve to be happy, Mer. Figuring out how to achieve such a state is the challenge before us."

Meredith gazed at her with a weak smile. "Max makes me laugh and fills my heart with joy."

"I know he does. You light up when he's in the room. But you have to be sure about whether you want to spend the rest of your lives together or you'll always be second-guessing the relationship."

"And you have to decide whether Zak's intentions are really centered on his feelings for you." She sipped her tea, contemplating Paulette. "Or is his interest in maneuvering close enough to discern our secrets so he can expose us all?"

"The only way I'll be able to tell is by spending more time with him." *Keep your friends close, your enemies closer.* "I'll be careful to not let him get too close."

<h1 style="text-align:center">Chapter Eleven</h1>

*I*f only more shoppers were crowded among the wide sidewalks of the open air mall, Paulette might relax. The basic tenet of safety, staying in well-populated areas, echoed in her mind. She strolled beside Zak along the concrete and brick path, maneuvering around potted trees and flower beds, his fingers laced with hers like besotted lovers. Meredith's caution echoed in her mind even as she enjoyed the bright sunshine and the friendly company. At least, he acted friendly. She pondered his true intentions as she scanned the endless row of clothing boutiques and snack food stores.

She spotted a children's clothing shop and hesitated to suggest exploring its offerings. Zak squeezed her hand and pulled her to a halt.

"Do you want to go in?" He took a step toward the store, pausing for her response.

"Yes, but I'd understand if you don't want to." She resisted weakly, spotting an adorable frilly dress on a child-sized mannequin in the window.

He grinned and tugged her closer, planting a kiss on her mouth. "I don't mind."

Opening the door, he ushered her inside the cool

interior. She paused to determine the layout and then headed for the infant clothes. Zak followed close behind. When she stopped to inspect a pale green onesie with dark green feet, his hand gravitated to her hip. The light pressure of his palm made it difficult to focus on the soft fabric in her fingers. Part of her attention remained on contemplating what he intended to do next. Deciding to buy the outfit, she draped it over her arm and moved away from Zak, a mixture of relief and disappointment filling her with the break in contact. She spied an adorable pant and top set and picked it up to check the size. Zak stopped beside her, his hand on her waist this time. She turned to look at him, raising her gaze to search his. He smiled and kissed her, a quick light press of lips.

"What are you doing?" Glancing around, she didn't see anyone shocked by his public display of affection other than perhaps herself.

"Kissing my girl." He grinned down at her, one brow cocked. "Okay?"

Was it? "I didn't know we were a couple."

"It's our second date, so by my definition we are."

"And if I don't agree with your definition?"

Another kiss followed. "Do you agree now?"

"No." Placing the outfit on the table along with the onesie, she made to leave, to put distance between them.

He caught her elbow and forced her to stop, look at him. "I'm sorry. I don't mean to rush this. It's just, well, I can't seem to stop thinking about you, touching you, and my God, kissing you."

His grasp detained her, the grip almost but not quite painful in his fervor. She longed to touch him as much as he wanted to touch her. But a great physical relationship didn't necessarily make a sound emotional one. Yes, he attracted her like lint to a black dress. But that kind of attraction could be easily severed. A bit of cold water in the right places would do the trick. She'd experienced such a relationship one too many times in her life. She had to be careful. Her baby's future rested in the balance. Zak regarded her, waiting for her comment. "I need some air."

She hurried outside, grateful for the warmth of the sun on her face, the bustle of a group of young women scurrying by. The lack of contact between them so she could think clearly. Foremost among her thoughts was the need to protect her family. Since she'd moved in with Meredith, her loved ones had become more important than ever before. Family first.

"Sweetheart, what's wrong?"

"Nothing, really." His puzzled frown revealed his confusion. She understood the feeling. "I guess I didn't expect you to be in such a hurry about us. If there even is an *us*."

He smiled ruefully. "I'll try to slow down, to make you feel more comfortable." He fell in step with her, gently linking hands, as they continued down the walkway, browsing the variety of shops. "But it'll be the most difficult task you could ever ask of me."

"Maybe so, but it's the only way I can do this." She fluttered a hand between them. "And even then, I have my doubts."

Zak took her hand, kissed her palm. "I'll do my best."

Exactly what she feared most.

After popping in and out of several more boutiques, her tummy started growling. "How about a burger for lunch?" She pointed to a sign advertising a local hamburger joint.

"Is there ever a time when a burger doesn't make for a good lunch?" Chuckling, he wrapped an arm around her waist and guided her toward the door. "And they have karaoke."

Glancing at him, she stepped through the door he held open. "You sing?"

"You might call it that." The door swung shut behind them, and he reached for her hand again as they walked up to the hostess station.

The hostess seated them at a table for two by the window overlooking a manmade lake. White ducks and swans drifted past on the choppy surface, the wind pushing long drooping weeping willow fronds into the waves. Several ambitious office workers on their lunch hour power walked around the perimeter on a winding path.

Zak slipped two menus from the holder and slid one across the small square table. He skimmed the contents on the page before setting it aside. "You are a beautiful woman, Paulette."

"Hmmm… I think I'll have a bacon cheeseburger." No point in responding to such blatant attempts at flattering her back into his good graces.

"I mean it." He snared her fingers from the menu. "You put all other women to shame."

"With fries." She freed her hand, laid the menu on the table and then placed both hands in her lap.

He chuckled. "Understood."

After the waiter took their order, she stared at the lazy circles the ducks made in the lake. "Sometimes I envy ducks."

"Why?" Zak rested his elbows on the table.

"They have such a simple life, swimming around, eating when they're hungry. No bills to pay." She indicated a group of brown ducks approaching the larger flock of white ones. Clouds scudded by, their shadows darkening the water. "Nothing to do but be out in nature among their fellow ducks. Such a peaceful, easy existence."

"Until they're shot by a hunter."

"True." She laughed at his observation. "We all have challenges of one kind or another." Unbidden, Grandpa Patrick's presence at Twin Oaks popped into her mind.

What was she to do about him? He seemed to think she needed him, but why?

"What's wrong?"

She shook her head. "Nothing for you to worry over." Or even know about if she had anything to say on the matter.

Their meals arrived and they fell silent for a couple minutes. The salty crunch of bacon blended with the gooey melted cheese and hot beef contrasted by the sweet tomato and bite of red onion. *Perfect.* Zak bit into his sandwich, though he studied her as she chewed, swallowed, and took another bite. Her face warmed under the scrutiny. To be sure a stray bit of food wasn't lingering in the wrong place, she wiped her mouth with the paper napkin, his eyes following her movements. Then something over her shoulder caught his attention and he shoved his napkin under the edge of his plate. An I-have-a-surprise-for-you smile lit his face.

"I'll be right back." He strode across the nearly empty dining room to the bar along the far wall.

She pivoted in her seat, saw him talk to a man—the manager?—and then head toward the raised stage. What did he intend? Anticipation and wonder stewed her lunch in her stomach. Was he really going to sing? He stepped up on the platform and spoke to the manager who had followed him. Music blared from the many speakers scattered around the podium and its lone microphone. Zak nodded in time to the beat of John Denver's "Sunshine on My Shoulders," one of her all-time favorite songs to sing. His deep baritone carried the warmth and sincerity of the lyrics, and she found herself singing along. Quietly, so only she could hear, but she smiled and waved back to Zak as he effortlessly maneuvered through the song.

She sang to express her joy in living, of life, in her future. Songs served that purpose, to express her happiness and elation. Some people sang the blues or soul to express deep feelings of hurt and pain, but for her, song equated to a joyful noise. Long suppressed memories surfaced to invade her mind and stir emotions in her heart. Performing with the high school choir and later with the cover band in Indianapolis where her spirits had soared as high as a bird when she sang. Hearing Zak's rich voice awoke her own need to express herself through song. Her heart raced with the rediscovered depth of her desire to sing, not merely for herself but for her child. When he finished, she joined in the scattered applause. Then she froze. Zak motioned to her to join him. The temptation proved too much and although nervous, having not sung in public in ages, she hurried to join him.

What should she choose? Would he have a song picked already? Would they sing a duet? The questions somersaulted in her mind as she dodged around tables and chairs and finally stepped onto the stage beside Zak. It had been too long since she stood on a stage.

"What do you want to sing?" Zak showed her the listing to choose from.

"A duet?" She leafed through the pages, scanning titles and artists.

"If you'd like." He leaned over her shoulder, so close she imagined she felt his heart beating.

"Something fun? Maybe 'Singin' in the Rain'?" She turned the page and spotted more show tunes. "Oh, how about 'Shall We Dance'?"

"I know that one, so that'll work." He punched in the code to start the background music and scroll the lyrics across the screen on the podium.

She'd never have guessed he sang, let alone be into show tunes like her. Perhaps she'd underestimated the man. Sneaking a peek, his quick grin shot a thrill of anticipation across her lower back, almost as if he'd caressed her with a look. Best to focus on the screen and not on him in order to be able to perform well. She lifted the mic from its holder and held it between them as they waited for their cue. The famous dancing scene of Yul Brynner and Deborah Kerr in *The King and I* floated in her mind's eye, the flouncy dress against the kingly attire a sharp contrast in styles and cultures.

One, two, three… She opened her mouth to let the words flow. Surprised delight wafted through her when Zak sang in harmony, taking the lower register and weaving a contrasting melody to the primary tune she sung. He slipped an arm around her waist, snugging her against him, and she almost dropped the microphone as a jolt of—what?—swept through her. She explored the sensation, sifting and sorting until she knew. But it couldn't be. Love? With Zak? She stumbled over the words gliding up the screen, but quickly recovered. He squeezed her to him, a silent acknowledgement of her showmanship. Focusing on the song, she pushed aside the newly discovered feelings, relishing the experience of performing.

When the song ended, she broke out in a laugh filled with the ecstasy of singing. When had she stopped? And why? She suspected it had something to do with her four-year affair with Johnny. She had put the flaming failure behind her. Sharing this moment with Zak elicited an indescribable joy infusing every cell of her body. The only damper was realizing her heart hadn't listened to her head. She peered up at him and smiled, unable to contain her happiness. He took advantage of the opportunity by kissing her, to the laughter and applause of the few patrons in the restaurant.

"Another?" Zak started flipping through the pages again and then glanced at her. "You're a real star at this."

"Thanks." She savored the moment of praise and excitement coursing in her veins, butterflies of happiness fluttering inside. "I think one's enough, though it was such fun to sing with you. I didn't realize you had such a great talent."

He shrugged and closed the book. "My mom insisted we do something musical. Grant plays sax mainly because he couldn't carry a tune if his life depended upon it. Singing comes more naturally to me."

"So we have something in common after all." She stepped down off the stage, a bounce in her stride as she made her way back to their table. No way would her stupid heart's decision rob her of enjoying sharing the stage with Zak. She firmly believed in not inflicting this child on another man. She could raise it, with her family's help, and he or she would be smart and loving.

"We have quite a bit in common, I think." Zak kept pace with her. "I'm overwhelmed by all of your wonderful gifts."

"Right. The gift of getting myself into sticky situations being first and foremost." She chuckled as she slid back onto the vinyl cushioned bench. She grabbed a fry and popped it into her mouth. The pure euphoria of the past few minutes blazed inside, warming her down to her toes.

Zak resumed his seat and then picked up his sandwich and took a bite, considering her as he chewed. After a few moments, he swallowed and stilled. "I'm very glad Mr. Starling led me to Roseville so I could meet you. If it weren't for a small owl symbol, our paths would never have crossed."

The solemnity with which he spoke made her look more closely at him. His eyes shone like the surface of a mountain lake on a rainy day. The thin jagged scar down his right jaw accentuated the sharp angles of his face, now with only a hint of the bruise from the explosion. His shoulders tensed and then fell into place as he continued to hold his sandwich in midair and the corners of his mouth slowly lifted into a smile.

"I guess that makes me 'for the birds' then, huh?" Keep it light. He acted too serious for a casual lunch. Another fry to chew on would keep her mouth closed.

"Not in my book." He took another bite, glancing out the window at the ducks on the pond. "You're an amazing woman, Paulette."

She had to find a way to lighten this conversation, steer him to more mundane and safe topics. "So what's your favorite music?"

He shrugged and swallowed. "Folk music. I find the stories behind the lyrics compelling."

She nodded, glad to have avoided a more serious conversation. She let her shoulders drop to their normal resting place instead of hugging her ears. "Mine is show tunes, all the wonderful songs from the musicals over the years." She bit into her burger.

"Paulette, I—" Clearing his throat, he set his sandwich down, mauled his napkin into a wad and tucked it under his plate. He peered at her, took a breath and let it out slowly. Taking her hand in his, he squeezed it lightly. He cleared his throat again. "Paulette, sweetheart, I realize this is sudden, and rushing things. But I have to tell you. I love you. Everything about you. You're smart, and sexy, and talented, and did I mention sexy? Will you... Will you marry me?"

Holy crap. Love? Marry? Burger, bacon, and bread sprayed the table and their joined hands. Too late, she covered her mouth with her free hand, appalled she'd actually spat out the bite in her surprise. He didn't. They couldn't. "Are you insane?"

His grip on her fingers tightened. "I'm serious."

"So am I." Pulling free from his grasp, she swabbed her napkin over the bits of her lunch splattered on the table. "I, um, like you, Zak, but I barely know you."

He splayed his hands, palms up. "What you see is what

you get. You know all that is important to know about me."

Shaking her head, she gaped at him. She'd made her choice months before and a wayward heart wasn't going to change her mind. "I know nothing about you. Your family. Your dreams. Your intentions."

"Now that, my intentions, you do know." He laid both hands on the table. "I intend to prove my love for you and to make you my wife, if you'll have me."

She gripped her belly and gaped at him. She found herself drawn to this man in so many ways, but it wasn't all about her or him. "What about the baby?"

"I'll love the child you carry as well. I promise I'll treat him or her as my own, because he's part of you."

"Honestly, Zak, even if I wanted to, I simply can't marry you." Her nails bit into her belly and she forced herself to relax. "I love you, sure, but now is not the time. Maybe in another timeline we could make this work, but right now I can't." What did he really want from her? Meredith may be right, the way he pushed to make them be more than they were. Did he merely want to be close enough to dig out the family skeletons and bring them to light?

"So your answer is no?" His unbelieving stare met her steady gaze. "Even though you love me?"

Oh crap. Do they make locks for loose lips? She'd done it yet again, let thoughts slip out without consideration. As a result, she created yet another mess. She nodded and placed her napkin beside her plate. The baby flipped, pushing hard until she felt queasy. Perfect timing. "I'm not feeling very well. Please, take me home."

"Your idea needs some work." Paulette moved around the dining room table later that evening, setting places for dinner. She sang softly as she worked, reliving the exaltation of performing again, while ignoring the letdown of Zak's proposal. No, not the proposal, but her answer. Should she have said yes in order to give her baby a father and her a husband? Or stay with her original plan, one that seemed lonely by comparison but safer for her heart.

"Max is a great judge of character." Meredith followed with forks and knives, aligning each handle to perfection. "He'll size up Zak, and then you'll know."

"Know what?" Brock strode into the large room, carrying a ceramic soup tureen.

"Put that on the sideboard, Dad." Paulette hurried to push the silver tea service to one side as Brock settled in place the large covered bowl bedecked with pink roses. Her mouth watered at the aroma of chicken corn chowder. "Meredith wants Max to determine whether I should marry Zak. I think not, but we'll see what he says."

"Marry Zak?" Brock's mouth fell open. "He's only been in town a week."

"Plus one day, actually." Meredith grinned. "He's a fast operator, but we wonder if he's on the up and up."

Familiar footfalls sounded in the hall. Paulette caught Meredith's eye, and they both waited for Max to reach the dining room doorway. When he filled the opening, Meredith hurried to greet him. Paulette wished she could feel such delight as her sister exhibited at that moment. Max kissed Meredith, tucking her into a hug as they walked into the room together.

"Thanks for inviting me to your family dinner, ladies." He nodded to Brock in silent greeting as Meredith moved away to finish laying the silverware in place.

"You're about to become family, so why not?" Brock shook hands with Max, clapping a hand twice on his upper arm at the same time.

Dina, decked out in black gaucho pants with a silver peasant blouse and sparkling silver earrings, led Grant and Zak into the room. "Have a seat, gentlemen."

Zak's sudden appearance sent tremors through her knees, especially when she noticed Max aiming to talk to the man. Zak had donned snug chocolate slacks and a soft red dress shirt that emphasized his muscular torso and made her mouth water. She forced herself to look away, but the image stayed in her mind. She took her place by the tureen, hoping her legs wouldn't buckle from their shaking. What outcome did she want from their exchange? She didn't want Max to not approve, but if he didn't like him, what would happen? Then again, if Max gave him a thumbs up, it meant she could trust him. Trust was one thing. But marry him?

Soon everyone had a bowl of steaming chowder before them, spooning the savory soup into eager mouths. She kept her own mouth full so she didn't blurt out anything stupid. Max took charge of the conversation, touching on a variety of topics, seeking Zak's opinion on county and state politics as well as national and global issues. Subjects she avoided since she had no control over their outcomes anyway. She occupied her mind with dress patterns and related research into period costumes while keeping an ear to the conversation.

"So, Zak, how is your research coming?" Max swallowed a spoonful of chowder.

"We're narrowing the options." Zak stirred his soup, glanced at Paulette, and then back to Max. "Still trying to figure out what the secret handshake might be."

"I'm sure you'll discover an answer," Max said. "With all your training and resources, it's only a matter of time."

"The sooner, the better." Grant shook his head and tapped his spoon three times on the edge of the bowl. "Time's running out and I should be heading home soon."

"Oh, have you heard from the doctors as to possible treatments?" Meredith split a roll in two and slathered butter on one half. "Surely they can do something to remove or at least shrink the tumors."

Grant shook his head as he looked around the table. "Looks like no good options have come to light yet."

One option they hadn't tried yet, one worth investigating given the paltry possibilities so far. Paulette tilted her head and shrugged. "Why not let Tara give it a go?"

All eyes turned to her.

"What? She's a healer." Paulette spooned soup into her mouth, reverting to her original plan of not uttering anything inane.

Grant gaped at her for the span of a sharp breath before guffawing. "That's a good one! I thought you were serious."

Oh well. It was worth a try. Meredith shrugged and bit into her roll, aware that Paulette had actually made a serious suggestion. Paulette smiled to camouflage her disappointment. "If nothing else, I'm always good for a joke."

Laughter rippled around the table and then the conversation turned to other subjects. She watched Zak smile and comment with practiced ease. Man, he was sexy, smart, and talented. She grinned to herself. He'd said something very similar to her earlier in the day. More things in common.

Suddenly, amidst a heated discussion on global warming, Grandpa Patrick appeared by the cold fireplace. Meredith choked on her chardonnay, staring at him with worried eyes. Paulette laid her spoon in the bowl and wiped her mouth with her cloth napkin. What was he doing? She hadn't seen him in days and had secretly hoped he'd grown bored and left. A futile wish, but still.

Grandpa Patrick moved to stand by Zak, peering at him from first one side, then the other. He glanced at Paulette, grinned, and then flicked the point of Zak's shirt collar. He laughed outright when Zak glanced down, startled, a frown between his brows. She chuckled at his discomfiture. Patrick flicked the collar again and laughed harder at Zak's repeat performance. Paulette shook her head to try to dissuade Patrick's hijinks and Zak lifted one questioning brow.

She sobered in the face of his steady regard. "Everything all right?"

He nodded slowly, then turned back to address Max. "We've certainly had odd weather this year, but still that doesn't mean anything."

"Sure it does." Grant motioned with his spoon, a milky yellow drop splatting on the gold tablecloth. "It proves mankind is messing with the balance of nature."

Patrick laughed again, leaning closer to Zak, finger poised.

"We don't have enough data to know the true nature of weather cycles." Zak spooned soup into his mouth, then stirred the remainder in his bowl.

"We already agreed you're not a weatherman," Grant said. "So I'll keep that in mind as you spew your opinions."

Another flick, but thankfully this time Zak ignored the misbehaving collar. Without a reaction, her grandpa would quickly lose interest in his pranks. Hopefully. She held her breath until, disenchanted with his target, Patrick moved on to hover near Brock where he leaned back, balancing the chair on two legs. A wicked grin split Patrick's face as he jerked on his son's chair, rocking it violently backward. Brock grabbed at the table as he yelped a curse, pulling the chair back to the floor.

"Brock!" Dina leapt to her feet beside him, glancing around the room.

Grant and Zak both jumped up, flinging napkins to the floor and chairs scraping behind them.

"What the hell...?" Brock released his death grip on the wooden table. Dina draped a protective arm around his shoulders, her left hand resting on his arm. Brock ran a hand through his hair. "Did we have an earthquake or something?"

"If we did, you're the only one who felt it." Max turned to Meredith. "Didn't you forget the fresh rolls, honey?"

Meredith stared at him and then blinked. "Oh. Right."

Meredith shoved back her own chair and stood. "Excuse me. I'll go get them."

She hurried past Brock, subtly motioning to Patrick to quit his antics and follow her. At her insistence, Patrick's shoulders drooped, but he trailed after her into the hallway and out of sight. Relief washed through Paulette when everyone resumed their seats and the conversation continued. Dismay soon followed, however, as the topic abruptly shifted to the one she wanted to avoid.

"I hear you've proposed to my future sister-in-law." Max studied Zak, a slow smile appearing. "I think you'd make a fine brother-in-law if she accepts your offer."

Brock nodded. "And a fine son-in-law." He looked at Paulette. "If she'll have you, of course. You two haven't known each other very long."

"Exactly." Paulette bobbed her head five times in quick succession. A reprieve. "That's what I told him."

"Long enough for me to know she's the woman I want to spend the rest of my days with." Zak's smile was aimed at her and she found herself returning one of her own. "I can't imagine loving anyone else as much as I love Paulette. Except maybe her child."

Dina dropped her spoon with a splash into the soup. "Am I the only one here who knew nothing about this proposal?"

Paulette shrugged lightly. "I'm sorry, Mom. He proposed over lunch. I told him 'no.'" She shot a glare at Zak, but he simply smiled.

Dina tilted her head and frowned. "Why?"

She huffed in surprise. "I barely know the man."

"Time doesn't dictate to the heart. I only knew your father a day before I realized he was the man for me."

She gawped at her mother, finding no quarter in the expectant countenance. "I don't even know his favorite color."

"Yellow." Zak lifted both brows and dropped them just as fast. "Any other questions?"

She let out a long breath and shook her head as she sifted through all the unanswered questions rattling around inside. "How many brothers and sisters do you have?"

"Grant is my only sibling." He quirked his brows twice and grinned.

"Thank goodness for small favors." Grant chuckled and then dipped another spoonful of chowder.

"See you know me better than you realize." Zak laid his spoon in his bowl. "Please, say yes."

Four pair of eyes turned to her, weighed on her, waiting. She knotted her napkin in her lap, twisting and pulling on it as she blinked at the anxious faces. Meredith returned with a basket of rolls and a container of butter that she plopped in front of Max and then took her place, thankfully leaving Patrick elsewhere. She swallowed, buying time. Zak reached across to take her hand, making her desist from her attempt to mangle the napkin and look at him. Handsome, sexy Zak Markel, one very fine hunk of a man she wouldn't mind gazing on forever. A few other actions came to mind as well, involving hands and feet and positions. Definitely attractive and smart. If only her situation were different. But his smile alone would be worth waking up to every morning.

He reached into his shirt pocket and she stopped breathing until he withdrew his hand. Fumbling with something in his fingers, he finally held up before her a gold ring boasting a solitary round cut diamond that reflected the chandelier and candle lights in flashes of color. When he cleared his throat, she swallowed in anticipation of his next words.

"Paulette, sweetheart, I love you. I believe you feel the same. I'll ask again, at the risk of embarrassing myself before all of your family and mine. Will you share the rest of your life with me as my wife and forever love?"

Chapter Twelve

The Wrangler bounced over a pot hole, making the woman beside him grab for the armrest with one hand as her other held her pregnant belly. Zak glanced at Paulette, pleased as a pup with a beefy bone to see the diamond ring on her left hand.

"Slow down or this babe may come today." She caught his grin and smiled self-consciously. "What?"

Sunshine haloed her hair, clear fall sky beyond the window emphasizing the perfection of his fiancée. He shook his head and focused on the road leading into Roseville.

"Why go back to the book store?" She released the armrest and rested both hands on her belly. "I'd think you would've run out of options by now."

The joy in his heart dimmed a trifle. He'd examined the recipes in the journal with Grant's help, and the directions continued to confuse both of them. Some instructions were written in what appeared to be some secret hieroglyphic code, interspersing symbols used like verbs with actual words. In other places, the directions seemed clear enough until the author totally changed the subject for a paragraph and then swerved back on topic. Yet it seemed as though some details had been omitted.

"I'm hoping for a miracle." He detected her puzzlement, one he shared. "I'm hoping the power of three in the form of three lovely women will work to reveal the solution to the mysterious instructions."

"I'm hoping you'll do like the lady says and slow this damn truck down before you toss me out the window." Grant's frown bounced in the rear view mirror.

"I'm sure he'd come back to pick you up." Paulette chuckled and then turned to watch the fields roll past as he steered through a winding section of the road. "Hey, Grant, did Meredith talk to you about her ideas for a memorial garden at Twin Oaks? If you're at loose ends while Zak's digging into his research, you might consider digging in the dirt with Sean. Interested?"

"Maybe. At least I'd have something more useful to do while I'm waiting on this ridiculous effort." He sighed loudly. "Really Zak, why would you think this elixir crap would have any effect on my condition?"

"I told you. Your expertise in geology is vital to solving this mystery." Zak negotiated a sharp curve. "What, you don't want to help me?"

"You're beyond help, if you ask me." Grant chuckled and then fell silent.

Zak ignored his brother's peevishness, knowing the root cause. He focused on the ribbon of pavement before him. He had developed a fondness for the area, made even stronger by meeting Paulette. Driving along the two-lane road brought peace to the internal drive for answers to ancient riddles. The low rolling hills sported a variety of low ranchers and bungalows, each nestled among a protective cluster of trees slowly shedding their colorful leaves, along the highway. Intermingled with the residences were the massive farms where immense fields of corn, cotton, soybeans, and wheat alternated in the growing season. Each farm's sky-high silos held the results of the farmer's efforts.

Lying brown and fallow, the ground rested after the crops had been harvested. Before long the barren and stubbled fields gave way to country neighborhoods and then to the outskirts of the small town. He parked down the block from the Golden Owl, hopped out of the Jeep, and then helped Paulette step safely to the sidewalk. Grant slipped from the back seat, rubbing his arm.

They sauntered down the sidewalk, Zak and Paulette arm in arm, Grant a stride behind. Zak smiled at passersby, happy to have his woman beside him. In the long run, solving the recipe's puzzle meant nothing compared to solving the loneliness of his heart. But for appearances sake, especially in the eyes of his brother, he'd press on until he figured out what he didn't understand about the alchemical writings. Hope lingered in his soul that this trip, begun to spend time with his brother, also yielded the miracle he sought. A cure before Grant indeed lost his vision.

"Do you want something to drink while I search?" He paused inside the front door of the store, holding it open for Paulette and Grant to pass through. The little bell announced their arrival, causing Roxie to look up from arranging books on top of the center set of shelves.

"If you don't mind." Paulette grasped his hand. "I'd rather chat with Tara for a spell."

"Literally, or figuratively?"

"Hush." She playfully swatted his arm. "That's not funny."

"Who's laughing?" But a grin erupted on his face despite his denial. "Go on. I'll try to be quick."

Grant caught Tara's eye as she worked behind the pastry counter. "I'll grab a coffee, too."

Zak nodded sagely, a knowing grin spreading over his lips. "I understand. You're abandoning me in my hour of need, all because of a dame."

Grant punched him in the arm and shook his head. "I'm following your lead."

Roxie approached, dusting her hands on her khakis. "Hi. What brings you all in today?"

"Zak seems to think there may be a book here he didn't find before." Paulette raised her hand to swipe a few stray tendrils back into place. "And Grant is along for the ride."

"Hold it." Roxie grabbed her wrist and pulled her left hand up to inspect the flashing diamond. "What's this?"

Zak beamed. "She said yes."

Roxie hugged Paulette. "Congratulations?"

Paulette hugged the taller woman and grinned at Zak. "Absolutely."

"Then I'm happy for you both." Roxie stepped back, propping a fist on each hip. She regarded Zak for a heartbeat. "You better not hurt her, sir, or you'll answer to me."

He sobered, detecting the depth of sincerity in Roxie's voice. Given that he had no clue as to what her abilities and powers may be, he'd take her at her word. "I'll never knowingly hurt her. You have my promise."

Roxie grinned and splayed her open palms. "Good. How can I help?"

Paulette waved her ring hand, indicating she was heading to the coffee bar. "Ta-ta. Grant and I will be waiting."

"Be sure to show Tara and Beth while you're over there." Roxie grinned at Paulette's retreating back, Grant striding beside her, then turned to address Zak. "So?"

He relayed his confusion with the alchemist's journal entries. From the distant look in her expression, he'd guess she was mentally searching the book store's inventory for a possible answer.

She blinked and then snapped her fingers. "I know what you need. Come on."

She led him to the history section, scanning the spines as she hurried down one aisle and then the next. Finally, she slid a thick book from the shelf and thrust it toward him.

Gripping the heavy tome, hope exploded in his chest, obliterating any doubt of success. "*The Historiography of Alchemy: Deciphering the Alchemist's Code.* Surely this holds the key."

"As I recall, the author is a historian of science but also a chemist, like you." She tapped the cover, pointing to the name beneath the title. "He managed to not only unravel the code but also recreate the techniques. The book even won prestigious awards for its cutting-edge content."

Would hugging the book be unmanly? The inanimate object felt alive in his hands, wriggling with secrets it was eager to reveal to him. He shook his head. Obviously, his imagination galloped away with him. "Why didn't I see this earlier?"

Roxie studied him, lips pursed as she considered her response. "Probably because you weren't open to receiving its message."

"And now I am?" He chuckled and tucked the book under one arm. "If you say so. Let me pay for this. I have a ton of reading to do."

"You may not believe me, but the world has a way of knowing when we're ready and when we're not." Roxie tilted her head and crossed her arms, contemplating him with a cross between a smile and a frown for several moments. "You've changed since coming to Roseville."

"If I have, it's all Paulette's doing." He shifted the book to secure a better grip on the glossy cover. Its contents held the answers he so fervently sought. Standing here chatting about nonsense only delayed solving the puzzle. With a nod toward the front of the store, he quirked one brow. "Shall we?"

As he paid for the book, Paulette sashayed toward him

with her usual sway. Not even pregnancy could eliminate her distinctive style. Sure, the baby probably limited the swagger her hips could tolerate, but she still had a very sexy walk, nonetheless. Imagine the turn on she'd be after the baby came.

Behind her, Grant lingered in a conversation with Tara. She reached out and laid a hand on his arm, a common gesture and yet different. He puzzled over the distinction, finally noting she was moving her hand lightly along Grant's long-sleeved shirt, as though searching for something. Grant laughed, and she raised her hand to lay it against his cheek, a brief inquisitive caress. Grant noticed Zak watching them. He addressed Tara briefly, and then strode toward Zak. Interesting exchange.

"Find what you were looking for?" Paulette leaned across his extended arm to peer at the cover. "A little light reading, I see. Guess I know what you'll be doing this afternoon."

Roxie handed him his card, and he placed it in his wallet, slipping the leather case into his back pocket. Lifting the book with the receipt tucked in the cover, he thanked Roxie and grasped Paulette's hand as Grant joined them. "Did you have a nice chat with Tara?"

Grant cut him a don't-ask look and walked to the door, pulling it open and waiting for Zak and Paulette.

Paulette nodded, assuming incorrectly that Zak had asked her the question as they strode toward the exit. "She was telling me some of the long list of items I'll need to have at hand when labor begins."

"Is she a nurse?" He took her arm as they strolled behind Grant back toward the Jeep.

"Better." She climbed into the passenger seat and clicked the seatbelt in place. She regarded him with a defensive challenge in her eyes. "She's a midwife."

Such a topic needed a different day for rational

discussion. She wasn't open to his logical arguments opposing such a course of action. Perhaps tomorrow she'd appreciate his reasoning, but not in her present mood. Keeping his own counsel, he started the engine, waited for Grant to close his door, and drove back to Twin Oaks.

As the threesome passed through the kitchen, Zak glanced at her when she dropped her purse on the table. "I'm going to sit in the parlor and read. What're you going to do?"

"Take a nap." She yawned to prove her point. "I'm exhausted all the time."

"Good idea." He led her toward the foot of the stairs, kissed her, then as she climbed to the second floor, he hurried into the double parlor.

"I need some air, so I'm going for a walk. Might check in with Sean. See you later." Grant continued down the hall and out the front door.

Zak watched him with questions swirling in his mind. Were he and Tara an item? Why had she touched him in such a peculiar fashion? He shook the niggling questions out of his thoughts and hurried into the parlor.

Ever since the lab explosion, he'd been working toward unraveling the secrets of the alchemist. He laid the weighty book on his thighs and flipped open the cover, paging quickly to the meat of its content. Before long the words and concepts captivated his attention until he lost himself in a myriad of revelations.

Alchemists used secrecy to protect their most valued items from being stolen by either competing alchemists who could profit from the recipe or from people deemed unworthy of the information. The complexity and secrecy made understanding the texts challenging if not impossible for centuries. He learned about a device employed by alchemical writers called *Decknamen*, a German term for a cover name. Essentially, the device involved inserting a metaphorical or literal link to the common name of an element, but one intended to obscure the meaning from the unworthy reader so only true alchemists could access the knowledge.

They also used allegories to further confuse and obscure the information. Most intriguing though was the use of dispersion, or interrupting the instructions with seemingly unrelated or unimportant information that redirected the reader to a false conclusion or impression. He reread the passage and smiled. Exactly what Starling had used in his journal. If the alchemist employed multiple of these techniques, the resulting journal would appear nonsensical. As it did currently. With the key before him, he could solve the puzzle.

He blinked and glanced at his watch. Later than he imagined. Almost time to dress for dinner. A noise at the door called his attention to a sexily rumpled Paulette. She closed the distance between them, sinking onto the settee, her thigh grazing his. He closed the book and put an arm around her shoulders as she snuggled up to him. Her head rested on his shoulder, her right hand covering his heart.

"Did you have a nice nap?" Excitement coursed through him and he held still with an effort, but one definitely worth making. His woman felt so right in his arms he'd stay in the slightly uncomfortable position forever if she desired it to be so. He laid the book on the side table, bumping the porcelain lamp, which wobbled then settled.

She moved her head up and down, rubbing her cheek across his chest. "I dreamed about you."

"Apparently, it was a good dream." She'd never curled up with him before. Her nearness worked its magic, stirring a need he knew well. Her fingers circled over his heart, alerting his groin of some very real possibilities. What position was safe for a pregnant woman?

She chuckled, low and throaty. "You'd donned an

outrageous costume of a wounded Confederate soldier. Complete with blood and torn uniform."

"Really?" Damn, her voice stoked the response initiated by her wandering fingers inspecting his shirt, drifting down to trace the edge of his belt. He swallowed, shifted. "Why would I be a soldier?"

Her hand paused at his buckle and she glanced up at him. "For the party in a few days, I'd imagine. Ask me about my costume."

"I have no clue." Not with her hand so close to his slowly throbbing package. Would she explore farther south? The anticipation was killing him. "Tell me."

"I wore a fabulous coffee brocade with seed pearls sewn across the bodice." She suppressed laughter, shoulders trembling with the effort. "But if it were a wedding dress, then somebody must have died because the headpiece and long flowing veil were both black lace. Can you believe?"

She pushed up to a sitting position, away from him, to laugh out loud. Deprived of her seeking fingers, disappointment battled with appreciation of the joyful sound on her lips. He shifted again, to hide his condition and ease the discomfort.

"Zak, don't you get it?" She kissed him, then retreated again. "Bride of a dead soldier. It's our costumes for the party. I have everything we'd need to make them. I'm excited to finally have a great idea for our costumes."

"I'm excited, too." Different reasons, but still. "The costumes sound fine, not too embarrassing and all that." He paused to draw her attention to him. "I figured out how to decipher the recipe accurately."

"So the book did hold the answer." She smoothed her hands on her slacks and chuckled. "It's been a good day for both of us. Somebody did know how to help you, and it didn't involve magic after all."

"Yeah, I guess the three sisters aren't witches."

"So no more threatening to spread rumors about them?"

"Absolutely. I wouldn't want to falsely accuse anyone, especially those three, since they're about to become family." He reached for her hand, satisfied when she met him half way. "They've been so helpful."

She squeezed his fingers, studying his expression. "They're my friends too."

"All the more reason then." Pulling her closer, he kissed her on the lips, drawing her ever nearer with his free hand on her arm. "I'm so lucky to have found you."

Paulette pulled away slowly, slipping her hand from his. She rose and then pulled him to his feet, clasping his hands between them. "I'm the lucky one. What would I do without you?"

He winked and kissed her again. "That's not something you need worry your beautiful mind about."

"I do love you, Zak. I didn't think it possible for another man to love me as you do, and to love this little one, too." She layered their hands on her belly and the baby kicked his palm. "Nothing will ever tear our family apart."

Twin Oaks transformed into a haunted house the night of the party. The usual furniture and rugs had been spirited away and replaced with sturdy tables covered with orange and black tablecloths sporting pillar candles in a variety of heights and surrounded by miniature black cats, pumpkins, broomsticks, and other decorations. Trays dotted the tables, filled with ghost-shaped sugar cookies, bat-shaped sandwiches of chicken salad on pumpernickel, deviled eggs, and even a pumpkin-shaped cheese ball with fresh veggies and crackers.

Meredith had chosen to be the greeter, making sure each person felt welcomed. She'd encouraged everyone to have fun. She surveyed the room and the many characters milling about, pride settling on her shoulders. Paulette's laugh, mingled with that of the children, drifted over the general hubbub and laughter. Apparently, the kiddie activities in the sewing room were a hit. Zak had insisted on helping with the games and crafts, but Meredith suspected he merely wanted to keep a close eye on his fiancée. The kids' costumes had made her laugh and smile as they paraded in with their parents: princesses, pirates, sheeted ghosts, a hobo, and even a Raggedy Ann doll. Next year, Paulette's baby would need a costume. She pictured the baby dressed in a pumpkin outfit and grinned wider.

"What's so funny?" Sean appeared at her side, dressed as a Zombie groom.

"The costumes. Like yours." She motioned to his outfit. "They're all so creative and fun."

"You look good as Wonder Woman yourself." He winked appreciatively. "Max can't keep his eyes off you."

She laughed and glanced toward the front parlor where Max, outfitted as Captain America, played bartender at a long table laden with colorful bottles of liquor and wine. The line of guests stretched toward the hall. Captain America chatted with Jack Sparrow, while behind him Betsy Ross laughed with a red devil, complete with forked tail and horns.

"Are you going to dance?" She pointed to the commotion to her left, and he shook his head.

The double parlor had become a crowded dance floor within minutes of the first guests' arrival. Meg, or rather Fairy Godmother, took on the role of DJ. Another of Paulette's great ideas, to include music and dancing. Here again, the combinations of characters made Meredith smile. A big black gorilla bebopped with a flapper from the roaring twenties. At the other end of the group, Thor and a lanky red fox moved in time with the rock and roll beat.

Even a Rubick's Cube gyrated rather awkwardly with the Wicked Witch of the West.

"Not tonight. Bum leg." He pointed to the fake blood down his left side and smiled.

She'd resisted Paulette's original idea to have a party, but eventually realized having an event increased the potential for future business. If folks had a wonderful time and experienced what Twin Oaks offered, they'd tell their friends and family, and voila! More guests, which ultimately translated into stability and security for Paulette's ventures. Everything rested on a successful party. She'd do whatever necessary to ensure everyone had a good time.

"Thanks for sending Grant out to lend a hand." Sean bobbed his head in time with the music. "His ideas for the sloping and drainage aspects will enhance the overall effect."

"Paulette's idea. He needed a focus." She folded her arms and grinned. "The garden will bring peace in a variety of ways, apparently."

His answering smile made her feel she'd finally managed to make him proud of her. "Every one of them positive as well."

Footsteps sounded behind her.

"Hey, Wonder Woman, sorry we're a tad late to the party."

Smiling at the familiar voice, Meredith spun to face the open double doors where three sexy witches smiled back at her. "Wow, you ladies are hot tonight."

"It's our favorite time of year." Roxie moved to hug Meredith, stepping back to let Tara and Beth follow suit.

"Let me look at those fab costumes." Meredith scanned the three women, their unique black dresses clearly made to order for their figures. Tara's boasted a handkerchief hemline, alternating points of silky fabric creating a floating jagged edge. Beth's dress featured a plunging neckline and scalloped hemline, angling from above her knees in front to dip to her calves in back. She seemed a touch uncomfortable wearing it, fidgeting with the drape of the skirt with surreptitious jerky movements. But Roxie's dress stood out with a scooped neckline and long fringe hanging from three-quarter sleeves and along the bottom hem. "No pointed hats?"

Beth scoffed at the idea. "No way. That's a Hollywood adaptation."

Meredith chuckled. "Max is serving up some Halloween brews, and help yourself to goodies scattered throughout. My favorites are the bat sandwiches."

Roxie leaned close to Meredith. "Is Grandpa here? I'd love to meet him."

Meredith grimaced. "No, and I hope he doesn't make an appearance."

Beth moved to the beat of the music blaring from the other room. "I've often wondered about what he attempted to recreate the day the explosion occurred that killed him. Recipes are my specialty, so maybe I'd give it a shot if I knew what it might be."

"Personally, I'd like to know why he had an affair at all." Tara shook her shoulders as though tossing off a bad thought. "But then, we wouldn't be here if he hadn't. I guess it doesn't really matter."

Meredith nodded. "My feelings exactly. I'd rather have you guys as cousins than not."

"Right. Let sleeping secrets lie." Roxie grinned. "Besides, we're here to party, not interrogate anyone."

The music changed and Tara clapped her hands. "I love that song. I'm going to dance." She hurried into the double parlor and spun onto the dance floor.

Roxie tossed her long hair, allowing it to settle between her shoulder blades. "Come on, Beth. Let's snare a drink and check out the costumes."

Meredith watched the two witches join the line. Grant, dressed like a scientist with an ink blot on his button-down shirt pocket and black rimmed glasses with tape on the nose piece, sauntered toward her. The black jeans he wore emphasized his slim waist and muscular thighs. His swagger emphasized his sexual masculinity. If she weren't engaged, she'd take a closer look at the sensual man before her.

"Was that Tara and her sisters? Dressed as witches?" He nodded to Meredith and then allowed his gaze to track the invisible path Tara had taken into the double parlor. A slight frown settled in place.

"Are you all right?" Meredith asked. "Still having headaches?"

"About the same," he murmured, keeping his eyes on the dancing woman. "They're more constant but not piercing."

"I hope something helps and soon. By the way, Sean seemed very pleased with your help the other day." Meredith's words didn't capture his attention as he followed Tara's gyrations. "I'm sure he appreciates your efforts."

Tara moved her hips to the strong beat of "Celebration" by Kool and the Gang, emphasizing the rhythm with her hands in the air. A mummy boogied up to her and matched her moves. Grant tensed. Meredith sensed his emotional reaction more so than a physical change. The air seemed to shimmer with his dislike of the mummy's hands so near to Tara's hips and arms as the two mirrored each other's dance moves.

"Excuse me." Grant strode into the double parlor and tapped the mummy's shoulder, cutting in.

Meredith smiled as the two danced and the mummy moped away. Suddenly a stream of kids washed around her, locusts to the snacks and desserts scattered on the various tables. Paulette and Zak, costumed as a mourning bride and a dead Confederate soldier respectively, hurried toward her.

"Interesting choice of costume, given you're engaged. Don't you think it's tempting fate a bit?"

Paulette laughed. "You don't believe in superstitions, surely. I'm parched after all the talking and laughing with those children. Do you want a drink, Zak? I'll get you something."

"No, I'm fine. Want me to retrieve it?" He turned as though to walk away but hesitated, waiting for her order.

"I'll do it. I want some water, though I'd die for a glass of wine."

"You wouldn't…" Meredith stepped toward her. Refraining from an occasional glass of wine proved challenging for her pregnant sister. It probably didn't help that the rest of the family continued with the nightly wine with dinner.

Paulette waved her off. "No, I know better. I'll behave."

While Paulette sashayed down the hall, Meredith glanced at Zak. "Having fun?"

He nodded. "I see Grant found Tara."

She spied the couple dancing to the beat, their bodies so close as to brush against each other with each sway of their hips. Tara placed both hands on Grant's cheeks and directed his gaze to her hips while she moved her lips, presumably singing along to the song. His eyes fastened on her, a wide bemused smile fixed on his face. After a moment, she dropped her hands and danced away, twirling to show off her costume.

"She's definitely on his radar." Meredith puzzled over Tara's actions, especially as she repeatedly laid her palms to his temples. Almost as if applying her healing skills to his head. "I wonder…"

"What?" Zak asked.

"Never mind." It simply wasn't possible. Even if it were possible, she couldn't prove it. Only time would answer the question. "It's nothing."

The song ended and Tara and Grant walked back to join them in the foyer. He didn't take her hand but merely escorted her away from the puppy dog eyes of the mummy staring after them.

"Hey Grant, you displayed moves I didn't know about." Zak lightly punched his brother in the arm.

Grant pointed at Tara, his face wreathed in a happy smile. "It's all her fault."

"Mine? I'll have you know I was fine dancing with Bert until you pushed in." Her smile softened her words to a joke.

"Thanks to Roxie, I found what I came here looking for." Zak patted a hand on his thigh and nodded in time with the motion.

"What?" Tara asked. "Paulette?"

Zak laughed. "Okay, so make that two things. Paulette, and the means to unlock a mystery so I can complete the task I began in Michigan."

"You did?" Grant pinned him with an intense stare. "Does that mean you want to go home?"

"Home?" The floor seemed to tilt beneath her feet, throwing Meredith off balance.

"Are you all right?" Zak gripped her elbow to steady her.

Would he take Paulette and the baby away? The thought hadn't entered her head before. All her plans to provide for and play with the child threatened to unravel before the baby even entered the world. Her growing family would shrink with her sister's departure. And, selfishly, she'd miss out on the joy of helping to raise a child given that she couldn't have any children of her own. Family had become ever more important to her since moving back to Twin Oaks.

Patrick chose that moment to make an appearance, descending the stairs without a foot touching a tread. Meredith blinked as he drew closer. He'd really spiffed up for the occasion, resplendent in his Army dress uniform bedecked with rows of medals and ribbons on the left breast. She glanced down the hall and cringed. Max's Aunt Jenny, fittingly attired as Betsy Ross, hurried into the foyer, blissfully unaware of the ghost on a collision course.

Max appeared at her side. "What's going on? You look like you've seen a ghost."

She nodded toward the stairs, forgetting Max couldn't see the apparition. Patrick shimmered then clarified into an opaque image. Suddenly she realized the distinct change in her grandfather's form. Max searched in the direction she indicated and then froze as he stared. Meredith frowned. "What do you see?"

His mouth opened but no sound emerged. His eyes grew round.

This couldn't be happening. Yet it was. She shook her head at Patrick, but he ignored her.

Aunt Jenny, naively oblivious to the situation, greeted the group then peered at her nephew. "Max, you look wonderful. This is such a great party, Meredith. You and Paulette have outdone yourselves. I can't wait to post pictures online for everyone to enjoy."

Patrick hovered behind Aunt Jenny and grinned at Max. Max finally closed his mouth when Meredith elbowed him.

"Meredith…" Paulette approached, hands gripping her belly, surprise in her expression.

Uh oh. Not now. "Paulette, look who's here." She flashed a look at Patrick, and Paulette blanched. "What's happened?"

"My water broke." Her knuckles glowed white from pressing them on her stomach. "But it's too soon. I need Tara."

"The baby is coming. How wonderful!" Patrick moved closer to Paulette, grinning. "I'm going to be a grandfather all over again."

Paulette nodded back, mute in the face of the disaster unfolding in front of her.

Aunt Jenny smiled at the specter. "It is wonderful, isn't it, Patrick?"

Meredith held her breath. How was it possible? Only she and Paulette had been able to see Patrick before. "Can you see him?"

Aunt Jenny chuckled. "Why of course dear. Why wouldn't I? It's his house after all." Suddenly realizing what she was saying, Aunt Jenny's smile disappeared as she blinked at Patrick. "Wait. This is not possible. You died. I went to your funeral."

"Such a lovely ceremony, it was too." Patrick crossed his arms and tilted his head. "Shouldn't someone be taking care of the mother-to-be though?"

"That was…1955. That means you're a…a…" Aunt Jenny screamed once, twice, three times, her high-pitched tones silencing the crowd.

Meredith covered her ears, watching as the crowd converged. *Crap. Crap. Crap.*

All eyes centered on the soldier hovering two feet above the foyer floor. Then, as if someone had flipped a switch, guests ran screaming through the wide open doors. The chaos of people frantically fleeing upturned chairs and tables, food and candles flying through the air. Meredith ducked as the remains of the sugar cookie ghosts peppered the wall behind her. Roxie hurried to douse the candles rolling on the floor. Zak pulled Paulette onto the stairs and hugged her to keep her safe from the panicked party-goers streaming through the wooden doors. Tara trailed into the hallway as the last of the panicked guests fled, stopping at the base of the stairs next to Paulette. At least their true friends stayed to face the apparition.

Meredith moved to stand in the open doorway. All her hopes for the night dashed like the cookies into crumbs across the floor. Tears hovered in her eyes. She blinked and one escaped down her cheek.

The costumed guests rushed down the front steps like a crazed river of frightened rabbits, hopping and jumping between the jack-o-lanterns and dried corn stalks. Raced down the sidewalk lined with the glow of metal coffee can luminaries sporting pictures of bats and ghosts and pumpkins. Jumped in their cars and pickups and created a squealing cloud of dust as taillights disappeared in the distance.

"That was fun." Max took Meredith's hand in his.

She gripped his fingers as she stared down the drive, her nails digging into his skin. All her plans disappeared along with the last pair of red lights.

Patrick floated beside them, chuckling.

"I guess that's that." She slowly shook her head, dismay reverberating through her. As silence fell around her, Meredith glared at Patrick. "There went your granddaughter's future."

Chapter Thirteen

*M*ild pain rippled across skin stretched like an overfilled balloon. Paulette supported her belly, trying to alleviate the discomfort. *It's too soon* repeated in her mind.

"Is it time?" Zak peered at her, one hand searching in his pocket. "I'll pull the Jeep around."

She shook her head, unable to utter words until the pain subsided. Dragging in a breath, she let it out slowly. "We have everything we need right here. Tara helped me prepare for the arrival of my baby last week."

Zak stilled, then frowned. "Where do you mean when you say 'here'?"

"It'll be fine. Don't worry." Tara touched Paulette's elbow. "You should walk a bit while you can. You have time before the little one will make his entrance."

Zak laid a hand on Paulette's arm, preventing her from following Tara's suggestion. "You can't be serious. You need to go to the hospital."

Paulette placed a hand on top of his. Seeing the depth of concern in his eyes only made her love him more. "I don't want to birth a child surrounded by the worst bacteria and germs of anywhere. Hospitals are notorious for harboring them."

"What if something goes wrong?" He swallowed, his Adam's apple sliding up, then down. A vein throbbed in his neck. "At your age, complications could arise. You might need urgent care."

"I'm a certified midwife. I'm qualified to handle any minor emergency and will anticipate anything major." Tara folded her arms. "I'm also a first responder, so in the unlikely event we need to transport her to a hospital, I'm trained to handle things until the EMTs and an ambulance arrive."

"But—"

"It's not your decision." Meredith closed the front doors and crossed to where the trio argued in the foyer. "Paulette's the one having the baby. She can do so wherever she feels most comfortable."

"But—"

Max laughed. "Come on, man, have a little faith."

Patrick hovered closer. "In my day, all women had babies in the hospital. Behind closed doors. Men were relegated to the waiting room."

Meredith glared at him. "You're no help."

"But—"

Paulette laughed at the stymied expression on Zak's face. A gasp followed as a stronger contraction seized hold. The intensity doubled her over. Zak's arms braced her, wrapping around from behind and holding on to each arm. As the grabbing pain eased, she let out the air trapped in her lungs. "It's time."

"Zak, help her upstairs. I'll grab my birthing bag out of the car and be right there." She hurried through the chaos of tables and sideways chairs toward the back door.

"But..." He hesitated, waiting for someone to cut him off yet again. He relaxed his hold on her arms and focused on Paulette's face. "Are you certain? I'll support you either way as long as this is really what you want."

Relief washed through her at his words. She hadn't even realized how much his opinion meant to her, how much his understanding and support meant. She kissed him quickly, before another contraction stole the moment. "Thank you." She considered the group standing at the bottom of the stairs. "You all should go change out of your costumes. The party's over."

"Or just beginning." Patrick chuckled again.

"Go away, Grandpa." Paulette shook her head. "You've done enough."

She turned to climb the stairs, gripping the handrail against a building pressure. Zak's arm wrapped around her waist, strong and snug. Okay, so he wanted to help her up to the birthing room. As another contraction ripped through her, she paused, gasping and fighting back the scream in her throat. She was glad to have his strength to steady her three steps from the top. Finally, the pain subsided enough to permit her to continue. She hurried the last few steps before she ended up trapped on the steps again.

"Thanks, Zak. I can manage from here." She gave him a quick peck on the lips. A puzzled frown appeared on his face before he slowly smiled, his expression clearing. "What?"

"I told you I'd support you and I meant it. I intend to be there when the little one is born, seeing as how I'll be his or her daddy."

"You don't have to bother. Tara will be there." But oh, what a lovely offer. His smile wilted at her words so she latched onto his arms and drew him closer for a kiss. The touch of his lips sparked a startlingly intense longing in the approximate area where a contraction began again. Breaking off the kiss, she studied him. "Unless you're serious?"

He nodded slowly and took her hand. "I'm not going

anywhere. I want to help bring your—*our* baby into the world. If you'll let me."

He'd stay with her and support her by doing as she asked even though it went against his own beliefs. The very idea of his unconditional assistance and caring sent waves of love and gratitude through her. She'd never been the recipient of a man's unwavering support before so it meant all the more to her.

"I'd like that." She tugged on his hand and led him along the hall to the right to the master suite Meredith had insisted Paulette use.

Zak hung back when she crossed the threshold of the bedroom. She kept hold of his hand and drew him with her across the large room with its quilt-covered queen bed and triple dresser and mirror occupying center stage. The door to the large bathroom stood open, and the old-fashioned claw foot tub beckoned to her. Soon the sanitized metal would be filled with luxuriously warm water to ease the strain of the delivery of her, or rather, their child. She loved the sound of that. Zak surprised her with his sincerity and desire to assist. She never would have anticipated his being in the room. *Wanting* to be in the room.

Tara strolled in, carrying a black backpack bulging with mysterious implements and supplies. She'd changed out of her sexy witch costume into scrubs and sensible shoes. Dropping the bag outside the bathroom, she unzipped it and left it yawning open as she assessed Paulette's stance. "How close are the contractions?"

"About five minutes, maybe." Another moved through her and she doubled over, Zak's hands providing support until she straightened.

"Let's get this show on the road then." Tara bustled in and started the water running in the tub.

"What can I do?" Zak asked.

"You're doing it." Tara sized him up. "The best thing

for you to do is to position yourself in front of her but outside of the tub. Paulette, change into your swimsuit top and we'll help you into the tub when you're ready."

Paulette went into the bedroom and rummaged in the overnight bag she'd left there earlier in the week. Tara had counseled her on the overall plan and they both hoped she wouldn't actually need everything it contained. If anything unexpected happened, then she'd need essentials at the hospital. Unzipping and then slipping out of the wedding gown, she laid the creamy lace on the bedspread. With a bit of stitching, the gown could be converted into a proper wedding gown. She trailed a finger across the elaborate lace skirt and then sucked in a breath as another spasm ripped her in two. A minute later, she hurried to finish changing clothes.

After a bit of a struggle with the halter top stretching over her enlarged breasts, Paulette wrapped a beach towel about her hips and sauntered into the bathroom. Zak, still in his Confederate uniform, wolf whistled and she grinned until another contraction had her doubled and hanging onto the edge of the tub for the duration. She concentrated on breathing until it subsided, then straightened.

"Ready?" Tara asked.

No. Yes. It suddenly hit her what would happen next. A little life to care for, who would change everything about her routine and her future. She'd have to teach it, bathe it, feed it. Her pent up breath whooshed from her as another urgent pressure ripped through her. After it eased, she glanced at Zak and then back to Tara.

"I'm ready for this pain to stop." Paulette sidled up to the tub and eased one leg over the edge, toes then foot then shin submerging into the body temperature water.

Zak took his position as she kneeled in the tub. Within a few moments, the buoyancy of the water reduced the strain on her abdomen and softened the intensity of the next contraction. She grabbed the rim and let out a long, low moan as the pain sped through her. Finally, she took a deep breath, only to have another contraction soon follow.

"That's it, you're doing fine." Zak laid his hands on top of hers.

She looked up at him, about to thank him for being with her, when the air behind him shimmered and Patrick materialized behind him. Thank goodness she wore a top and Zak and the tub blocked his view of the rest of her. "Get out of here."

Zak reared back like a cobra prepared to strike, eyes wide and brows arched. "I thought you wanted me here." He made as if to rise, but she grabbed hold, nails digging in.

"Not you." She glared at Patrick. "You."

"Why are you taking a bath at a time like this?" Patrick frowned and moved closer for a better view.

"Go away."

"You have hold of my hands." Zak tried to look over his shoulder but she wouldn't let him. "Do you want me to leave?"

"No! My grandfather is behind you again." Another pain grabbed hold and worked through her, stealing her breath and making Zak grunt when her nails dug into his flesh.

"What—"

"With the time between contractions, it will be a little while yet." Tara shot Patrick a dark look until he closed his mouth, while she arranged a stack of towels and receiving blankets on a table situated under the window. "Your baby will soon be here to meet you."

After the pain eased, Paulette glared at her grandfather, silently telling him she didn't want him to witness the birth.

"As you wish, my dear. I'm here for you, never forget that." With a snap of a salute, he winked as he slowly disappeared.

About time. She sure as hell didn't need more eyes on her pregnant body, and definitely not during the delivery. She rested against the high tub walls, gripping the rim with both hands. Over the next several hours, she endured the worst pain of her life. Tara reassured her that everything progressed as expected. But it took so very long she worried if she'd have the strength to keep her head above the water. Zak talked to her, keeping her calm even as the contractions came faster and faster. Tara released some of the cooling water and replaced it with more warm. Finally, at Tara's direction, Paulette shifted into a squatting position and let out another moan as the pains consumed her attention. After about thirty minutes, she gave one last push accompanied by a loud groan. With a splash, the baby slid from her and Zak lifted it up and into Paulette's waiting arms.

She cuddled the infant, checking his hands and feet, counting his fingers and toes. Dark eyes blinked open and looked at her. Love, hot and intense, bloomed in her chest. She smiled at her son. He blinked at her. That was all it took to cement the bond between them forever. All her doubts and worries about being a mother dissipated into the scented air.

"He's perfect, sweetheart." Zak sank onto his heels, elbows resting on the edge of the tub. "Do you know what you'll call him?"

Tara intervened to tend to the cord and check on Paulette's condition. The baby cried at the interruption, stretching out fisted hands and tiny toes in protest. Tara chuckled and continued her task. When she finished, she retreated to allow the new mother and child some time together.

Paulette's son squirmed in her arms, his lips parting into another cry. She sang to him, a simple lullaby, "You Are My Sunshine." Joy filled the song with fierce emotion. His scrunched-up features made her heart smile. Keeping her focus on the child, she finished the song.

With utter certainty, she finally understood her grandfather's purpose in her mysterious need. Without him, she wouldn't have gone to the Golden Owl the very day Zak arrived in town. Wouldn't have discovered her cousins. And most importantly, wouldn't have rediscovered her joy so she could sing to her child.

She let her son wrap his little fingers around her finger. "What do you think of calling him Johnny Patrick? Johnny after his father, and Patrick after his grandfather."

"Do you think that's such a good idea? Naming him after that particular relative?" Tara helped wrap the boy in a receiving blanket and then moved about, cleaning up after the previous activities in the deep water. "That won't entice him to…" She nodded at Zak and let her words die away.

"Maybe you're right, but I think he'd be honored." She flicked a look at Zak's puzzled expression. "If he were still alive, of course."

Zak tensed. "He's not alive? Then how—?"

Paulette laid a finger on his lips, hushing him. "I'll explain later."

She contemplated the trusting face in her arms, tucking the soft fabric more snugly around him. Calling him Johnny every day would remind her too much of the father who abandoned his son. "I think I'll call him Pat."

Which brought up the next question of how she went about banishing the boy's namesake. Especially after the fiasco of the night before, he needed to go back to wherever it was he came from. Little Pat gazed at her, a tiny dimple in his precious chin. His pale blond hair and dark eyes more like hers than his father's. At least she wouldn't see Johnny every time she looked at her son. "He's such a happy, normal baby."

Cuddling him closer, she smiled down on Pat's perfect

little face and his perfect little nose. Normal. Every bit of him. Or was he? Worry inched from her back down her extremities. With the gifts of her ancestors, how normal could he be? Would he have special abilities like she and Meredith possessed? Did she want him to? No, she didn't. This supposed gift caused more trouble than it solved.

Zak's smile comforted her fears. "I suppose we should marry sooner than we thought."

She nodded, the water around her cooling. Zak epitomized the best kind of man, husband, dad. "Did you want to hold your son while I step out?"

"Yes. Please." Zak grinned and reached for the baby, cradling him snug against his chest as though he'd performed the very act multiple times. "Thanks. I didn't want to presume to call him my son."

Paulette eased out of the tub, wriggling her toes in the plush bath mat. Tara held out a large towel and wrapped it around her. The soft fibers returned warmth to her chilled flesh. "We're a family, in reality if not legally. Nothing will ever change that."

Rain beat against the window. Paulette blinked awake in her own bed, smiling as she recalled the events of the previous day. Pat slept in the cradle nearby, still content after his latest early-morning feeding. She'd worried about her ability to nurse, but he had latched on and found satisfaction without causing too much discomfort. Though if he continued to eat so frequently she'd be raw by the end of the day.

She pushed out of bed, humming a cheery tune as she wrapped a heavy robe over her nightgown. Moving slowly, cautiously, she left her son sleeping and made her way downstairs. Coffee was her first order of business.

Meredith sat at the little table, reading the newspaper

with her mug hovering over the page. She looked up when Paulette walked by. "Did you sleep well?"

"Not much." She yawned and then poured coffee in a mug and sipped. "He's a hungry sucker, literally."

Meredith chuckled and set her cup down. "Where's the little guy?"

"He's sleeping, finally. I might have time for some breakfast before he awakens ravenous."

Zak strode into the room, the kitchen door swinging shut behind him. Apparently refreshed and happy, he crossed to Paulette and kissed her. "Good morning, beautiful."

She smiled up at him, a deep-seated love filling every pore of her body. "Morning. You must be blind if you think this old ratty thing is beautiful."

"It's not the wrapping I care about." He kissed her again and then laid a hand on his stomach. "I left Grant with your folks in the dining room. Where's breakfast?" He glanced around the empty countertops. "Did we miss it?"

Meredith rose and refilled her mug. "Meg should be here any minute with today's feast." She leaned against the counter, and shook her head. "I've never understood why she prefers to cook in her little bungalow instead of this gourmet kitchen."

A noise at the back door prompted Meredith to hurry to open it. Meg balanced an immense covered tray as she entered the room. The delicious aromas of bacon and cinnamon mingled in the air. Paulette breathed deeply, savoring the scents of Meg's famous breakfast with anticipation.

Meg scurried across the kitchen and butt bumped the swinging door open. "Come and get it while it's hot."

"Right behind you." Zak caught Paulette's elbow and escorted her toward the door, Meredith falling in behind them.

Three irregularly spaced knocks on the back door had

them all turning around. Meredith being closest moved to answer the tentative summons. Paulette froze. A tall, sandy-haired man filled the doorway, light blue eyes zeroing in on her as he removed his wide-brimmed hat. She must look a mess. In her bathrobe of all things. She swallowed and pulled the lapels together.

"What are you doing here?" Paulette's voice came out harsher than she'd intended. But really, he had no right to come back so tall and handsome the day after her—*their*—son entered this world.

He ambled toward her, a hesitant hitch in his usually confident stride. His gaze moved to Zak and back to her. "I've missed you. I need to talk to you."

Zak tensed, the grip on her elbow intensifying before he released it. Reaching out the same hand, he approached the visitor. "Zak Markel. And you are?"

"Johnny Anderson." He accepted the handshake then focused on her.

The two men she loved. One from the past, the other from the present. Love and dread choked her. "You shouldn't have come here, Johnny. It's over between us."

He shook his head. "It can't be. You said you carried our child." His gaze dropped to her bulging tummy, though flatter than before. "You've had it?"

"Not that you deserve to know, but yes."

He stepped closer to her, examining her expression. "Did you marry him?" He flicked a glance at Zak.

"Not yet." She folded her arms, hugging herself as emotions ricocheted through her. Embarrassment as to her ratty bathrobe. Surprise at his sudden appearance. But most of all, fear. What did he intend?

"Then I'm not too late." His shoulders relaxed and a smile crept onto his lips.

A chill spread across her back. "For what?"

"I want us to be a real family. I didn't realize how much

I needed you. I've come all the way from Anchorage with one thought in mind. Marry me, Paulette."

Oh. My. God. He didn't just say that. The words she'd longed to hear for years flowed from his mouth. Pale blue eyes searched hers, his fine lips parted. She'd loved the man for years and the lure of their past tugged on her resolve. They'd planned a future of sorts, though an incomplete one. She had thought they'd grow old together at one point in time. Now? What was he really offering her? The baby crying distracted her.

Johnny's gaze followed the sound. "Is that our child?"

"I have to go." She spun and hurried from the tense tableau in the kitchen. Climbing to the second floor, three little words echoed in her mind. Marry him? After all he'd done, walking away when she'd told him about her condition. Shaking her head, she hurried into her room and scooped up the wee infant.

Behind her several sets of footsteps approached. She turned to face the door as Pat began rooting for his breakfast. Zak ushered Johnny into the room. Johnny ignored the rumpled twin beds and discarded clothes tossed onto a chair during her late night feedings. Zak's feelings about the other man's presence were impossible to decipher. His usual open expression had turned shuttered and dark. Johnny zeroed in on Pat as he strode closer.

She snuggled the bundled little boy. Still, the man before her was the boy's father. Johnny Patrick was conceived out of love, one which had departed on an airplane months ago. "Why now, Johnny?"

"I've thought about nothing but how stupid I was to fly off to Alaska and leave you behind." A forgive-me-for-being-a-jerk smile flowed onto his lips. "I was wrong to abandon you, especially since you carried my child. Can you forgive me?"

"I forgave you a long time ago." She searched his eyes,

finding hope flare in their depths. "That doesn't mean I've forgotten what you did. I'm engaged to marry Zak now."

Zak crossed his arms, but hesitation weighed down the corners of his smile.

"I'm sure he's a nice guy. You've always been good at judging a person's character." Johnny shrugged apologetically at Zak, then flashed his heart-stopping, come-kiss-me smile at her. "But I'm the boy's biological father, so perhaps you and I should raise our son, instead of a stranger. I love you and need you, Paulette. I didn't realize how much until I found myself thousands of miles away and couldn't concentrate on anything but missing your smile, your wit, your laugh."

"You had your precious career to care about and focus on. That was more important than I ever was to you."

"I thought so at the time." He shrugged. "I was wrong. I admit that. Please, marry me. Give our son both his parents. I've come to appreciate how important family is after working this job for the last few months." He smiled down at the baby but kept his hands to himself. *Smart man.*

She should simply brush off the absurd idea. Except the more she considered what he'd said the more sense the idea held. Johnny had a point. She'd loved him once, enough to create this perfect little bundle of boy. But her feelings for Johnny didn't even remotely approach the depth of love for the dark-haired man on the opposite side of the room. Zak appeared to have swallowed his tongue for all the verbal support he offered. Standing mute by the open door, he watched with a tortured expression. No help there.

"Say something, Zak." Her words sounded like a plea for mercy, willing him to participate in this horrific conversation.

He cleared his throat, and swallowed. His gaze swung from her to Johnny, who stared back at him, and then to her. A frown creased his brow. "I'm sorry, sweetheart. I'll love you 'til the day I die."

No. He wouldn't.

He swallowed again. "But I think it's in the best interests of your son to be raised by you and his true father." He glanced at Johnny and then zeroed in on her, his Adam's apple working furiously. "Marry him."

Chapter Fourteen

ootsteps thudded down the stairs, followed shortly by the back door slamming shut. Meredith set down her toast. The group at the table paused in the process of eating their poached eggs and bacon. Brock held a slice of wheat toast just shy of taking a bite.

"I'll be right back." Meredith pinned Max with what she prayed was a deterring look. "And don't steal my bacon while I'm gone."

"I'll try to keep my hands to myself, but don't be long." He winked as he walked his fingers closer to her plate. "Don't know how long I can resist the temptation."

Chuckling, she stepped out of the dining room and glanced up and down the hallway. Who had left in such a hurry? Best to go up and check on Paulette and the baby. She hurried to the stairs. Entering Paulette's room, she found her sister cuddling her son.

"What happened?" She sank down onto the mussed bed beside her sister. "Where's Zak?"

"He left." Paulette raised bloodshot eyes to look at Meredith. Tears leaked down her cheeks.

"And Johnny? Where's he?"

"I made him leave too." She shook her head and

contemplated the tiny fair head in her arms. "Those two deserve each other."

Meredith tilted her head and considered her next words. "What happened?"

"Zak told me to marry Johnny. Of all the crazy ideas." She sobbed, choking on her tears.

Meredith wrapped an arm around quaking shoulders and waited for the gulps to subside. When they did, she squeezed Paulette once and then released her. "Care to start at the beginning?"

Paulette dragged in a breath and let it escape through open lips. Slowly, she stood and carried the sleeping baby to his cradle. After settling him in his bed, she turned to face Meredith. "Zak said Pat should be raised by his biological parents."

Shocked at her pronouncement, Meredith stared at her sobbing companion. "I don't believe it. I thought he loved you."

She nodded, wiping away the water marks from her face with one hand. "He said he does. If that's true, how can he leave me?"

Meredith shook her head, perplexed at the turn of events. What was Zak thinking? "Are you going to marry Johnny when you don't love him?"

"No!" She glanced at the cradle then back at Meredith. "Hell, I don't know."

"I wish life would settle down from all this drama surrounding us all the time." Meredith stood and crossed to hug Paulette. "It will, right?"

"Please, let your words come true." A smile tried to form on her lips but failed to linger for more than a moment. "This all started when Grandpa showed up so unexpectedly. He even tried to witness Pat's birth."

"What? You didn't tell me that." Meredith walked over to the cradle, needing to see her nephew sleeping peacefully, hoping some sense of peace would wrap around her heart and soul.

"I had to threaten him with Mom's 'behave yourself' look, the one she used on us when we were kids. He needs to go away. I don't need him here, acting out and causing mischief."

"Maybe he'll tell me how to make that a reality. I can ask, anyway." Meredith contemplated Paulette as her sister silently started making the twin bed. "You okay?"

Paulette huffed a laugh. "No, but I will be. I just need time to think over my options and make a decision." She tucked the quilt under the pillow, smoothing the surface with a practiced swipe of her hand. Straightening, she faced Meredith. "Thanks for your concern, but I don't need a sitter. Go on about your day. I'll be fine."

Someone needed to speak with Patrick before he caused more trouble. The next task for her day. "All right. I have a few things to take care of myself, but if you need anything, give me a shout. I'll be around."

She left Paulette to change into more appropriate attire, and went in search of Patrick. She found him in the double parlor. Dressed in his fine suit again, he lay stretched out on the settee, hat over his eyes. She cleared her throat and he lifted the brim and peered at her.

"You've caused quite a bit of trouble in the last few days, Grandpa." She strode into the room, appraising his expression as it shifted from welcome to wary. Good, he should be concerned. "Don't you think it's time for you to go back to be with Grandma?"

"Sure, but as I keep saying, only Paulette can make that happen, and she keeps shooing me away." He sat up, slipping his hat onto the settee beside him.

A sigh flowed from her. He had no shame about his actions whatsoever. "You're impossible, that's why she wants you to leave. But she doesn't merely want you to leave the room, she wants you to leave the house. We want you to go rest in peace or whatever it is you do."

"She yelled at me the last time." A slow grin spread onto his face. "All I wanted was to see her child."

Meredith crossed her arms and glared at him. "Really? Like the actual moment of his birth seemed the right time and place for you to see him?" She shook her head and shifted her weight to the other foot. "So tell me what she needs to do to send you on your way."

"She's in no condition after birthing a babe. Give her a few weeks to recuperate." Shifting to a relaxed position, he smirked at her. "I'm perfectly content to wait."

"We're not. Let's go. Up!" She marched toward him, though she had no idea how she was going to make him budge. He didn't move, merely smirked wider, if possible. "Show me. You know you don't belong here, so help me help you."

"I can tell you, but only Paulette can send me home and only after she realizes why she needed me in the first place. Meet me in the attic and I'll point out the spell in my book of secrets. But only if you say 'pretty please with a cherry on top.'" He winked and placed his hat on his head.

Before she could respond, he dematerialized, leaving behind only a dent in the cushion to confirm he existed. Shaking her head, she hurried toward the doorway. As she stepped into the foyer, the front doorbell rang. Now what? Hopefully not a nosy neighbor or someone selling magazine subscriptions.

She yanked open the door, a foreboding sense of urgency to meet her grandfather upstairs making her agitated. She blinked at the uniformed officer standing on the wide front porch. Bits and pieces of smashed pumpkins and shredded corn stalks evidenced the panicked escape by the party guests the night before. Maybe she should have cleaned the mess up, but with the other events occurring, she'd not had a moment to think about doing so. "Can I help you?"

"Are you Meredith Reed?" The officer stood casually though fully alert as he waited for her response.

"Yes. What's wrong?"

"We received several reports of strange events here and, well, we're required to investigate claims of disturbances." He slipped a pen from his shirt pocket and flipped open the small notebook in his hands.

Damn. Patrick, see what you've caused? "Strange events?"

He shrugged and lifted one brow, as though sharing a joke. If only. "Miss Jenny seems to think the place is haunted."

Wait until I get hold of him. "How ridiculous." She forced a smile to stiff lips. "We had a Halloween party the other night. She may have had a few too many drinks and mistook our, um, decorations and sound effects as something supernatural."

"Something spooked the guests. Young Jeremy even mentioned the disturbance. You didn't see anything odd?" He studied her, weighing her comments with her countenance. Then he made a note in the book before peering at her, waiting for her response.

She held her tongue, afraid to say more and make the situation worse. She sensed Patrick hovering behind her. She didn't dare peek over her shoulder, but she waved a hand behind her to shoo him away. His burst of laughter confirmed his presence, and she waved harder.

"This is humorous." Patrick had the audacity to chuckle.

Her wrist would break if she waved more forcefully. Gritting her teeth, she plastered a tight smile on her lips and trained it on the officer. "No, nothing out of the ordinary."

"Mind if I take a look around, make sure everything is all right?" He stepped forward as though to brush past her. "For the report."

No way. Sidling in front of him, she blocked his path. "I'm sorry, but my sister just delivered a baby and is resting. I wouldn't want to disturb her with such a nonsensical mission as to look for ghosts. I'm sure you understand."

She looked over her shoulder and glared at Patrick. Silently she mouthed, "Go to the attic."

Patrick winked and disappeared.

Relieved, she focused on the officer again. Retreating two steps, the officer gazed at her for an endless moment.

"I suppose Miss Jenny may have had a bit too much fun, like you said." He flipped closed his small notebook and returned the pen to his shirt pocket. "Ghosts. What a hoot. Thanks for your time, ma'am." He turned to leave, took three steps, and then hesitated as he surveyed the porch. Slowly, he lifted his gaze to meet hers. "Does kinda look like things got out of hand here though."

That's putting it mildly. "A good time was had by all. No worries." She smiled and prayed he'd vacate her damn porch. "Have a good day!"

He studied her for the span of three frantic breaths. He couldn't search the house and find Patrick. Who knew what mischief he'd cause if so? Finally, the officer made a decision.

"I'd clean up the pumpkins before they draw yellow jackets to your front door." He saluted her with a grin and a tug on his hat brim. "Happy Halloween." With that, he walked down the remaining steps and slipped into his cruiser.

She didn't move to close the door until his tail lights receded down the driveway. If Patrick weren't already dead, she'd kill him.

Zak followed Johnny to his rental car, catching up to him as he opened the door. "May I have a word?"

"Okay." Johnny rested his elbow on the top of the door, his body poised to slide into the driver's seat.

How to start. He cleared his throat and swallowed. "I want you to know that if you do anything to hurt Paulette, anything at all, you'll answer to me."

"Is that so?"

"Yes."

"You dare to make threats?" Johnny regarded him with cold eyes. "To me?"

"Treat her and Pat right and you won't have any problems." Zak resisted the temptation to land a fist in the middle of the man's gloating face.

"Fair enough. But I don't expect you'll know one way or the other, seeing as how she'll be my wife and living in Anchorage."

The frigid tone of the man's voice chilled Zak. "She won't like living in the cold climates. You know that."

"Yeah, but that's where my job is, so that's where we'll go." Johnny shook his head. "She'll be fine once she adjusts to the temps."

"You'd force her to go live in a place she will hate?" Zak glared at the selfish bastard.

Johnny tapped his hand on the door. "She'll survive."

"Don't be a prick. Raising a child up there will be tough. Let her stay here with her sister to help her. She'd be happier and you could do your work. It would be better all around."

"She's not staying near you." He shook his head. "You think I'm stupid?"

"It's not about me, but about her clients and prospects here." A sense of panic threatened to consume the oxygen in his lungs. Paulette couldn't be taken from him, but he'd already given her away to Johnny, the man who prepared to destroy everything she'd worked so hard to put into place. "I'm thinking of her wellbeing and her future."

"You don't have a say in her future. Not anymore." Johnny smirked as he gripped the metal door. "I'll be back later to pick up her and the boy to fly back to Alaska with me. My work awaits, and I cannot stay in this whole lot of nothing area and keep my sanity. If you'll excuse me."

The door slammed shut and the engine roared to life. Spitting gravel behind him, Johnny tore down the driveway followed by a rising cloud of white dust.

Zak stared after him, worry a fist in his gut. What had he done?

Chapter Fifteen

G olden light warmed Zak as he hiked up the winding trail. Adjusting his shades to block the afternoon sun, he checked to make sure that Grant was keeping up with him. Although curious, the man had the sense not to ask Zak about his sudden need to be outside. Towering pines dotted the hills rising and falling around them. Zak unzipped his jacket, the cool air blowing away the warmth growing inside, but not the anger nor the entrenched disappointment.

"Hold up, bro." Grant paused to bend down to retie his hiking bootlaces. After he straightened up, he scanned the low mountains ranging to the horizon under the pale sky arched overhead. "Why are we here?"

"You know why." Zak surveyed the fall foliage wearing various shades of red, yellow and brown scattered among the evergreens. Despite the variety, the trees lacked color similar to the sky. Everything seemed pale and uninteresting. He looked back at Grant, noting his clear and pain-free expression. Ever since the party, Zak had been pleased to see that Grant acted normally, no more pains or headaches. "The damn dirt."

Grant nodded and screwed his mouth to one side in thought. "She broke it off?"

Zak scanned his surroundings, envisioning nothing but Paulette's tortured stare and the smirk on Johnny's face before he drove away. He couldn't stand for him to take her to a place where he'd never see her again. All because of his own words and actions. *Damn.* He refused to wallow. Better to redirect his energies back to what he came here for. Everything else would fall into place. He hoped. "Glad you're feeling better, bro."

"It's funny, but ever since I danced with Tara I've felt really good. The best ever."

"Let's hope it lasts. At least one of the goals of our excursion, to find relief for your condition, will have been achieved." After consulting the topographical map in his backpack, Zak pulled his compass from his pocket and then pointed at a narrow dirt track disappearing into the dense woods. "But in case we end up needing the elixir, this way should lead us to our destination which is apparently at the top of the hill. Ready?"

"Figures it has to be up to the top of a mountain, even if it is an old eroded one." Grant adjusted his daypack, his water jug sloshing as it jostled. "Daylight's wasting."

Zak headed up the faint trail, one most likely made by deer. Paulette's words rambled around his brain, mixing with the visual of her body language. She hadn't argued with his statement, as blunt and yet sharp as it tumbled from his mouth. Why had he given her away? Why hadn't he fought for her? The answer simply remained that a boy needed a father, even if the father wasn't much of one. His own dad failed as father of the year. Still, he'd done his best to guide his boys. Surely, Johnny would do the same. In Zak's place. His heart jerked at the thought.

He trudged up the slope, automatically stepping over roots and rocks jutting from the ground. When he'd practically demanded she marry Pat's father, her pretty little mouth had fallen open, reminding him of the mouth of a beaker, her lips so round. Her eyes had widened with shock. Tears had glistened in the corners, threatening to cascade down pale cheeks. She had clutched Pat close, fingers sinking into the light blue blanket. He should have gone to her and taken back his words.

"How much farther?" Grant asked.

Drawn back to the present, Zak slipped the folded map from his jacket pocket. He stopped to triangulate their location relative to their destination. He pointed to where the trail curved to the right and ended at the base of a rushing waterfall. "Should be off to the left of the falls."

"Wait. We have to cross the river?" Grant studied the landscape, eyeing the distance and the width of the rapids.

"According to the map, there should be a path under the falls. Come on."

He hoped the topo proved accurate, or they'd end up very wet. The trail steepened to climb toward the falls. Water rushed down toward the valley, flowing over and around rocks. A double rainbow arched in the spray. The screech of a red-tailed hawk pierced the quiet. He sighed and kept walking. Another day, another time, he'd appreciate the beauty of his surroundings.

Reaching the plateau beside the pool of water churning from the river dropping into it, he waited for Grant to join him. He inspected the area for the purported path behind the falls. *There.* Practically invisible to a casual observer. As he neared the bank of the flowing river, he could make out where the soil had been compacted by other hikers.

"Good eye, bro." Grant stopped beside him. "I would have missed it."

"Let's get this over with." He dodged behind the falls and found himself in a cool cave. Hurrying through, he tread carefully across the water-slick rock floor, emerging back into the afternoon light on the other side.

Grant cussed behind him, finally bolting from under the

falls, wet and eyes blazing. "You could have warned me about the water."

Zak chuckled humorlessly. "I knew you'd figure it out." He checked the notes on the back of the topo map, where he'd copied the location coordinates from the soil analysis. Calculating with the help of the map and the compass, he pinpointed the area he had determined most promising. "Over there."

Dropping his backpack, he removed his jacket and hung it on a bare tree branch. Leaning over, he unzipped the largest compartment and withdrew a folding spade. He clicked the handle into place and stood. "Pull out the sample jars while I start digging."

Grant wiggled from his pack and lowered it to the ground. "Sure thing."

Zak jabbed the hard-packed earth and began loosening the soil. He kept digging until he reached the depth indicated by the report. His muscles ached from the unaccustomed exercise, burning with each thrust and lift. A mound of dirt grew to one side with his efforts. After he located the right mix of dirt, crystal, manganese, and acidity, he'd be free to go back to Michigan. Back to his home. Back where he could try to forget Paulette.

He jammed the spade deep into the ground, his shoulders rebelling at the vibration traveling up the wood handle when the blade struck something unyielding. *Damn.* He repositioned the tip and shoved the tool beside and then under the object. Dumping the load on the ground, he smiled. "Pay dirt."

Grant used a hand shovel to scoop the pile into a jar. "How much do you need?"

"I'm not sure, that's why I gave you six jars." Zak rested on his heels, squatting by the wide hole he'd dug. "Let's fill them and get back. We can head home tonight if we hurry."

Grant speared him with a frown. "Leave? But…"

"This is why we came." Zak propped his elbows on his knees. Grant's frown changed to what could only be called a pout. "What?"

"Tara…" He swallowed and shook his head. "Nothing. If you want to go, we can."

Zak studied the carefully nonchalant expression on his brother's face. "You like her, don't you?"

Grant shrugged and scooped dirt into a second jar. "She's okay."

"Yeppers. You do like her." Standing, he resumed shoveling, adding to the pile Grant worked to put in the capped containers. "We can stay if you want to take her out or something. I'd hate to come between you and true love."

Scoffing, Grant shook his head. "Nah. My real life and my real nightmare are up north. I need to get back and start the treatments after this trip. She'd be a distraction."

"All the more reason." Zak added another shovelful to the pile, then paused to ponder Grant's movements. "Are you sure you want to walk away from the possibility?"

Grant twisted the last lid closed. Rising from where he had kneeled, he considered Zak. "Are you sure you want to walk away from Paulette?"

His heart pinched, but he started filling in the hole so he didn't have to look at Grant. "No choice. The real father showed up."

"That wasn't my question." Grant nestled the glass jars back into the bubble wrap padded backpack. Pausing, he regarded Zak. "You should fight for her. You know you want to."

Zak unlocked the jointed handle and folded the spade. "My feelings don't seem to matter." He jammed the tool into his pack and zipped it with a jerk.

"It's obvious to everyone but you apparently that Paulette loves you, not that simpleton." Grant secured the last jar, zipped the pack, and stood to slip it on his shoulders. "You need to make him realize what he's proposing won't work in the long run."

"She loved him before." Zak scanned the work site to make sure he'd left the area as he found it sans a bit of dirt. Satisfied, he shrugged at Grant. "She will again. Come on, we've a ways to go and the sun is starting to go down."

He followed Grant as they retraced their steps. Paulette may not initially agree with his decision, but she'd grow to love Johnny again eventually. Pat's dimpled chin and blond hair swam in his mind, steady eyes seeming to recognize him when he neared. He'd miss the little guy when Paulette moved away. When he moved back home. He'd never see either of them again.

The thought stabbed through him, making him place his foot wrong. He quick stepped to catch his balance only to have his left foot land on a loose pine cone and unbalance him. Yelping, he tumbled to the ground with a thud. He lay there for a moment to catch the breath which rushed from him, and in that moment realized he couldn't let her go. Couldn't let Pat go.

"You okay?" Grant hurried back to offer him a hand up.

Zak accepted the help as his mind whirled with new plans. "Yeah. That was a wakeup call. You're right. We're not leaving yet." He started walking, hurrying now with purpose fueling his pace.

"What's the matter?" Grant's footsteps hurried behind him. "Why the rush?"

"I shouldn't have left when I did." Zak increased the length of his stride. "I've got to get back, because I'm going to have a little talk with Johnny."

Male laughter drew Zak toward the double parlor doorway. Brock and Johnny sat facing each other on the matching overstuffed chairs, a glass of amber liquid in hand. The laughter died when Johnny noticed him. Grant sauntered up to wait beside his brother. To Johnny's credit, the blond man with the cleft chin like his son's rose and motioned for the late arrivals to join the festivities, such as they were. Brock shot Zak a look, but he couldn't decipher its meaning. Did he resent his presence or welcome it? Either way, he needed to speak to Johnny. If Brock stayed, then so be it.

"Come in. What's your poison?" Brock stood and moved to the decanters situated on the cherry buffet to the left of the fireplace.

"Bourbon and water." Grant grinned as he settled onto the sofa facing the matching chairs. He stretched out his long legs and relaxed. "I'm glad to be back in civilization."

Zak opted for a seat on the small sofa facing the fireplace. At least he'd have someplace to look other than at the other men. "Do you have any scotch?"

"Absolutely. Did you have success today?" Brock poured the two drinks. He handed each a rock glass containing dark reddish brown liquor and then resumed his seat.

"Cheers." Zak saluted Brock, Grant, and then Johnny with his glass. He sipped the liquid fire which seared a path down his parched throat. "Yes, we did."

"Zak here's been trying to solve a bit of a mystery. That's what brought him to Roseville in the first place," Brock said for Johnny's edification.

"What kind of mystery?" Johnny swirled his drink as he contemplated Zak.

The ancient recipe no longer intrigued him. Grant appeared normal, healed, as though he'd already received the miracle they had sought. Oh, he may still eventually attempt to create it since they'd collected the samples, but Zak's wake up stumble pointed out his priorities. Only Paulette mattered to him. "Trying to unravel a coded recipe and its precise ingredients. But that's not why I'm here, now, with you."

Johnny contemplated him as he put his glass to his lips and then swallowed, his expression becoming guarded. "And that reason?"

The air sizzled around him, tension producing an electric current similar to a Taser. Out of the corner of his eye the air shimmered. Odd. He blinked to clear his vision. He focused on the intruder, the interloper, the bastard studying him.

"I need to know your real intentions regarding Paulette." At Johnny's raised brows, Zak cleared his throat. "And Pat."

"We discussed this earlier." Johnny sloshed the liquor against the sides of the glass, lips pursing. He tossed back a gulp and set the glass on the table. "Why is it your concern?"

Annoyance bristled along Zak's spine. "I love her enough to walk away. But I need to know you'll take care of her and the boy, that you'll love them and not abandon either of them. Ever."

He had the nerve to chuckle. "I'm not a fortune teller. After I give the boy a last name—as in mine—we'll see how things work out."

"What? Do you love her?" He couldn't believe what he was hearing. "You said you did, and you want to be with her, that you missed her. I heard you."

Johnny chuckled again, deeper with a hint of sinister undertones. "She has to trust me enough to let me back."

"Don't you hurt her, or I'll—"

He laughed outright. "You'll what? Beat me up? That won't make her love you more. In fact, she'd probably willingly go with me." He picked up his glass and a smirk inched onto his lips. "Turns out I need a family in order to be promoted in my new job, a detail my boss neglected to tell me before I started."

The man's cold appraisal chilled him. "What of Paulette?"

"Yes, Johnny, what of my daughter's feelings?" Brock glared at the man across from him, the glass dangling in his right hand.

"She loved me before." Johnny sipped his drink, the smirk returning. "She'll love me again, I'm sure, whether or not I return the sentiment."

The emotions he'd been tamping down for the past day flared into anger. The selfish bastard. Zak lunged to his feet, scotch sloshing onto the oriental carpet. He slammed the glass down on the table and had the bastard's polo shirt collar in both fists before anyone could react. "Now you hear me, you S.O.B." His voice was low, almost a whisper, but with a deadly intent all its own.

"Hey, get your hands off me!" Johnny struggled against the sofa back, attempting to pry Zak's stronger hands off his clothing.

Zak shook him once, heard teeth click. *Good. Damn the man.* "Here's what is going to happen. First, you're going to tell her you've realized it would be wrong for her to marry you when she loves me."

Johnny made as if to speak and Zak shook him again. Grant tensed, pulling his feet under him so he could react if necessary, but didn't come to either man's aid.

"Don't hurt him, Zak," Brock said. "If he hurts Paulette, teaching him a lesson will be my pleasure."

Johnny shot frantic yet silent appeals for help to the three men staring at him. "But…"

Zak shook his head slowly, tightening his grip to pull the resisting man closer. "Second, that you really can't give up your job in Alaska, and you realized how much she'd hate living there."

Johnny's Adam's apple bobbed three times as he worked to stay calm.

"Third, you'll stay involved in Pat's life but only from a distance."

The man's eyes bulged and his face turned increasingly darker shades of red.

"Finally, you will set up a trust fund Pat can use to go to trade school or college as he chooses." He gave the collar another jerk. "Any questions?"

Johnny shook his head, his hair winging out like a maple seed spiraling to the ground.

"I'm glad we understand each other." Zak hauled him to his feet. "Let's go tell her about the change in plans."

"She's in the kitchen with Meredith and the baby." Brock rose to his feet and trailed after Zak as he ushered Johnny none too gently from the room. "I'm coming with you."

"I have to see this," Grant said from the back of the little procession.

Zak remained focused on the trembling man in front of him, one hand clenched on the bastard's upper arm, as they marched down the hallway and through the swinging door. The baby carrier sat on the little table nestled in the bay window, Paulette in a chair facing him. Meredith sat opposite but swiveled in her chair to determine who entered the room. Both women's brows arched in question.

"Gentlemen, what brings you all to the kitchen?" Meredith asked.

"They ma—" Johnny's whine stopped as Zak's grip tightened.

"Paulette, I'm afraid Johnny-boy has some news to share with you," Zak said, giving the man in question a little jerk. "Go ahead."

He hesitated and Zak glared at him until he complied. "I—um—I changed my mind about us marrying, Paulette."

"What? Why?" She glanced suspiciously between Zak and Johnny.

Johnny let his expression soften. "I realized you love him more than you ever loved me. The two of you would make better parents, therefore."

"And?" Zak goaded. "Don't stop there."

Johnny swiped a hand over his jaw. "I miss my job in Alaska, my life there. The cold suits me."

"You can say that again," Brock muttered. "Go on. Tell her the rest."

"There's more?" Her expression had changed from wary and suspicious to open and hopeful.

"A little more." Zak released his hold and then poked Johnny. "Go on."

Johnny winced and shrugged. "I want to be a part of Pat's life, but from a distance. He should know I'm his biological father, and I'll always care about him. Which is why I'm going to set up a trust fund for his education."

Paulette's lips parted as she blinked at him. "Is that all, or is there more?"

Zak grinned. "That's it."

She grinned back at him then flashed a smile at Johnny. "Why are you really doing this, Johnny? These ideas don't really sound like they're yours."

Another poke from Zak had the ex-fiancé clearing his throat as he rubbed his side. "I'm trying to do the right thing here, no matter whose ideas they are."

Johnny didn't even glance at Zak, for which Zak remained grateful. Let her think it was a committee decision and not just his.

"That does leave one open question," Grant interjected. Everyone turned to him and he smiled. "Zak?"

He went to stand beside her. Taking her hand, he dropped to one knee. He looked at Pat, asleep and thus oblivious to the events surrounding him. Love combined with a need to protect the infant swelled inside. He smiled at the expectation evident on Paulette's face. "Paulette, my sweetheart, the love of my life. For the third time, will you marry me?"

She threw her arms around his neck and kissed him.

Cheers rose around him, but her lips on his were the only thing he cared about. Pat stirred and they broke off the kiss to gaze at him, cheek to cheek. After a moment, Zak turned to her. "When do you want to tie the knot?"

She kissed him, a quick peck. "I have something I need to take care of before we do."

"What?" Another kiss passed between them.

"You don't really want to know." She winked at Meredith. "It'll be okay. Let's celebrate our re-engagement, shall we?"

"I have some champagne left over from the party." Meredith pushed away from the table and crossed to the fridge.

Johnny stood to one side, watching everyone congratulate Paulette and Zak. Brock popped the corks of the two chilled bottles and poured the bubbly into Disney themed juice glasses.

Brock raised his Pluto glass. "To Paulette and Zak, may their love for each other grow deeper every day."

Grant sidled up to Zak and tapped glasses with him, Mickey and Aladdin ringing in salute. "I see you took my suggestion."

Zak shrugged. "Now it's your turn."

"Since we're not leaving tonight, I may do so." Grant tapped Aladdin against Mickey again. "Looks like things are back to normal for you two and a wedding looms in the near future."

He nodded, drinking in his beautiful fiancée. He'd move heaven and earth to be with her. He loved and trusted her with all of his being. She smiled in his direction and he realized that though he'd asked, she hadn't answered as to her secret errand. He frowned. What was she keeping from him?

Chapter Sixteen

The book of secrets lay open on top of the stack of footlockers. Beside it, a candle burned, its flame flickering in the soft light. Paulette breathed in sandalwood and frankincense burning in the small dish beside the candle. The sound of low voices drifted into the room, murmurings of Roxie, Tara, and Beth as they moved through the house doing some secret witch ceremony to prepare the house for what she must do.

She let her gaze rest on the words staring back at her, humming a hymn. She finally understood why he'd come in the first place. When Johnny had left the first time for Alaska, the joy in her heart had left as well. She'd stopped singing altogether. In her attempt to discover the method for returning her grandpa, she'd met Zak, who ultimately brought the joy and singing back into her life. She'd needed to find her joy so she could be whole and happy.

According to what Meredith had told her, the words before her would banish their grandfather from the house. He'd return to wherever she pulled him from and they'd never see him again. She swallowed a sob, forcing herself to stay clear on her mission. Despite his tendency to show up at the wrong place and time, and his love of playing pranks on folks, she'd miss him.

She scanned the room, the tune shifting to a John Denver song. What was it called? Something about going home… Right. "Back Home Again." Exactly where she found herself. His ballads were among her favorites growing up. Back when she used to sing no matter what else she did. Not just in the shower either. Singing soprano in the high school choir had occupied much of her time. So many friends she'd let slip away after graduation in order to pursue her dreams. She sighed. Dreams which never materialized until she moved to Twin Oaks.

Precisely what her grandpa thought she needed. To reconnect with music. She had been humming and even singing more since he arrived. Had he opened her to the possibility of love with Zak? Or had loving Zak opened her up to music? She smiled. Who cared, so long as music had returned to stay?

Incorporating singing around Pat would be a natural progression. An excuse if she needed one to use her voice for more than conversation. Her heart soared with the idea.

She glanced at Meredith as she hesitantly walked into the attic, peering behind the door as though someone might be hiding there. Which, knowing Patrick, there could be. Satisfied, Meredith strolled to the center of the shadowy room. Grizabella trotted in behind her, slowing to a mincing walk when Meredith stopped.

"They should be here soon to complete the deed. Ready?" Meredith linked her hands together in front of her blue jeans. Griz wound about her ankles before sitting, her tail slowly sweeping the wood floor.

"I suppose so, but I'm kinda sorry he can't stay longer." Paulette scanned the room then studied Meredith's expression. "You're going to miss him, too, aren't you?"

"Yes and no, but it's time. I understand your desire to

know Grandpa, but you have to realize his time here is over." She pointed to the banishing spell. "It's up to you to help him go back."

"Doesn't he need to be present for this to work?"

She shook her head and moved closer. "We know he's somewhere in the house. He told me these are the words to send him on."

Paulette peered at the text, each red letter handwritten on the linen paper with fancy flourishes, giving the page the appearance of a work of art rather than of witchcraft. The lines blurred and danced, and she swiped at the tears hovering in her eyes. She lifted her gaze to Meredith. The setting sun shot its last rays through the window, illuminating the dust particles floating around them. Tiny bits swirling, rising, sinking in a chaotic dance among the many boxes and bags and trunks. Time seemed to stand still among the memories contained within the attic. Yet Patrick deserved to be at peace, not a restless grandpa causing trouble and anxiety for the living.

She blinked then focused on her sister. "When they get here, I'll be ready."

"Patrick said you would know what to do when the time came." Meredith crossed her arms and cocked her head to one side. "Do you?"

Paulette nodded as footsteps announced the arrival of the three sisters. They filed into the room, not looking like witches at all. Dressed in everyday clothes—slacks or jeans with a pullover sweater or blouse—they looked like any other group of women off the street. Tara moved to stand by the window while Beth walked behind Paulette. Roxie stationed herself by the door. Silence lasted for two heart beats.

Roxie spoke first. "When you're ready, Paulette, focus on your intent, to make sure the words carry the weight of what you're trying to achieve."

Paulette nodded and studied the page, considering each word individually and then as a whole thought. "My intent, in this case, is to send Grandpa to rest in peace with Grandma."

"Go on, then." Meredith stepped back from the book. "Before somebody wonders where we are and comes looking."

Paulette took a deep breath and released it as she counted to five. She met each woman's eyes and then focused on the book. "Here goes everything."

"We're here with you," Tara said. "You'll be fine."

Beth stood with feet apart, arms crossed. "Whenever you're ready."

The sound of the candle flickering filled the ensuing silence as Paulette steeled herself to banish her grandfather. She felt like she was killing him all over again. She parted her lips to read the spell and then chose to sing the words instead, making up her own tune as she went.

"Let my words protect this living space.

"Send the summoned spirit to rest in peace,

"Back to its own time and place.

"My words shall bring us peace."

As when he arrived, a cold wind rushed through the room, extinguishing the candle and rifling the pages of the book of secrets. Paulette braced herself from being blown sideways. The other women fought the force of the gale, feet stuttering on the wood floor as they struggled to remain standing during the onslaught. Grizabella arched at the commotion and hissed. Patrick suddenly materialized before Paulette, forcing a gasp and tears to smart her eyes. Hovering a couple feet from the ground, he smiled and winked.

"Thank you, my dear, first for needing me and now for singing me home."

"Good-bye, Grandpa." She reached toward him and he extended his hand toward hers. "I'll miss you."

"As long as I'm in your thoughts and heart, you'll always have me close by." He winked again and then looked at Meredith. "I've enjoyed knowing you, too."

"Good-bye, Grandpa. Rest easy knowing we'll be fine."

He swept over to the three sisters, touching their cheeks lightly as he passed by each of them. Hesitant smiles graced their faces as he hovered in front of them. "My lovely granddaughters. I love each of you. Take care."

The wind began to ease, the pages settling. Keeping her balance became easier. Patrick's image faded along with the ever gentling breeze until he vanished. Grizabella relaxed her back, the hairs on her spine easing down from where they had stood at attention.

"What just happened?"

Paulette along with the other women turned at the sound of Zak's question from the open door. She laughed at his evident astonishment. Hurrying to him, she stopped and peered up into his eyes. "What are you doing here?"

"I was worried about you." He shook his head even as he searched her face and then glanced at each of the women moving closer to them. "Was this your secret errand?"

She bobbed her head. "We needed to help our grandfather go home."

"So it's true. Twin Oaks really is haunted." His words emerged as bemused statements of fact. He gripped her upper arms with fingers of steel. "Are you okay? Is Pat safe?"

"Of course." She grinned at him, loving him more for his concern. "Grandpa would never have hurt his family."

His countenance cleared as he lowered his hands to shove them into his jeans pockets. "Good point. Now what?"

Meredith scooped up the cat and strode over to stand beside Paulette. "Now we live our lives ghost free, I hope."

Tara and Beth caught up to Roxie as she stopped on Paulette's other side. "Nice job, cuz. We'll finish up outside and then we'll be on our way."

"Outside?" Zak's puzzlement met with more laughter.

Tara tapped his arm twice. "Don't worry about it. See ya, Paulette."

The three sisters eased past Zak and headed back down the stairs.

Meredith crossed the room to close the book of secrets, cradling Griz in one arm. "I'll finish up in here if you want to get Zak something cold to drink. He looks like he could use a beer."

"Or something stronger." Paulette tugged on Zak's arm until he slid one hand into hers. "Come on, babe, and I'll fill you in."

An hour and two scotches later, Paulette could tell Zak had finally accepted the fact that she and Meredith could see ghosts. He'd acted smug when she confessed their cousins did indeed practice witchcraft. But one big question loomed like the blade of Damocles.

"Do you still want to marry me?" She swallowed and tried to not look away when he slowly blinked as though in a trance of some kind.

Silence stretched between them like taffy, slow and sticky with tension.

"Zak? Say something, please." She waited as he inspected her expression and then smiled a heart-swelling grin, causing her pulse to throb in her ears and making her weak at the knees.

"Of course, sweetheart." He leaned forward and pressed hungry lips to hers. "My love for you hasn't wavered just because you're a ghost whisperer with witches for cousins."

A cough at the arched doorway of the double parlor

drew their attention to where Max stood with a bouquet of fresh flowers. "Ghost whisperers?"

Grant appeared beside him, freshly shaved and dressed for a night on the town. "Witches for cousins? You mean, Tara?"

Paulette nodded and waved them into the room. "Want a drink?"

"I want an answer." Max strode to a chair and peered at her. "Are you and Meredith really able to see ghosts? I hoped that was a marketing ploy. You know, smoke and mirrors kind of thing."

"Sorry, Max." She flicked a look at Zak and then smiled at Max and Grant. "I guess the truth is stranger than fiction."

Grant flopped into the other chair. "I'll take that drink now. Double scotch, neat."

"I'll get it." Zak went to the sideboard and poured two glasses and refilled his own. "It's been quite an afternoon."

He handed out the glasses and then sat down beside Paulette again. He sipped and then stretched one arm along the sofa to rest behind her. "I always knew you were special."

"Just not how." Grant shook his head. "Tara, a witch? That's hard to swallow but maybe explains why I've felt so good ever since she touched me while we danced."

Paulette snuggled closer to Zak. "She's not evil, Grant. There are many Wiccans in the world who have very strong beliefs and capabilities."

The three men looked at her with raised brows and she chuckled.

"Not me, silly. But I did research the religion and a lot of it makes sense to me. Educate yourselves before you judge my cousins."

"Who's judging our cousins?" Meredith strode into the room, carrying a tray of sliced cheeses and a variety of crackers. Grizabella trailed behind her. "I thought you might like something to snack on since dinner will be a bit late."

"Where's Meg?" Max removed the flower vase from the middle of the coffee table centered between the sofas.

"Our little exercise this afternoon shooed everyone away from the property. She's just starting to sauté the onions, celery, and garlic for the beef stroganoff." Situating the platter on the table, she snagged a cracker and popped it into her mouth. Grizabella hopped onto a vacant overstuffed chair and curled up for a nap. Chewing, Meredith gazed at each person in turn before swallowing. "I've been thinking…"

"Uh oh, watch out now," Paulette sniped as she grabbed a buttery cracker and topped it with smoked Gouda. Her tummy rumbled in anticipation.

"Ha. Ha." Meredith propped fists on her hips. "Do you want to hear this or not?"

"Shoot." Zak grabbed a wheat cracker and pepper jack and popped it whole into his mouth.

Meredith quirked a brow at Paulette. "Well?"

"Go on. I'm all ears."

"What if we have a double wedding instead of planning two events?"

"So you do want to go through with our wedding?" Max rose to kiss her. "You had me worried you were getting cold feet."

"They were chilly for a while, but have warmed to the idea." She kissed him and smiled. "I do love you."

"Right back at ya."

"I love the idea!" Paulette jumped to her feet and hurried to hug her sister, pushing Max out of the way. "Oh, Meredith, we'd be able to share our very special day together."

"And, Zak, we'd have each other to help us remember our anniversary." Max laughed at his own joke.

"True." Zak chuckled as he nodded. He snapped his fingers, drawing everyone's attention. "What if we get married on Halloween? I mean, given your revelations today, the day would fit the spooky theme of this courtship."

"That's only four days from now." Could it be done? "The house is still decorated, so that would be one thing we wouldn't have to figure out."

"Are you serious?" Meredith stared at her. "Plan a double wedding in four days? What about food? Dresses? Tuxes? Music? Oh, and don't forget invitations to the guests."

"I'll pull some strings at the court house for the licenses." Max sipped his drink. "I know people who owe me a few favors."

"We don't need a big wedding, do we? And the Halloween theme would be unique. Our costumes could be modified to be wedding dresses and suits and would fit the theme perfectly," Paulette mused. "Meg can throw something together for food. CDs for music. E-mail invitations to those closest to us. Good thing Mom and Dad stayed longer than first planned." She paused in her tumble of words and grinned at each of them. "We can do this."

"I came here looking for dirt and I found myself a ghost whisperer wife." Zak shook his head and smiled. "Who'd've thunk?"

Paulette laughed at his slang and then kissed him. "Meredith, make one of your infamous lists of who's doing what and let's begin, shall we?"

The second floor ballroom brimmed with guests early Friday afternoon. Three rows of folding chairs stretched across the dance floor with a center aisle for the wedding party to march down. The few empty white cushioned seats reminded Paulette of oversized pillow mints as she stood at the back of the room with Meredith. The white stood out from the black cats affixed to the columns and bats dangling from the high ceiling, orange pumpkins scattered around, and clusters of red pillar candles sending their cranberry scent into the air from tall gold holders. Before the wide windows, the minister stood facing the crowd on a dais, Max and Zak at his left facing him.

Roxie eased closer to Paulette, examining her dress to ensure the skirt and train lay correctly and the black veil draped smoothly. "Stop fidgeting. You look lovely."

"The minister's not very happy about our theme, I have to tell you." She winked at her friend. "I do love your sexy witch costumes, though."

Tara chuckled as she joined them. "It's rather fun, isn't it?"

Meredith, dressed not as Wonder Woman but in a white flowing gown with halter top and white cape tied around her neck, hugged Roxie, then Tara, and finally Beth. She'd been inspired by Daenerys Targaryen on the TV series *Game of Thrones* to wear something almost toga like in its simplicity. In one hand, she held a bouquet of white and yellow roses tied with a white satin ribbon hanging to her ankles. "Thanks again for being our bridesmaids."

"Yes, it means so much to have you stand with us today." Paulette hugged them in turn with her bouquet hand.

"Places, ladies," Roxie said with a wink. "The minister is about to begin."

"Here we go." Meredith moved to stand behind Paulette as the three cousins filed in front of them.

She faced the open doorway, the guests half turned in their seats and craning their necks to be the first to glimpse the brides. At the front, her parents sat together, Dina holding Pat in his little devil costume. Hopefully, he wouldn't grow up to earn such a reputation. She grinned wider at the thought.

At the minister's nod, Sean pressed a button on the stereo and the sound of the wedding march filled the room while their friends and family surged to their feet.

Gripping her bouquet of red and white roses with trembling hands, she began the slow walk down the aisle behind the three ladies dressed as vixen witches. Meredith followed a few steps behind.

At first she nodded at the guests, acknowledging their joy. Then Zak's appreciative gaze caught hers and she couldn't look away. She smiled at the zombie groom tux he wore, though he had removed the fake blood for the occasion. His attire, though, had no effect on the emotion pulsating through her pores and veins, every inch attuned to him.

He stepped forward when she neared and took her hand, moving with her to stand in front of the minister. Out of the corner of her eye, she saw Max join Meredith and take their position beside them.

The minister began reading the greeting and then the meaning of marriage. She tried to listen through the roar of excitement in her ears, the joy ricocheting in her core, as the time drew closer when she and Zak would become man and wife. Pat would be their son, if in spirit only. She doubted Johnny would give up his rights as father, but that didn't preclude Zak from being a great dad.

"Paulette O'Connell, do you take Zachary Markel to be your husband so long as you both shall live?"

Finally. "I do." She searched Zak's eyes as he held both her hands.

"Zachary Markel, do you take Paulette O'Connell to be your wife so long as you both shall live?"

"And beyond." The minister cleared his throat, and Zak squeezed her hands. "I do."

She assumed the minister turned next to Meredith and Max and asked them the same questions. Zak's mouth descended to hers and obliterated any other thoughts. The connection and longing for Zak was why she married him, to have him all to herself to cherish forever. He ended the kiss, a reluctant grin on his lips as he pulled away but didn't release her hands. Laughter rippled through the guests and her neck and cheeks warmed.

"I now pronounce you both man and wife." The minister shook his head. "*Now* you may kiss your brides, gentlemen."

Applause erupted accompanied by laughter as Zak and Max bent to accomplish their individual missions. Music sounded from the speakers.

"I love you so much, Zachary Markel." She could only hope her eyes showed the extent of the love and exaltation flooding her at being his wife.

"I love you, Mrs. Markel."

"Congratulations, Zak. I guess this makes us brothers." Max shook hands with him and then kissed Paulette on the lips. "Congratulations on landing him, Paulette."

"Hey, that's my wife you're kissing." Zak said good-naturedly. "Congratulations to you and Meredith too. Do I get to kiss her?" He lifted a brow in Meredith's direction.

"No way." Max hugged Meredith to him. "Let's run the gauntlet and then we can party. I want to dance with my wife."

They made their way back down the aisle, accepting the many congratulatory wishes from their family and friends. They'd elected to skip a formal receiving line due to space constraints and their own impatience with the stuffy feel a line created. But they still had to take time to visit with each guest.

Before long they escaped the ballroom and hurried downstairs to where the reception party waited. Their guests trailed after them, laughing and chatting while flowing down the steps and mingling in the parlor and sewing room as well as the kitchen and foyer. Once again the double parlor had been transformed into a dance floor with Grant acting as DJ.

The two couples walked onto the floor and the guests ringed around them as "Unchained Melody," the theme song from the movie *Ghost*, played. A musical nod to what brought them together. Paulette rejoiced when Zak snuggled her to his hard body and they moved to the slow song. The smile she wore would never fade as long as he stayed in her life.

Over Zak's shoulder, Paulette saw Grant ask Tara to dance. She hesitated, but placed her hand in his and followed him onto the hardwood. So cute together, but it couldn't last. Not with him going back to Michigan since Zak had agreed to stay in Roseville. They both enjoyed the warmer climates, and he had resigned his professor job so now had no reason to return.

"I'm sure Tara will miss your brother." Moving to the slow rhythm, she peered up at her husband.

"If he goes. He said something about hanging around for a little while longer." Zak kissed her nose. "Maybe help Sean with the landscaping. Who knows what he'll uncover when he starts digging."

"Good." She watched the other couple sway to the music. "Very good."

"I love you with every molecule of my being." He kissed her nose again, then her lips, drawing her closer.

"Looks like you were right, Zak. You do always get what you want."

"Did you, Mrs. Markel?" He searched her expression, a smile tugging on his lips.

She glanced around the room filled with her family and friends, her son, and her husband. She'd never be alone and unloved again.

Smiling into Zak's eyes, she nodded. "Oh yes, Mr. Markel. Yes, indeed."

The End

Thanks so much for reading *Haunted Melody*! I hope you enjoyed Paulette and Zak's story. Grant and Tara tangle in the next story in the Secrets of Roseville series, *The Touchstone of Raven Hollow*.

To find out about new releases and upcoming appearances, please sign up for my newsletter via my website at www.bettybolte.com. I send out a monthly newsletter with book news to share with my readers, upcoming events and signings, and even a few favorite recipes, puzzles, and other doings!

I'd love to hear from you! Feel free to send me an email at betty@bettybolte.com, find me on Facebook at AuthorBettyBolte, follow me on BookBub, or connect with me on Twitter @BettyBolte.

You can always find an updated list of the titles in this series, as well as all of my other books on my website, at www.bettybolte.com/books/.

Thanks again for reading!

9 780999 816253